THE GOTHIC TALES
—of—
SHERIDAN LE FANU

THE GOTHIC TALES
—of—
SHERIDAN LE FANU

Edited by Xavier Aldana Reyes

THE BRITISH LIBRARY

This collection first published in 2020 by
The British Library
96 Euston Road
London NW1 2DB

Introduction © Xavier Aldana Reyes 2020

Cataloguing in Publication Data
A catalogue record for this publication is available from the British Library

ISBN 978 0 7123 5396 0

Text design and typesetting by Tetragon, London
Printed in Scotland by Bell and Bain, Ltd.

CONTENTS

Introduction   vii

The Fortunes of Sir Robert Ardagh (1838)   1
Passage in the Secret History of an Irish Countess (1838)   31
A Chapter in the History of a Tyrone Family (1839)   73
Schalken the Painter (1839, rev. 1851)   119
Ultor De Lacy: A Legend of Cappercullen (1861)   143
Squire Toby's Will (1868)   173
Stories of Lough Guir (1870)   211
Madam Crowl's Ghost (1870)   225

INTRODUCTION

Joseph Thomas Sheridan Le Fanu (1814–1873) was a leading Victorian journalist, magazine editor and prolific mystery writer who, despite having penned more than ten novels and published many more short stories in literary magazines, is mostly known to twenty-first-century readers only for his *In a Glass Darkly* (1872). This fictional collection of the papers of occult detective Dr. Hesselius included the oft-anthologised stories 'Green Tea' (1869), the story of a man haunted by a monkey-like demon invisible to everyone else; a revised version of 'The Watcher' (1847), retitled 'The Familiar', about a man stalked by a dwarfish figure from the past; and his best-known work, the vampiric novella *Carmilla* (1871–1872). The latter was not just an influence on Bram Stoker's *Dracula* (1897) but also inspired countless adaptations the world over, most notably Carl Theodor Dreyer's experimental film *Vampyr* (1932), Hammer Films' titillating *The Vampire Lovers* (1970) and the Canadian YouTube web series *Carmilla* (2014–2016). Some readers may also be familiar with Le Fanu's mystery novels in the Female Gothic tradition—*Uncle Silas* (1864), adapted to film, and *The Wyvern Mystery* (1869)—and with his novella in two parts *Spalatro* (1843). Despite the fact that he was also a tremendous writer of ghost tales, Le Fanu has tended to fly under the radar, often overlooked in favour of the likes of M. R. James. Ironically, James was an indebted enthusiast who, at a meeting of the Royal Institution of Great Britain, compared Le Fanu to Edgar Allan Poe and praised his skilful use of the narrative crescendo. Aiming to firmly position Le Fanu alongside other canonical horror writers published by the British Library, this anthology focuses on some of his lesser-known stories, especially those that specifically engage with the Gothic tradition.

Four of the stories in the present volume—'The Fortunes of Sir Robert Ardagh' (1838), 'Passage in the Secret History of an Irish Countess' (1838), 'Strange Event in the Life of Schalken the Painter' (1839) and 'A Chapter in the History of a Tyrone Family' (1839)— are some of Le Fanu's earliest and were initially published in *Dublin University Magazine* (1833–1882). They were also posthumously collected in the three-volume collection *The Purcell Papers* in 1880, which purported to be extracted from the manuscript papers of a Catholic priest, Father Purcell. Perhaps because the volumes are a bit of a motley crew, with some tales veering more clearly towards comedy and historical fiction, they are yet, at the time of writing, to be reprinted *in toto* by a major publisher. 'The Fortunes of Sir Robert Ardagh', set in Limerick in the eighteenth century, circles around the strange death of the last heir of a noble family. It is told twice, a particularly disconcerting narrative choice, since both versions seem just as unlikely and point to the workings of dark magic. Just who was Sir Robert's confidant and what role did he play in the latter's demise? In 'Passage in the Secret History of an Irish Countess', an orphaned woman writes an account of the persecution she suffered at the hands of her inheritance-hungry uncle, previously a murder suspect, and his cruel minions. The story, which would eventually be expanded into *Uncle Silas*, includes all of the motifs of the Female Gothic; Margaret could even be read as a Victorian update of Ann Radcliffe's brave heroines. 'A Chapter in

INTRODUCTION

the History of a Tyrone Family', a story reminiscent of the Bluebeard fairy tale, even anticipates the captivity and marital abuse in Charlotte Brontë's *Jane Eyre* (1847). In fact, its blind Dutchwoman, one of Lord Glenfallen's wives who is manipulated into murder, clearly precedes Bertha Mason as an earlier archetype of the 'madwoman in the attic'. Finally, 'Schalken the Painter', presented here in its revised and retitled version for *Ghost Stories of Tales and Mystery* (1851), relies for its shock effect on the character of the Gothic lover from beyond the grave, in this case an eccentric man with a 'demoniac' countenance who buys the hand of Gerard Douw's young daughter. Based on real historical figures, this brilliant story was masterfully adapted for British television in 1979.

The Gothic in Le Fanu manifests primarily in the tropes that drive events forward, from apparent Faustian bargains and foretold deaths to the tribulations of damsels in distress persecuted by avuncular tyrants. The background and aesthetics play a similar role, with ruinous castles and manor houses providing the necessary gloomy atmospherics to sustain suspense. Yet the Gothic is also evoked in the author's retrojection of events to foregone centuries, which, the reader is told at one point, 'afforded a soil much more convenient' to the growth of superstition. Setting marvellous events in the remote past and presenting them as entertaining exponents from Ireland's 'wild extraordinary traditions' allow him to imbue the action with both wonder and credibility. As Father Purcell admonishes his readers at the end of 'The Fortunes of Sir Robert Ardagh',

> The events which I have recorded are not imaginary. They are FACTS; and there lives one whose authority none would venture to question, who could vindicate the accuracy of every statement which I have set down, and that, too, with all the circumstantiality of an eye-witness.

INTRODUCTION

To an extent, whether things did or did not actually happen is irrelevant: in Le Fanu's hands, dark fables become embellished myth, the stuff of Gothic legend. Oftentimes, the intervention of supernatural entities appears more plausible and satisfying than the collection of confused and irreconcilable statements that make up the 'real' version of events. The result is carefully calculated: we are left with a sense of uncertainty and dread, so shaken as to feel the compulsion to return to the text in search of small details we may have overlooked on a first read.

A similar effect is at the heart of the ghost story, a horror subgenre Le Fanu perfected. The stories selected for the second half of the collection—'Ultor de Lacy: A Legend of Cappercullen' (1861), 'Squire Toby's Will' (1868), 'Stories of Lough Guir' (1870) and 'Madame Crowl's Ghost' (1870)—are all taken from *Madame Crowl's Ghost and Other Tales of Mystery*, a 1923 anthology of until then uncollected short stories edited by M. R. James. These illustrate some of Le Fanu's most intrinsic preoccupations as a ghost story writer: his preference for the physical, unforgiving spirit and his interest in folklore. Le Fanu's apparitions are solid entities recorded by multiple witnesses, something that precludes their existence from any possible ambiguity. His are not potentially internal or subjective ghosts, more typical of the Victorian period and best encapsulated by Henry James's *The Turn of the Screw* (1898), even though their impact is specific and channelled by personal emotion. Both 'Ultor de Lacy', about a haunted castle and a curse visited upon the descendants of a particular family, and 'Squire Toby's Will', about a man who cheats his brother out of the manor that rightfully belongs to him despite supernatural warnings, offer good examples of the retributive ghoul. Here the dead, who take on the gloomy shape of a man with a stained cheek and a pair of figures in mourning, are bent on nasty revenge. There is, naturally, some room for manoeuvre, and I have chosen 'Madame Crowl's Ghost' because the ghost sighting in it does not lead to the death of the protagonist but to the resolution of a horrific mystery. The past is still unlocked here, but the outcome is patently different: the discovery serves to rationalise the feelings of disgust and fear felt towards an elderly woman. Finally, I have favoured 'Stories of Lough Guir' over other equally interesting ones, such as 'The White Cat of Drumgunniol' (1870) and 'Sir Dominick's Bargain: A Legend of Dunoran' (1872), because it best displays Le Fanu's fascination with Irish folklore, an area that received steady attention in the early nineteenth century from the likes of the antiquarian Thomas Crofton Croker (1798–1854). In his late years Le Fanu befriended Patrick Kennedy (1801–1873), a bookseller and collector of folk tales who would regularly send him stories for publication in *Dublin University Magazine*. This relationship may well have further sparked his interest in the ties between history and tradition, between specific landscapes and the supernatural. The vignettes in 'Stories of Lough Guir' are less scary than amusing, but they point to the connections between the Gothic and the imagery of the folk tale. Its sunken castle, banshee and alleged shape-shifting earl (the third Earl of Desmond, chief of Justice for Ireland in 1367) are all drawn from the region's oral tradition and beautifully capture Le Fanu's most vernacular side.

XAVIER ALDANA REYES is Reader in English Literature and Film at Manchester Metropolitan University and a member of the Manchester Centre for Gothic Studies. He has edited *Horror: A Literary History* (2016) and *Promethean Horrors: Classic Tales of Mad Science* (2019) for British Library Publishing, along with collections of stories by Algernon Blackwood, William Hope Hodgson and H. P. Lovecraft.

I would like to dedicate this collection to my good friend Sorcha Ní Fhlainn.

'Is maith an scáthán súil charad.'

—1838—

THE FORTUNES OF
SIR ROBERT ARDAGH

*Being a second Extract from
the Papers of the late Father Purcell*

> 'The earth hath bubbles as the water hath—
> And these are of them.'

I N the south of Ireland, and on the borders of the county of Limerick, there lies a district of two or three miles in length, which is rendered interesting by the fact that it is one of the very few spots throughout this country, in which some vestiges of aboriginal forest still remain. It has little or none of the lordly character of the American forest, for the axe has felled its oldest and its grandest trees; but in the close wood which survives, live all the wild and pleasing peculiarities of nature: its complete irregularity, its vistas, in whose perspective the quiet cattle are peacefully browsing; its refreshing glades, where the grey rocks arise from amid the nodding fern; the silvery shafts of the old birch trees; the knotted trunks of the hoary oak, the grotesque but graceful branches which never shed their honours under the tyrant pruning-hook; the soft green sward; the chequered light and shade; the wild luxuriant weeds; the lichen and the moss—all, all are beautiful alike in the green freshness of spring, or in the sadness and sere of autumn. Their beauty is of that kind which makes the heart full with joy—appealing to the affections with a power which belongs to nature only. This wood runs up, from below the base, to the ridge of a long line of irregular hills, having perhaps, in primitive times, formed but the skirting of some mighty forest which occupied the level below.

But now, alas! whither have we drifted? whither has the tide of civilisation borne us? It has passed over a land unprepared for it—it has left nakedness behind it; we have lost our forests, but our marauders remain; we have destroyed all that is picturesque, while we have retained everything that is revolting in barbarism. Through the midst of this woodland there runs a deep gully or glen, where the stillness of the scene is broken in upon by the brawling of a mountain-stream, which, however, in the winter season, swells into a rapid and formidable torrent.

There is one point at which the glen becomes extremely deep and narrow; the sides descend to the depth of some hundred feet, and are so steep as to be nearly perpendicular. The wild trees which have taken root in the crannies and chasms of the rock have so intersected and entangled, that one can with difficulty catch a glimpse of the stream, which wheels, flashes, and foams below, as if exulting in the surrounding silence and solitude.

This spot was not unwisely chosen, as a point of no ordinary strength, for the erection of a massive square tower or keep, one side of which rises as if in continuation of the precipitous cliff on which it is based. Originally, the only mode of ingress was by a narrow portal in the very wall which overtopped the precipice, opening upon a ledge of rock which afforded a precarious pathway, cautiously intersected, however, by a deep trench cut with great labour in the living rock; so that, in its original state, and before the introduction of artillery into the art of war, this tower might have been pronounced, and that not presumptuously, almost impregnable.

The progress of improvement and the increasing security of the times had, however, tempted its successive proprietors, if not to adorn, at least to enlarge their premises, and at about the middle of the last century, when the castle was last inhabited, the original square tower formed but a small part of the edifice.

The castle, and a wide tract of the surrounding country, had from time immemorial belonged to a family which, for distinctness, we shall call by the name of Ardagh; and owing to the associations which, in Ireland, almost always attach to scenes which have long witnessed alike the exercise of stern feudal authority, and of that savage hospitality which distinguished the good old times, this building has become the subject and the scene of many wild and extraordinary traditions. One of them I have been enabled, by a personal acquaintance with an eye-witness of the events, to trace to its origin; and yet it is hard to say whether the events which I am about to record appear more strange or improbable as seen through the distorting medium of tradition, or in the appalling dimness of uncertainty which surrounds the reality.

Tradition says that, sometime in the last century, Sir Robert Ardagh, a young man, and the last heir of that family, went abroad and served in foreign armies; and that, having acquired considerable honour and emolument, he settled at Castle Ardagh, the building we have just now attempted to describe. He was what the country people call a *dark* man; that is, he was considered morose, reserved, and ill-tempered; and, as it was supposed from the utter solitude of his life, was upon no terms of cordiality with the other members of his family.

The only occasion upon which he broke through the solitary monotony of his life was during the continuance of the racing season, and immediately subsequent to it; at which time he was to be seen among the busiest upon the course, betting deeply and unhesitatingly, and invariably with success. Sir Robert was, however, too well known as a man of honour, and of too high a family, to be suspected of any unfair dealing. He was, moreover, a soldier, and a man of an intrepid as well as of a haughty character; and no one cared to hazard a surmise, the consequences of which would be felt most probably by its originator only.

Gossip, however, was not silent; it was remarked that Sir Robert never appeared at the race-ground, which was the only place of public resort which he frequented, except in company with a certain strange-looking person, who was never seen elsewhere, or under other circumstances. It was remarked, too, that this man, whose relation to Sir Robert was never distinctly ascertained, was the only person to whom he seemed to speak unnecessarily; it was observed that while with the country gentry he exchanged no further communication than what was unavoidable in arranging his sporting transactions, with this person he would converse earnestly and frequently. Tradition asserts that, to enhance the curiosity which this unaccountable and exclusive preference excited, the stranger possessed some striking and unpleasant peculiarities of person and of garb—she does not say, however, what these were—but they, in conjunction with Sir Robert's secluded habits and extraordinary run of luck—a success which was supposed to result from the suggestions and immediate advice of the unknown—were sufficient to warrant report in pronouncing that there was something *queer* in the wind, and in surmising that Sir Robert was playing a fearful and a hazardous game, and that, in short, his strange companion was little better than the devil himself.

Years, however, rolled quietly away, and nothing novel occurred in the arrangements of Castle Ardagh, excepting that Sir Robert parted with his odd companion, but as nobody could tell whence he came, so nobody could say whither he had gone. Sir Robert's habits, however, underwent no consequent change; he continued regularly to frequent the race meetings, without mixing at all in the convivialities of the gentry, and immediately afterwards to relapse into the secluded monotony of his ordinary life.

It was said that he had accumulated vast sums of money—and, as his bets were always successful, and always large, such must have been the case. He did not suffer the acquisition of wealth, however, to influence his hospitality or his housekeeping—he neither purchased land, nor extended his establishment; and his mode of enjoying his money must have been altogether that of the miser—consisting merely in the pleasure of touching and telling his gold, and in the consciousness of wealth.

Sir Robert's temper, so far from improving, became more than ever gloomy and morose. He sometimes carried the indulgence of his evil dispositions to such a height that it bordered upon insanity. During these paroxysms he would neither eat, drink, nor sleep. On such occasions he insisted on perfect privacy, even from the intrusion of his most trusted servants; his voice was frequently heard, sometimes in earnest supplication, sometime as if in loud and angry altercation with some unknown visitant; sometimes he would, for hours together, walk to and fro throughout the long oak wainscoted apartment, which he generally occupied, with wild gesticulations and agitated pace, in the manner of one who has been roused to a state of unnatural excitement by some sudden and appalling intimation.

These paroxysms of apparent lunacy were so frightful, that during their continuance even his oldest and most faithful domestics dared not approach him; consequently, his hours of agony were never intruded upon, and the mysterious causes of his sufferings appeared likely to remain hidden for ever.

On one occasion a fit of this kind continued for an unusual time, the ordinary term of their duration—about two days—had been long past, and the old servant who generally waited upon Sir Robert after these visitations, having in vain listened for the well-known tinkle of his master's hand-bell, began to feel extremely anxious; he feared that his master might have died from sheer exhaustion, or perhaps put an end to his own existence during his miserable depression. These fears at length became so strong, that having in vain urged some of his brother servants to accompany him, he determined to go up alone, and himself see whether any accident had befallen Sir Robert.

He traversed the several passages which conducted from the new to the more ancient parts of the mansion, and having arrived in the old hall of the castle, the utter silence of the hour, for it was very late in the night, the idea of the nature of the enterprise in which he was engaging himself, a sensation of remoteness from anything like human companionship, but, more than all, the vivid but undefined anticipation of something horrible, came upon him with such oppressive weight that he hesitated as to whether he should proceed. Real uneasiness, however, respecting the fate of his master, for whom he felt that kind of attachment which the force of habitual intercourse not unfrequently engenders respecting objects not in themselves amiable, and also a latent unwillingness to expose his weakness to the ridicule of his fellow-servants, combined to overcome his reluctance; and he had just placed his foot upon the first step of the staircase which conducted to his master's chamber, when his attention was arrested by a low but distinct knocking at the hall-door. Not, perhaps, very sorry at finding thus an excuse even for deferring his intended expedition, he placed the candle upon a stone block which lay in the hall, and approached the door, uncertain whether his ears had not deceived him. This doubt was justified by the circumstance that the hall entrance had been for nearly fifty years disused as a mode of ingress to the castle. The situation of this gate also, which we have endeavoured to describe, opening upon a narrow ledge of rock which overhangs a perilous cliff, rendered it at all times, but particularly at night, a dangerous entrance. This shelving platform of rock, which formed the only avenue to the door, was divided, as I have already stated, by a broad chasm, the planks across which had long disappeared by decay or otherwise, so that it seemed at least highly improbable that any man could have found his way across the passage in safety to the door, more particularly on a night like that, of singular darkness. The old man, therefore, listened attentively, to ascertain whether the first application should be followed by another. He had not long to wait; the same low but singularly distinct knocking was repeated; so low that it seemed as if the applicant had employed no harder or heavier instrument than his hand, and yet, despite the immense thickness of the door, with such strength that the sound was distinctly audible.

The knock was repeated a third time, without any increase of loudness; and the old man, obeying an impulse for which to his dying hour he could never account, proceeded to remove, one by one, the three great oaken bars which secured the door. Time and damp had effectually corroded the iron chambers of the lock, so that it afforded little resistance. With some effort, as he believed, assisted from without, the old servant succeeded in opening the door; and a low, square-built figure, apparently that of a man wrapped in a large black cloak, entered the hall. The servant could not see much of this visitant with any distinctness; his dress appeared foreign, the skirt of his ample cloak was thrown over one shoulder; he wore a large felt hat, with a very heavy leaf, from under which escaped what appeared to be a mass of long sooty-black hair; his feet were cased in heavy riding-boots. Such were the few particulars which the servant had time and light to observe. The stranger desired him to let his master know instantly that a friend had come, by appointment, to settle some business with him. The servant hesitated, but a slight motion on the part of his visitor, as if to possess himself of the candle, determined him; so, taking it in his hand, he ascended the castle stairs, leaving his guest in the hall.

On reaching the apartment which opened upon the oak-chamber he was surprised to observe the door of that room partly open, and the room itself lit up. He paused, but there was no sound; he looked in, and saw Sir Robert, his head and the upper part of his body reclining on a table, upon which burned a lamp; his arms were stretched forward on either side, and perfectly motionless; it appeared that, having been sitting at the table, he had thus sunk forward, either dead or in a swoon. There was no sound of breathing; all was silent, except the sharp ticking of a watch, which lay beside the lamp. The servant coughed twice or thrice, but with no effect; his fears now almost amounted to certainty, and he was approaching the table on which his master partly lay, to satisfy himself of his death, when Sir Robert slowly raised his head, and throwing himself back in his chair, fixed his eyes in a ghastly and uncertain gaze upon his attendant. At length he said, slowly and painfully, as if he dreaded the answer:

'In God's name, what are you?'

'Sir,' said the servant, 'a strange gentleman wants to see you below.'

At this intimation Sir Robert, starting on his feet and tossing his arms wildly upwards, uttered a shriek of such appalling and despairing terror that it was almost too fearful for human endurance; and long after the sound had ceased it seemed to the terrified imagination of the old servant to roll through the deserted passages in bursts of unnatural laughter. After a few moments Sir Robert said:

'Can't you send him away? Why does he come so soon? O God! O God! let him leave me for an hour; a little time. I can't see him now; try to get him away. You see I can't go down now; I have not strength. O God! o God! let him come back in an hour; it is not long to wait. He cannot lose anything by it; nothing, nothing, nothing. Tell him that; say anything to him.'

The servant went down. In his own words, he did not feel the stairs under him till he got to the hall. The figure stood exactly as he had left it. He delivered his master's message as coherently as he could. The stranger replied in a careless tone:

'If Sir Robert will not come clown to me, I must go up to him.'

The man returned, and to his surprise he found his master much more composed in manner. He listened to the message, and though the cold perspiration rose in drops upon his forehead faster than he could wipe it away, his manner had lost the dreadful agitation which had marked it before. He rose feebly, and casting a last look of agony behind him, passed from the room to the lobby, where he signed to his attendant not to follow him. The man moved as far as the head of the staircase, from whence he had a tolerably distinct view of the hall, which was imperfectly lighted by the candle he had left there.

He saw his master reel, rather than walk down the stairs, clinging all the way to the banisters. He walked on, as if about to sink every moment from weakness. The figure advanced as if to meet him, and in passing struck down the light. The servant could see no more; but there was a sound of struggling, renewed at intervals with silent but fearful energy. It was evident, however, that the parties were approaching the door, for he heard the solid oak sound twice or thrice, as the feet of the combatants, in shuffling hither and thither over the floor, struck upon it. After a slight pause he heard the door thrown open with such violence that the leaf seemed to strike the side-wall of the hall, for it was so dark without that this could only be surmised by the sound. The struggle was renewed with an agony and intenseness of energy that betrayed itself in deep-drawn gasps. One desperate effort, which terminated in the breaking of some part of the door, producing a sound as if the door-post was wrenched from its position, was followed by another wrestle, evidently upon the narrow ledge which ran outside the door, overtopping the precipice. This proved to be the final struggle, for it was followed by a crashing sound as if some heavy body had fallen over, and was rushing down the precipice, through the light boughs that crossed near the top. All then became still as the grave, except when the moan of the night wind sighed up the wooded glen.

The old servant had not nerve to return through the hall, and to him the darkness seemed all but endless; but morning at length came, and with it the disclosure of the events of the night. Near the door, upon the ground, lay Sir Robert's sword-belt, which had given way in the scuffle. A huge splinter from the massive door-post had been wrenched off by an almost superhuman effort—one which nothing but the gripe of a despairing man could have severed—and on the rock outside were left the marks of the slipping and sliding of feet.

At the foot of the precipice, not immediately under the castle, but dragged some way up the glen, were found the remains of Sir Robert, with hardly a vestige of a limb or feature left distinguishable. The right hand, however, was uninjured, and in its fingers were clutched, with the fixedness of death, a long lock of coarse sooty hair—the only direct circumstantial evidence of the presence of a second person. So says tradition.

This story, as I have mentioned, was current among the dealers in such lore; but the original facts are so dissimilar in all but the name of the principal person mentioned and his mode of life, and the fact that his death was accompanied with circumstances of extraordinary mystery, that the two narratives are totally irreconcilable (even allowing the utmost for the exaggerating influence of tradition), except by supposing report to have combined and blended together the fabulous histories of several distinct bearers of the family name. However this may be, I shall lay before the reader a distinct recital of the events from which the foregoing tradition arose. With respect to these there can be no mistake; they are authenticated as fully as anything can be by human testimony; and I state them principally upon the evidence of a lady who herself bore a prominent part in the strange events which she related, and which I now record as being among the few well-attested tales of the marvellous which it has been my fate to hear. I shall, as far as I am able, arrange in one combined narrative the evidence of several distinct persons who were eye-witnesses of what they related, and with the truth of whose testimony I am solemnly and deeply impressed.

Sir Robert Ardagh, as we choose to call him, was the heir and representative of the family whose name he bore; but owing to the prodigality of his father, the estates descended to him in a very impaired condition. Urged by the restless spirit of youth, or more probably by a feeling of pride which could not submit to witness, in the paternal mansion, what he considered a humiliating alteration in the style and hospitality which up to that time had distinguished his family, Sir Robert left Ireland and went abroad. How he occupied himself, or what countries he visited during his absence, was never known, nor did he afterwards make any allusion or encourage any inquiries touching his foreign sojourn. He left Ireland in the year 1742, being then just of age, and was not heard of until the year 1760—about eighteen years afterwards—at which time he returned. His personal appearance was, as might have been expected, very greatly altered, more altered, indeed, than the time of his absence might have warranted one in supposing likely. But to counterbalance the unfavourable change which time had wrought in his form and features, he had acquired all the advantages of polish of manner and refinement of taste which foreign travel is supposed to bestow. But what was truly surprising was that it soon became evident that Sir Robert was very wealthy—wealthy to an extraordinary and unaccountable degree; and this fact was made manifest, not only by his expensive style of living, but by his proceeding to disembarrass his property, and to purchase extensive estates in addition. Moreover, there could be nothing deceptive in these appearances, for he paid ready money for everything, from the most important purchase to the most trifling.

Sir Robert was a remarkably agreeable man, and possessing the combined advantages of birth and property, he was, as a matter of course, gladly received into the highest society which the metropolis then commanded. It was thus that he became acquainted with the two beautiful Miss F——ds, then among the brightest ornaments of the highest circle of Dublin fashion. Their family was in more than one direction allied to nobility; and Lady D——, their elder sister by many years, and sometime married to a once well-known nobleman, was now their protectress. These considerations, beside the fact that the young ladies were what is usually termed heiresses, though not to a very great amount, secured to them a high position in the best society which Ireland then produced. The two young ladies differed strongly, alike in appearance and in character. The elder of the two, Emily, was generally considered the handsomer—for her beauty was of that impressive kind which never failed to strike even at the first glance, possessing as it did all the advantages of a fine person and a commanding carriage. The beauty of her features strikingly assorted in character with that of her figure and deportment. Her hair was raven-black and richly luxuriant, beautifully contrasting with the perfect whiteness of her forehead—her finely pencilled brows were black as the ringlets that clustered near them—and her blue eyes, full, lustrous, and animated, possessed all the power and brilliancy of brown ones, with more than their softness and variety of expression. She was not, however, merely the tragedy queen. When she smiled, and that was not seldom, the dimpling of cheek and chin, the laughing display of the small and beautiful teeth—but, more than all, the roguish archness of her deep, bright eye, showed that nature had not neglected in her the lighter and the softer characteristics of woman.

Her younger sister Mary was, as I believe not unfrequently occurs in the case of sisters, quite in the opposite style of beauty. She was light-haired, had more colour, had nearly equal grace, with much more liveliness of manner. Her eyes were of that dark grey which poets so much admire—full of expression and vivacity. She was altogether a very beautiful and animated girl—though as unlike her sister as the presence of those two qualities would permit her to be. Their dissimilarity did not stop here—it was deeper than mere appearance—the character of their minds differed almost as strikingly as did their complexion. The fair-haired beauty had a large proportion of that softness and pliability of temper which physiognomists assign as the characteristics of such complexions. She was much more the creature of impulse than of feeling, and consequently more the victim of extrinsic circumstances than was her sister. Emily, on the contrary, possessed considerable firmness and decision. She was less excitable, but when excited her feelings were more intense and enduring. She wanted much of the gaiety, but with it the volatility of her younger sister. Her opinions were adopted, and her friendships formed more reflectively, and her affections seemed to move, as it were, more slowly, but more determinedly. This firmness of character did not amount to anything masculine, and did not at all impair the feminine grace of her manners.

Sir Robert Ardagh was for a long time apparently equally attentive to the two sisters, and many were the conjectures and the surmises as to which would be the lady of his choice. At length, however, these doubts were determined; he proposed for and was accepted by the dark beauty, Emily F———d.

The bridals were celebrated in a manner becoming the wealth and connections of the parties; and Sir Robert and Lady Ardagh left Dublin to pass the honeymoon at the family mansion, Castle Ardagh, which had lately been fitted up in a style bordering upon magnificent. Whether in compliance with the wishes of his lady, or owing to some whim of his own, his habits were henceforward strikingly altered; and from having moved among the gayest if not the most profligate of the votaries of fashion, he suddenly settled down into a quiet, domestic, country gentleman, and seldom, if ever, visited the capital, and then his sojourns were as brief as the nature of his business would permit.

Lady Ardagh, however, did not suffer from this change further than in being secluded from general society; for Sir Robert's wealth, and the hospitality which he had established in the family mansion, commanded that of such of his lady's friends and relatives as had leisure or inclination to visit the castle; and as their style of living was very handsome, and its internal resources of amusement considerable, few invitations from Sir Robert or his lady were neglected.

Many years passed quietly away, during which Sir Robert's and Lady Ardagh's hopes of issue were several times disappointed. In the lapse of all this time there occurred but one event worth recording. Sir Robert had brought with him from abroad a valet, who sometimes professed himself to be French, at others Italian, and at others again German. He spoke all these languages with equal fluency, and seemed to take a kind of pleasure in puzzling the sagacity and balking the curiosity of such of the visitors at the castle as at any time happened to enter into conversation with him, or who, struck by his singularities, became inquisitive respecting his country and origin. Sir Robert called him by the French name, JACQUE, and among the lower orders he was familiarly known by the title of 'Jack, the devil,' an appellation which originated in a supposed malignity of disposition and a real reluctance to mix in the society of those who were believed to be his equals. This morose reserve, coupled with the mystery which enveloped all about him, rendered him an object of suspicion and inquiry to his fellow-servants, amongst whom it was whispered that this man in secret governed the actions of Sir Robert with a despotic dictation, and that, as if to indemnify himself for his public and apparent servitude and self-denial, he in private exacted a degree of respectful homage from his so-called master, totally inconsistent with the relation generally supposed to exist between them.

This man's personal appearance was, to say the least of it, extremely odd; he was low in stature; and this defect was enhanced by a distortion of the spine, so considerable as almost to amount to a hunch; his features, too, had all that sharpness and sickliness of hue which generally accompany deformity; he wore his hair, which was black as soot, in heavy neglected ringlets about his shoulders, and always without powder—a peculiarity in those days. There was something unpleasant, too, in the circumstance that he never raised his eyes to meet those of another; this fact was often cited as a proof of his being something not quite right, and said to result not from the timidity which is supposed in most cases to induce this habit, but from a consciousness that his eye possessed a power which, if exhibited, would betray a supernatural origin. Once, and once only, had he violated this sinister observance: it was on the occasion of Sir Robert's hopes having been most bitterly disappointed; his lady, after a severe and dangerous confinement, gave birth to a dead child. Immediately after the intelligence had been made known, a servant, having upon some business passed outside the gate of the castle-yard, was met by Jacque, who, contrary to his wont, accosted him, observing, 'So, after all the pother, the son and heir is still-born.' This remark was accompanied by a chuckling laugh, the only approach to merriment which he was ever known to exhibit. The servant, who was really disappointed, having hoped for holiday times, feasting and debauchery with impunity during the rejoicings which would have accompanied a christening, turned tartly upon the little valet, telling him that he should let Sir Robert know how he had received the tidings which should have filled any faithful servant with sorrow; and having once broken the ice, he was proceeding with increasing fluency, when his harangue was cut short and his temerity punished, by the little man raising his head and treating him to a scowl so fearful, half-demoniac, half-insane, that it haunted his imagination in nightmares and nervous tremors for months after.

To this man Lady Ardagh had, at first sight, conceived an antipathy amounting to horror, a mixture of loathing and dread so very powerful that she had made it a particular and urgent request to Sir Robert, that he would dismiss him, offering herself, from that property which Sir Robert had by the marriage settlements left at her own disposal, to provide handsomely for him, provided only she might be relieved from the continual anxiety and discomfort which the fear of encountering him induced.

Sir Robert, however, would not hear of it; the request seemed at first to agitate and distress him; but when still urged in defiance of his peremptory refusal, he burst into a violent fit of fury; he spoke darkly of great sacrifices which he had made, and threatened that if the request were at any time renewed he would leave both her and the country for ever. This was, however, a solitary instance of violence; his general conduct towards Lady Ardagh, though at no time uxorious, was certainly kind and respectful, and he was more than repaid in the fervent attachment which she bore him in return.

Some short time after this strange interview between Sir Robert and Lady Ardagh; one night after the family had retired to bed, and when everything had been quiet for some time, the bell of Sir Robert's dressing-room rang suddenly and violently; the ringing was repeated again and again at still shorter intervals, and with increasing violence, as if the person who pulled the bell was agitated by the presence of some terrifying and imminent danger. A servant named Donovan was the first to answer it; he threw on his clothes, and hurried to the room.

Sir Robert had selected for his private room an apartment remote from the bed-chambers of the castle, most of which lay in the more modern parts of the mansion, and secured at its entrance by a double door. As the servant opened the first of these, Sir Robert's bell again sounded with a longer and louder peal; the inner door resisted his efforts to open it; but after a few violent struggles, not having been perfectly secured, or owing to the inadequacy of the bolt itself, it gave way, and the servant rushed into the apartment, advancing several paces before he could recover himself. As he entered, he heard Sir Robert's voice exclaiming loudly—'Wait without, do not come in yet;' but the prohibition came too late. Near a low truckle-bed, upon which Sir Robert sometimes slept, for he was a whimsical man, in a large armchair, sat, or rather lounged, the form of the valet Jacque, his arms folded, and his heels stretched forward on the floor, so as fully to exhibit his misshapen legs, his head thrown back, and his eyes fixed upon his master with a look of indescribable defiance and derision, while, as if to add to the strange insolence of his attitude and expression, he had placed upon his head the black cloth cap which it was his habit to wear.

Sir Robert was standing before him, at the distance of several yards, in a posture expressive of despair, terror, and what might be called an agony of humility. He waved his hand twice or thrice, as if to dismiss the servant, who, however, remained fixed on the spot where he had first stood; and then, as if forgetting everything but the agony within him, he pressed his clenched hands on his cold damp brow, and dashed away the heavy drops that gathered chill and thickly there.

Jacque broke the silence.

'Donovan,' said he, 'shake up that drone and drunkard, Carlton; tell him that his master directs that the travelling carriage shall be at the door within half-an-hour.'

The servant paused, as if in doubt as to what he should do; but his scruples were resolved by Sir Robert's saying hurriedly, 'Go—go, do whatever he directs; his commands are mine; tell Carlton the same.'

The servant hurried to obey, and in about half-an-hour the carriage was at the door, and Jacque, having directed the coachman to drive to B——n, a small town at about the distance of twelve miles—the nearest point, however, at which post-horses could be obtained—stepped into the vehicle, which accordingly quitted the castle immediately.

Although it was a fine moonlight night, the carriage made its way but very slowly, and after the lapse of two hours the travellers had arrived at a point about eight miles from the castle, at which the road strikes through a desolate and heathy flat, sloping up distantly at either side into bleak undulatory hills, in whose monotonous sweep the imagination beholds the heaving of some dark sluggish sea, arrested in its first commotion by some preternatural power. It is a gloomy and divested spot; there is neither tree nor habitation near it; its monotony is unbroken, except by here and there the grey front of a rock peering above the heath, and the effect is rendered yet more dreary and spectral by the exaggerated and misty shadows which the moon casts along the sloping sides of the hills.

When they had gained about the centre of this tract, Carlton, the coachman, was surprised to see a figure standing at some distance in advance, immediately beside the road, and still more so when, on coming up, he observed that it was no other than Jacque whom he believed to be at that moment quietly seated in the carriage; the coachman drew up, and nodding to him, the little valet exclaimed:

'Carlton, I have got the start of you; the roads are heavy, so I shall even take care of myself the rest of the way. Do you make your way back as best you can, and I shall follow my own nose.'

So saying, he chucked a purse into the lap of the coachman, and turning off at a right angle with the road, he began to move rapidly away in the direction of the dark ridge that lowered in the distance.

The servant watched him until he was lost in the shadowy haze of night; and neither he nor any of the inmates of the castle saw Jacque again. His disappearance, as might have been expected, did not cause any regret among the servants and dependants at the castle; and Lady Ardagh did not attempt to conceal her delight; but with Sir Robert matters were different, for two or three days subsequent to this event he confined himself to his room, and when he did return to his ordinary occupations, it was with a gloomy indifference, which showed that he did so more from habit than from any interest he felt in them. He appeared from that moment unaccountably and strikingly changed, and thenceforward walked through life as a thing from which he could derive neither profit nor pleasure. His temper, however, so far from growing wayward or morose, became, though gloomy, very—almost unnaturally—placid and cold; but his spirits totally failed, and he grew silent and abstracted.

These sombre habits of mind, as might have been anticipated, very materially affected the gay housekeeping of the castle; and the dark and melancholy spirit of its master seemed to have communicated itself to the very domestics, almost to the very walls of the mansion.

Several years rolled on in this way, and the sounds of mirth and wassail had long been strangers to the castle, when Sir Robert requested his lady, to her great astonishment, to invite some twenty or thirty of their friends to spend the Christmas, which was fast approaching, at the castle. Lady Ardagh gladly complied, and her sister Mary, who still continued unmarried, and Lady D—— were of course included in the invitations. Lady Ardagh had requested her sisters to set forward as early as possible, in order that she might enjoy a little of their society before the arrival of the other guests; and in compliance with this request they left Dublin almost immediately upon receiving the invitation, a little more than a week before the arrival of the festival which was to be the period at which the whole party were to muster.

For expedition's sake it was arranged that they should post, while Lady D——'s groom was to follow with her horses, she taking with herself her own maid and one male servant. They left the city when the day was considerably spent, and consequently made but three stages in the first day; upon the second, at about eight in the evening, they had reached the town of K——k, distant about fifteen miles from Castle Ardagh. Here, owing to Miss F——d's great fatigue, she having been for a considerable time in a very delicate state of health, it was determined to put up for the night. They, accordingly, took possession of the best sitting-room which the inn commanded, and Lady D—— remained in it to direct and urge the preparations for some refreshment, which the fatigues of the day had rendered necessary, while her younger sister retired to her bed-chamber to rest there for a little time, as the parlour commanded no such luxury as a sofa.

Miss F——d was, as I have already stated, at this time in very delicate health; and upon this occasion the exhaustion of fatigue, and the dreary badness of the weather, combined to depress her spirits. Lady D—— had not been left long to herself, when the door communicating with the passage was abruptly opened, and her sister Mary entered in a state of great agitation; she sat down pale and trembling upon one of the chairs, and it was not until a copious flood of tears had relieved her, that she became sufficiently calm to relate the cause of her excitement and distress. It was simply this. Almost immediately upon lying down upon the bed she sank into a feverish and unrefreshing slumber; images of all grotesque shapes and startling colours flitted before her sleeping fancy with all the rapidity and variety of the changes in a kaleidoscope. At length, as she described it, a mist seemed to interpose itself between her sight and the ever-shifting scenery which sported before her imagination, and out of this cloudy shadow gradually emerged a figure whose back seemed turned towards the sleeper; it was that of a lady, who, in perfect silence, was expressing as far as pantomimic gesture could, by wringing her hands, and throwing her head from side to side, in the manner of one who is exhausted by the over indulgence, by the very sickness and impatience of grief, the extremity of misery. For a long time she sought in vain to catch a glimpse of the face of the apparition, who thus seemed to stir and live before her. But at length the figure seemed to move with an air of authority, as if about to give directions to some inferior, and in doing so, it turned its head so as to display, with a ghastly distinctness, the features of Lady Ardagh, pale as death, with her dark hair all dishevelled, and her eyes dim and sunken with weeping. The revulsion of feeling which Miss F——d experienced at this disclosure—for up to that point she had contemplated the appearance rather with a sense of curiosity and of interest, than of anything deeper—was so horrible, that the shock awoke her perfectly. She sat up in the bed, and looked fearfully around the room, which was imperfectly lighted by a single candle burning dimly, as if she almost expected to see the reality of her dreadful vision lurking in some corner of the chamber. Her fears were, however, verified, though not in the way she expected; yet in a manner sufficiently horrible—for she had hardly time to breathe and to collect her thoughts, when she heard, or thought she heard, the voice of her sister, Lady Ardagh, sometimes sobbing violently, and sometimes almost shrieking as if in terror, and calling upon her and Lady D——, with the most imploring earnestness of despair, for God's sake to lose no time in coming to her. All this was so horribly distinct, that it seemed as if the mourner was standing within a few yards of the spot where Miss F——d lay. She sprang from the bed, and leaving the candle in the room behind her, she made her way in the dark through the passage, the voice still following her, until as she arrived at the door of the sitting-room it seemed to die away in low sobbing.

As soon as Miss F——d was tolerably recovered, she declared her determination to proceed directly, and without further loss of time, to Castle Ardagh. It was not without much difficulty that Lady D—— at length prevailed upon her to consent to remain where they then were, until morning should arrive, when it was to be expected that the young lady would be much refreshed by at least remaining quiet for the night, even though sleep were out of the question. Lady D—— was convinced, from the nervous and feverish symptoms which her sister exhibited, that she had already done too much, and was more than ever satisfied of the necessity of prosecuting the journey no further upon that day. After some time she persuaded her sister to return to her room, where she remained with her until she had gone to bed, and appeared comparatively composed. Lady D—— then returned to the parlour, and not finding herself sleepy, she remained sitting by the fire. Her solitude was a second time broken in upon, by the entrance of her sister, who now appeared, if possible, more agitated than before. She said that Lady D—— had not long left the room, when she was roused by a repetition of the same wailing and lamentations, accompanied by the wildest and most agonised supplications that no time should be lost in coming to Castle Ardagh, and all in her sister's voice, and uttered at the same proximity as before. This time the voice had followed her to the very door of the sitting-room, and until she closed it, seemed to pour forth its cries and sobs at the very threshold.

Miss F——d now most positively declared that nothing should prevent her proceeding instantly to the castle, adding that if Lady D—— would not accompany her, she would go on by herself. Superstitious feelings are at all times more or less contagious, and the last century afforded a soil much more congenial to their growth than the present. Lady D—— was so far affected by her sister's terrors, that she became, at least, uneasy; and seeing that her sister was immovably determined upon setting forward immediately, she consented to accompany her forthwith. After a slight delay, fresh horses were procured, and the two ladies and their attendants renewed their journey, with strong injunctions to the driver to quicken their rate of travelling as much as possible, and promises of reward in case of his doing so.

Roads were then in much worse condition throughout the south, even than they now are; and the fifteen miles which modern posting would have passed in little more than an hour and a half, were not completed even with every possible exertion in twice the time. Miss F——d had been nervously restless during the journey. Her head had been constantly out of the carriage window; and as they approached the entrance to the castle demesne, which lay about a mile from the building, her anxiety began to communicate itself to her sister. The postillion had just dismounted, and was endeavouring to open the gate—at that time a necessary trouble; for in the middle of the last century porter's lodges were not common in the south of Ireland, and locks and keys almost unknown. He had just succeeded in rolling back the heavy oaken gate so as to admit the vehicle, when a mounted servant rode rapidly down the avenue, and drawing up at the carriage, asked of the postillion who the party were; and on hearing, he rode round to the carriage window and handed in a note, which Lady D—— received. By the assistance of one of the coach-lamps they succeeded in deciphering it. It was scrawled in great agitation, and ran thus:

> 'My Dear Sister—My Dear Sisters both,—In God's name lose no time, I am frightened and miserable; I cannot explain all till you come. I am too much terrified to write coherently; but understand me—hasten—do not waste a minute. I am afraid you will come too late.
>
> 'E. A.'

The servant could tell nothing more than that the castle was in great confusion, and that Lady Ardagh had been crying bitterly all the night. Sir Robert was perfectly well. Altogether at a loss as to the cause of Lady Ardagh's great distress, they urged their way up the steep and broken avenue which wound through the crowding trees, whose wild and grotesque branches, now left stripped and naked by the blasts of winter, stretched drearily across the road. As the carriage drew up in the area before the door, the anxiety of the ladies almost amounted to agony; and scarcely waiting for the assistance of their attendant, they sprang to the ground, and in an instant stood at the castle door. From within were distinctly audible the sounds of lamentation and weeping, and the suppressed hum of voices as if of those endeavouring to soothe the mourner. The door was speedily opened, and when the ladies entered, the first object which met their view was their sister, Lady Ardagh, sitting on a form in the hall, weeping and wringing her hands in deep agony. Beside her stood two old, withered crones, who were each endeavouring in their own way to administer consolation, without even knowing or caring what the subject of her grief might be.

Immediately on Lady Ardagh's seeing her sisters, she started up, fell on their necks, and kissed them again and again without speaking, and then taking them each by a hand, still weeping bitterly, she led them into a small room adjoining the hall, in which burned a light, and, having closed the door, she sat down between them. After thanking them for the haste they had made, she proceeded to tell them, in words incoherent from agitation, that Sir Robert had in private, and in the most solemn manner, told her that he should die upon that night, and that he had occupied himself during the evening in giving minute directions respecting the arrangements of his funeral. Lady D—— here suggested the possibility of his labouring under the hallucinations of a fever; but to this Lady Ardagh quickly replied:

'Oh! no, no! Would to God I could think it. Oh! no, no! Wait till you have seen him. There is a frightful calmness about all he says and does; and his directions are all so clear, and his mind so perfectly collected, it is impossible, quite impossible.' And she wept yet more bitterly.

At that moment Sir Robert's voice was heard in issuing some directions, as he came downstairs; and Lady Ardagh exclaimed, hurriedly:

'Go now and see him yourself. He is in the hall.'

Lady D—— accordingly went out into the hall, where Sir Robert met her; and, saluting her with kind politeness, he said, after a pause:

'You are come upon a melancholy mission—the house is in great confusion, and some of its inmates in considerable grief.' He took her hand, and looking fixedly in her face, continued: 'I shall not live to see to-morrow's sun shine.'

'You are ill, sir, I have no doubt,' replied she; 'but I am very certain we shall see you much better to-morrow, and still better the day following.'

'I am *not* ill, sister,' replied he. 'Feel my temples, they are cool; lay your finger to my pulse, its throb is slow and temperate. I never was more perfectly in health, and yet do I know that ere three hours be past, I shall be no more.'

'Sir, sir,' said she, a good deal startled, but wishing to conceal the impression which the calm solemnity of his manner had, in her own despite, made upon her, 'Sir, you should not jest; you should not even speak lightly upon such subjects. You trifle with what is sacred—you are sporting with the best affections of your wife—'

'Stay, my good lady,' said he; 'if when this clock shall strike the hour of three, I shall be anything but a helpless clod, then upbraid me. Pray return now to your sister. Lady Ardagh is, indeed, much to be pitied; but what is past cannot now be helped. I have now a few papers to arrange, and some to destroy. I shall see you and Lady Ardagh before my death; try to compose her—her sufferings distress me much; but what is past cannot now be mended.'

Thus saying, he went upstairs, and Lady D—— returned to the room where her sisters were sitting.

'Well,' exclaimed Lady Ardagh, as she re-entered, 'is it not so?—do you still doubt?—do you think there is any hope?'

Lady D—— was silent.

'Oh! none, none, none,' continued she; 'I see, I see you are convinced.' And she wrung her hands in bitter agony.

'My dear sister,' said Lady D——, 'there is, no doubt, something strange in all that has appeared in this matter; but still I cannot but hope that there may be something deceptive in all the apparent calmness of Sir Robert. I still must believe that some latent fever has affected his mind, or that, owing to the state of nervous depression into which he has been sinking, some trivial occurrence has been converted, in his disordered imagination, into an augury foreboding his immediate dissolution.'

In such suggestions, unsatisfactory even to those who originated them, and doubly so to her whom they were intended to comfort, more than two hours passed; and Lady D—— was beginning to hope that the fated term might elapse without the occurrence of any tragical event, when Sir Robert entered the room. On coming in, he placed his finger with a warning gesture upon his lips, as if to enjoin silence; and then having successively pressed the hands of his two sisters-in-law, he stooped sadly over the fainting form of his lady, and twice pressed her cold, pale forehead, with his lips, and then passed silently out of the room.

Lady D——, starting up, followed to the door, and saw him take a candle in the hall, and walk deliberately up the stairs. Stimulated by a feeling of horrible curiosity, she continued to follow him at a distance. She saw him enter his own private room, and heard him close and lock the door after him. Continuing to follow him as far as she could, she placed herself at the door of the chamber, as noiselessly as possible, where after a little time she was joined by her two sisters, Lady Ardagh and Miss F——d. In breathless silence they listened to what should pass within. They distinctly heard Sir Robert pacing up and down the room for some time; and then, after a pause, a sound as if some one had thrown himself heavily upon the bed. At this moment Lady D——, forgetting that the door had been secured within, turned the handle for the purpose of entering; when some one from the inside, close to the door, said, 'Hush! hush!' The same lady, now much alarmed, knocked violently at the door; there was no answer. She knocked again more violently, with no further success. Lady Ardagh, now, uttering a piercing shriek, sank in a swoon upon the floor. Three or four servants, alarmed by the noise, now hurried upstairs, and Lady Ardagh was carried apparently lifeless to her own chamber. They then, after having knocked long and loudly in vain, applied themselves to forcing an entrance into Sir Robert's room. After resisting some violent efforts, the door at length gave way, and all entered the room nearly together. There was a single candle burning upon a table at the far end of the apartment; and stretched upon the bed lay Sir Robert Ardagh. He was a corpse—the eyes were open—no convulsion had passed over the features, or distorted the limbs—it seemed as if the soul had sped from the body without a struggle to remain there. On touching the body it was found to be cold as clay—all lingering of the vital heat had left it. They closed the ghastly eyes of the corpse, and leaving it to the care of those who seem to consider it a privilege of their age and sex to gloat over the revolting spectacle of death in all its stages, they returned to Lady Ardagh, now a widow. The party assembled at the castle, but the atmosphere was tainted with death. Grief there was not much, but awe and panic were expressed in every face. The guests talked in whispers, and the servants walked on tiptoe, as if afraid of the very noise of their own footsteps.

The funeral was conducted almost with splendour. The body, having been conveyed, in compliance with Sir Robert's last directions, to Dublin, was there laid within the ancient walls of St. Audoen's Church—where I have read the epitaph, telling the age and titles of the departed dust. Neither painted escutcheon, nor marble slab, have served to rescue from oblivion the story of the dead, whose very name will ere long moulder from their tracery—

'Et sunt sua fata sepulchris.'*

The events which I have recorded are not imaginary. They are FACTS; and there lives one whose authority none would venture to question, who could vindicate the accuracy of every statement which I have set down, and that, too, with all the circumstantiality of an eye-witness.†

---

* This prophecy has since been realised; for the aisle in which Sir Robert's remains were laid has been suffered to fall completely to decay; and the tomb which marked his grave, and other monuments more curious, form now one indistinguishable mass of rubbish.

† This paper, from a memorandum, I find to have been written in 1803. The lady to whom allusion is made, I believe to be Miss Mary F——d. She never married, and survived both her sisters, living to a very advanced age.

—1838—

PASSAGE IN THE SECRET HISTORY OF AN IRISH COUNTESS

Being a Fifth Extract from the Legacy of the late Francis Purcell, P.P. of Drumcoolagh

THE following paper is written in a female hand, and was no doubt communicated to my much-regretted friend by the lady whose early history it serves to illustrate, the Countess D——. She is no more—she long since died, a childless and a widowed wife, and, as her letter sadly predicts, none survive to whom the publication of this narrative can prove 'injurious, or even painful.' Strange! two powerful and wealthy families, that in which she was born, and that into which she had married, have ceased to be—they are utterly extinct.

To those who know anything of the history of Irish families, as they were less than a century ago, the facts which immediately follow will at once suggest *the names* of the principal actors; and to others their publication would be useless—to us, possibly, if not probably, injurious. I have, therefore, altered such of the names as might, if stated, get us into difficulty; others, belonging to minor characters in the strange story, I have left untouched.

My dear friend,—You have asked me to furnish you with a detail of the strange events which marked my early history, and I have, without hesitation, applied myself to the task, knowing that, while I live, a kind consideration for my feelings will prevent your giving publicity to the statement; and conscious that, when I am no more, there will not survive one to whom the narrative can prove injurious, or even painful.

My mother died when I was quite an infant, and of her I have no recollection, even the faintest. By her death, my education and habits were left solely to the guidance of my surviving parent; and, as far as a stern attention to my religious instruction, and an active anxiety evinced by his procuring for me the best masters to perfect me in those accomplishments which my station and wealth might seem to require, could avail, he amply discharged the task.

My father was what is called an oddity, and his treatment of me, though uniformly kind, flowed less from affection and tenderness than from a sense of obligation and duty. Indeed, I seldom even spoke to him except at meal-times, and then his manner was silent and abrupt; his leisure hours, which were many, were passed either in his study or in solitary walks; in short, he seemed to take no further interest in my happiness or improvement than a conscientious regard to the discharge of his own duty would seem to claim.

Shortly before my birth a circumstance had occurred which had contributed much to form and to confirm my father's secluded habits— it was the fact that a suspicion of *murder* had fallen upon his younger brother, though not sufficiently definite to lead to an indictment, yet strong enough to ruin him in public opinion.

This disgraceful and dreadful doubt cast upon the family name, my father felt deeply and bitterly, and not the less so that he himself was thoroughly convinced of his brother's innocence. The sincerity and strength of this impression he shortly afterwards proved in a manner which produced the dark events which follow. Before, however, I enter upon the statement of them, I ought to relate the circumstances which had awakened the suspicion; inasmuch as they are in themselves somewhat curious, and, in their effects, most intimately connected with my after-history.

My uncle, Sir Arthur T——n, was a gay and extravagant man, and, among other vices, was ruinously addicted to gaming; this unfortunate propensity, even after his fortune had suffered so severely as to render inevitable a reduction in his expenses by no means inconsiderable, nevertheless continued to actuate him, nearly to the exclusion of all other pursuits; he was, however, a proud, or rather a vain man, and could not bear to make the diminution of his income a matter of gratulation and triumph to those with whom he had hitherto competed, and the consequence was, that he frequented no longer the expensive haunts of dissipation, and retired from the gay world, leaving his coterie to discover his reasons as best they might.

He did not, however, forego his favourite vice, for, though he could not worship his great divinity in the costly temples where it was formerly his wont to take his stand, yet he found it very possible to bring about him a sufficient number of the votaries of chance to answer all his ends. The consequence was, that Carrickleigh, which was the name of my uncle's residence, was never without one or more of such visitors as I have described.

It happened that upon one occasion he was visited by one Hugh Tisdall, a gentleman of loose habits, but of considerable wealth, and who had, in early youth, travelled with my uncle upon the Continent;

the period of his visit was winter, and, consequently, the house was nearly deserted excepting by its regular inmates; it was therefore highly acceptable, particularly as my uncle was aware that his visitor's tastes accorded exactly with his own.

Both parties seemed determined to avail themselves of their suitability during the brief stay which Mr. Tisdall had promised; the consequence was, that they shut themselves up in Sir Arthur's private room for nearly all the day and the greater part of the night, during the space of nearly a week, at the end of which the servant having one morning, as usual, knocked at Mr. Tisdall's bedroom door repeatedly, received no answer, and, upon attempting to enter, found that it was locked; this appeared suspicious, and, the inmates of the house having been alarmed, the door was forced open, and, on proceeding to the bed, they found the body of its occupant perfectly lifeless, and hanging half-way out, the head downwards, and near the floor. One deep wound had been inflicted upon the temple, apparently with some blunt instrument which had penetrated the brain; and another blow, less effective, probably the first aimed, had grazed the head, removing some of the scalp, but leaving the skull untouched. The door had been double-locked upon the *inside*, in evidence of which the key still lay where it had been placed in the lock.

The window, though not secured on the interior, was closed—a circumstance not a little puzzling, as it afforded the only other mode of escape from the room; it looked out, too, upon a kind of courtyard, round which the old buildings stood, formerly accessible by a narrow doorway and passage lying in the oldest side of the quadrangle, but which had since been built up, so as to preclude all ingress or egress; the room was also upon the second story, and the height of the window considerable. Near the bed were found a pair of razors belonging to the murdered man, one of them upon the ground, and both of them open.

The weapon which had inflicted the mortal wound was not to be found in the room, nor were any footsteps or other traces of the murderer discoverable.

At the suggestion of Sir Arthur himself, a coroner was instantly summoned to attend, and an inquest was held; nothing, however, in any degree conclusive was elicited; the walls, ceiling, and floor of the room were carefully examined, in order to ascertain whether they contained a trapdoor or other concealed mode of entrance—but no such thing appeared.

Such was the minuteness of investigation employed, that, although the grate had contained a large fire during the night, they proceeded to examine even the very chimney, in order to discover whether escape by it were possible; but this attempt, too, was fruitless, for the chimney, built in the old fashion, rose in a perfectly perpendicular line from the hearth to a height of nearly fourteen feet above the roof, affording in its interior scarcely the possibility of ascent, the flue being smoothly plastered, and sloping towards the top like an inverted funnel, promising, too, even if the summit were attained, owing to its great height, but a precarious descent upon the sharp and steep-ridged roof; the ashes, too, which lay in the grate, and the soot, as far as it could be seen, were undisturbed, a circumstance almost conclusive of the question.

Sir Arthur was of course examined; his evidence was given with clearness and unreserve, which seemed calculated to silence all suspicion. He stated that, up to the day and night immediately preceding the catastrophe, he had lost to a heavy amount, but that, at their last sitting, he had not only won back his original loss, but upwards of four thousand pounds in addition; in evidence of which he produced an acknowledgment of debt to that amount in the handwriting of the deceased, and bearing the date of the fatal night. He had mentioned the circumstance to his lady, and in presence of some of the domestics; which statement was supported by *their* respective evidence.

One of the jury shrewdly observed, that the circumstance of Mr. Tisdall's having sustained so heavy a loss might have suggested to some ill-minded persons accidentally hearing it, the plan of robbing him, after having murdered him in such a manner as might make it appear that he had committed suicide; a supposition which was strongly supported by the razors having been found thus displaced, and removed from their case. Two persons had probably been engaged in the attempt, one watching by the sleeping man, and ready to strike him in case of his awakening suddenly, while the other was procuring the razors and employed in inflicting the fatal gash, so as to make it appear to have been the act of the murdered man himself. It was said that while the juror was making this suggestion Sir Arthur changed colour.

Nothing, however, like legal evidence appeared against him, and the consequence was that the verdict was found against a person or persons unknown; and for some time the matter was suffered to rest, until, after about five months, my father received a letter from a person signing himself Andrew Collis, and representing himself to be the cousin of the deceased. This letter stated that Sir Arthur was likely to incur not merely suspicion, but personal risk, unless he could account for certain circumstances connected with the recent murder, and contained a copy of a letter written by the deceased, and bearing date, the day of the week, and of the month, upon the night of which the deed of blood had been perpetrated. Tisdall's note ran as follows:

'Dear Collis,

'I have had sharp work with Sir Arthur; he tried some of his stale tricks, but soon found that *I* was Yorkshire too: it would not do—you understand me. We went to the work like good ones, head, heart and soul; and, in fact, since I came here, I have lost no time. I am rather fagged, but I am sure to be well paid for my hardship; I never want sleep so long as I can have the music of a dice-box, and wherewithal to pay the piper. As I told you, he tried some of his queer turns, but I foiled him like a man, and, in return, gave him more than he could relish of the genuine *dead knowledge*.

'In short, I have plucked the old baronet as never baronet was plucked before; I have scarce left him the stump of a quill; I have got promissory notes in his hand to the amount of—if you like round numbers, say, thirty thousand pounds, safely deposited in my portable strongbox, alias double-clasped pocket-book. I leave this ruinous old rat-hole early on to-morrow, for two reasons—first, I do not want to play with Sir Arthur deeper than I think his security, that is, his money, or his money's worth, would warrant; and, secondly, because I am safer a hundred miles from Sir Arthur than in the house with him. Look you, my worthy, I tell you this between ourselves—I may be wrong, but, by G——, I am as sure as that I am now living, that Sir A—— attempted to poison me last night; so much for old friendship on both sides.

'When I won the last stake, a heavy one enough, my friend leant his forehead upon his hands, and you'll laugh when I tell you that his head literally smoked like a hot dumpling. I do not know whether his agitation was produced by the plan which he had against me, or by his having lost so heavily—though it must be allowed that he had reason to be a little funked, whichever way his thoughts went; but he pulled the bell, and ordered two bottles of champagne. While the fellow was bringing them he drew out a promissory note to the full amount, which he signed, and, as the man came in with the bottles and glasses, he desired him to be off; he filled out a glass for me, and, while he thought my eyes were off, for I was putting up his note at the time, he dropped something slyly into it, no doubt to sweeten it; but I saw it all, and, when he handed it to me, I said, with an emphasis which he might or might not understand:

"'There is some sediment in this; I'll not drink it.'

"'Is there?' said he, and at the same time snatched it from my hand and threw it into the fire. What do you think of that? have I not a tender chicken to manage? Win or lose, I will not play beyond five thousand to-night, and to-morrow sees me safe out of the reach of Sir Arthur's champagne. So, all things considered, I think you must allow that you are not the last who have found a knowing boy in

'Yours to command,

'Hugh Tisdall.'

Of the authenticity of this document I never heard my father express a doubt; and I am satisfied that, owing to his strong conviction in favour of his brother, he would not have admitted it without sufficient inquiry, inasmuch as it tended to confirm the suspicions which already existed to his prejudice.

Now, the only point in this letter which made strongly against my uncle, was the mention of the 'double-clasped pocket-book' as the receptacle of the papers likely to involve him, for this pocket-book was not forthcoming, nor anywhere to be found, nor had any papers referring to his gaming transactions been found upon the dead man. However, whatever might have been the original intention of this Collis, neither my uncle nor my father ever heard more of him; but he published the letter in Faulkner's newspaper, which was shortly afterwards made the vehicle of a much more mysterious attack. The passage in that periodical to which I allude, occurred about four years afterwards, and while the fatal occurrence was still fresh in public recollection. It commenced by a rambling preface, stating that 'a *certain person* whom *certain* persons thought to be dead, was not so, but living, and in full possession of his memory, and moreover ready and able to make *great* delinquents tremble.' It then went on to describe the murder, without, however, mentioning names; and in doing so, it entered into minute and circumstantial particulars of which none but an *eye-witness* could have been possessed, and by implications almost too unequivocal to be regarded in the light of insinuation, to involve the '*titled gamble*' in the guilt of the transaction.

My father at once urged Sir Arthur to proceed against the paper in an action of libel; but he would not hear of it, nor consent to my father's taking any legal steps whatever in the matter. My father, however, wrote in a threatening tone to Faulkner, demanding a surrender of the author of the obnoxious article. The answer to this application is still in my possession, and is penned in an apologetic tone: it states that the manuscript had been handed in, paid for, and inserted as an advertisement, without sufficient inquiry, or any knowledge as to whom it referred.

No step, however, was taken to clear my uncle's character in the judgment of the public; and as he immediately sold a small property, the application of the proceeds of which was known to none, he was said to have disposed of it to enable himself to buy off the threatened information. However the truth might have been, it is certain that no charges respecting the mysterious murder were afterwards publicly made against my uncle, and, as far as external disturbances were concerned, he enjoyed henceforward perfect security and quiet.

A deep and lasting impression, however, had been made upon the public mind, and Sir Arthur T——n was no longer visited or noticed by the gentry and aristocracy of the county, whose attention and courtesies he had hitherto received. He accordingly affected to despise these enjoyments which he could not procure, and shunned even that society which he might have commanded.

This is all that I need recapitulate of my uncle's history, and I now recur to my own. Although my father had never, within my recollection, visited, or been visited by, my uncle, each being of sedentary, procrastinating, and secluded habits, and their respective residences being very far apart—the one lying in the county of Galway, the other in that of Cork—he was strongly attached to his brother, and evinced his affection by an active correspondence, and by deeply and proudly resenting that neglect which had marked Sir Arthur as unfit to mix in society.

When I was about eighteen years of age, my father, whose health had been gradually declining, died, leaving me in heart wretched and desolate, and, owing to his previous seclusion, with few acquaintances, and almost no friends.

The provisions of his will were curious, and when I had sufficiently come to myself to listen to or comprehend them, surprised me not a little: all his vast property was left to me, and to the heirs of my body, for ever; and, in default of such heirs, it was to go after my death to my uncle, Sir Arthur, without any entail.

At the same time, the will appointed him my guardian, desiring that I might be received within his house, and reside with his family, and under his care, during the term of my minority; and in consideration of the increased expense consequent upon such an arrangement, a handsome annuity was allotted to him during the term of my proposed residence.

The object of this last provision I at once understood: my father desired, by making it the direct, apparent interest of Sir Arthur that I should die without issue, while at the same time he placed me wholly in his power, to prove to the world how great and unshaken was his confidence in his brother's innocence and honour, and also to afford him an opportunity of showing that this mark of confidence was not unworthily bestowed.

It was a strange, perhaps an idle scheme; but as I had been always brought up in the habit of considering my uncle as a deeply-injured man, and had been taught, almost as a part of my religion, to regard him as the very soul of honour, I felt no further uneasiness respecting the arrangement than that likely to result to a timid girl, of secluded habits, from the immediate prospect of taking up her abode for the first time in her life among total strangers. Previous to leaving my home, which I felt I should do with a heavy heart, I received a most tender and affectionate letter from my uncle, calculated, if anything could do so, to remove the bitterness of parting from scenes familiar and dear from my earliest childhood, and in some degree to reconcile me to the measure.

It was during a fine autumn that I approached the old domain of Carrickleigh. I shall not soon forget the impression of sadness and of gloom which all that I saw produced upon my mind; the sunbeams were falling with a rich and melancholy tint upon the fine old trees, which stood in lordly groups, casting their long, sweeping shadows over rock and sward. There was an air of neglect and decay about the spot, which amounted almost to desolation; the symptoms of this increased in number as we approached the building itself, near which the ground had been originally more artificially and carefully cultivated than elsewhere, and whose neglect consequently more immediately and strikingly betrayed itself.

As we proceeded, the road wound near the beds of what had been formally two fish-ponds, which were now nothing more than stagnant swamps, overgrown with rank weeds, and here and there encroached upon by the straggling underwood; the avenue itself was much broken, and in many places the stones were almost concealed by grass and nettles; the loose stone walls which had here and there intersected the broad park were, in many places, broken down, so as no longer to answer their original purpose as fences; piers were now and then to be seen, but the gates were gone; and, to add to the general air of dilapidation, some huge trunks were lying scattered through the venerable old trees, either the work of the winter storms, or perhaps the victims of some extensive but desultory scheme of denudation, which the projector had not capital or perseverance to carry into full effect.

After the carriage had travelled a mile of this avenue, we reached the summit of rather an abrupt eminence, one of the many which added to the picturesqueness, if not to the convenience of this rude passage. From the top of this ridge the grey walls of Carrickleigh were visible, rising at a small distance in front, and darkened by the hoary wood which crowded around them. It was a quadrangular building of considerable extent, and the front which lay towards us, and in which the great entrance was placed, bore unequivocal marks of antiquity; the time-worn, solemn aspect of the old building, the ruinous and deserted appearance of the whole place, and the associations which connected it with a dark page in the history of my family, combined to depress spirits already predisposed for the reception of sombre and dejecting impressions.

When the carriage drew up in the grass-grown court yard before the hall-door, two lazy-looking men, whose appearance well accorded with that of the place which they tenanted, alarmed by the obstreperous barking of a great chained dog, ran out from some half-ruinous out-houses, and took charge of the horses; the hall-door stood open, and I entered a gloomy and imperfectly lighted apartment, and found no one within. However, I had not long to wait in this awkward predicament, for before my luggage had been deposited in the house, indeed, before I had well removed my cloak and other wraps, so as to enable me to look around, a young girl ran lightly into the hall, and kissing me heartily, and somewhat boisterously, exclaimed:

'My dear cousin, my dear Margaret—I am so delighted—so out of breath. We did not expect you till ten o'clock; my father is somewhere about the place, he must be close at hand. James—Corney—run out and tell your master—my brother is seldom at home, at least at any reasonable hour—you must be so tired—so fatigued—let me show you to your room—see that Lady Margaret's luggage is all brought up—you must lie down and rest yourself—Deborah, bring some coffee—up these stairs; we are so delighted to see you—you cannot think how lonely I have been—how steep these stairs are, are not they? I am so glad you are come—I could hardly bring myself to believe that you were really coming—how good of you, dear Lady Margaret.'

There was real good-nature and delight in my cousin's greeting, and a kind of constitutional confidence of manner which placed me at once at ease, and made me feel immediately upon terms of intimacy with her. The room into which she ushered me, although partaking in the general air of decay which pervaded the mansion and all about it, had nevertheless been fitted up with evident attention to comfort, and even with some dingy attempt at luxury; but what pleased me most was that it opened, by a second door, upon a lobby which communicated with my fair cousin's apartment; a circumstance which divested the room, in my eyes, of the air of solitude and sadness which would otherwise have characterised it, to a degree almost painful to one so dejected in spirits as I was.

After such arrangements as I found necessary were completed, we both went down to the parlour, a large wainscoted room, hung round with grim old portraits, and, as I was not sorry to see, containing in its ample grate a large and cheerful fire. Here my cousin had leisure to talk more at her ease; and from her I learned something of the manners and the habits of the two remaining members of her family, whom I had not yet seen.

On my arrival I had known nothing of the family among whom I was come to reside, except that it consisted of three individuals, my uncle, and his son and daughter, Lady T——n having been long dead. In addition to this very scanty stock of information, I shortly learned from my communicative companion that my uncle was, as I had suspected, completely retired in his habits, and besides that, having been so far back as she could well recollect, always rather strict, as reformed rakes frequently become, he had latterly been growing more gloomily and sternly religious than heretofore.

Her account of her brother was far less favourable, though she did not say anything directly to his disadvantage. From all that I could gather from her, I was led to suppose that he was a specimen of the idle, coarse-mannered, profligate, low-minded *'squirearchy'*—a result which might naturally have flowed from the circumstance of his being, as it were, outlawed from society, and driven for companionship to grades below his own—enjoying, too, the dangerous prerogative of spending much money.

However, you may easily suppose that I found nothing in my cousin's communication fully to bear me out in so very decided a conclusion.

I awaited the arrival of my uncle, which was every moment to be expected, with feelings half of alarm, half of curiosity—a sensation which I have often since experienced, though to a less degree, when upon the point of standing for the first time in the presence of one of whom I have long been in the habit of hearing or thinking with interest.

It was, therefore, with some little perturbation that I heard, first a slight bustle at the outer door, then a slow step traverse the hall, and finally witnessed the door open, and my uncle enter the room. He was a striking-looking man; from peculiarities both of person and of garb, the whole effect of his appearance amounted to extreme singularity. He was tall, and when young his figure must have been strikingly elegant; as it was, however, its effect was marred by a very decided stoop. His dress was of a sober colour, and in fashion anterior to anything which I could remember. It was, however, handsome, and by no means carelessly put on; but what completed the singularity of his appearance was his uncut, white hair, which hung in long, but not at all neglected curls, even so far as his shoulders, and which combined with his regularly classic features, and fine dark eyes, to bestow upon him an air of venerable dignity and pride, which I have never seen equalled elsewhere. I rose as he entered, and met him about the middle of the room; he kissed my cheek and both my hands, saying:

'You are most welcome, dear child, as welcome as the command of this poor place and all that it contains can make you. I am most rejoiced to see you—truly rejoiced. I trust that you are not much fatigued—pray be seated again.' He led me to my chair, and continued: 'I am glad to perceive you have made acquaintance with Emily already; I see, in your being thus brought together, the foundation of a lasting friendship. You are both innocent, and both young. God bless you— God bless you, and make you all that I could wish.'

He raised his eyes, and remained for a few moments silent, as if in secret prayer. I felt that it was impossible that this man, with feelings so quick, so warm, so tender, could be the wretch that public opinion had represented him to be. I was more than ever convinced of his innocence.

His manner was, or appeared to me, most fascinating; there was a mingled kindness and courtesy in it which seemed to speak benevolence itself. It was a manner which I felt cold art could never have taught; it owed most of its charm to its appearing to emanate directly from the heart; it must be a genuine index of the owner's mind. So I thought.

My uncle having given me fully to understand that I was most welcome, and might command whatever was his own, pressed me to take some refreshment; and on my refusing, he observed that previously to bidding me good-night, he had one duty further to perform, one in whose observance he was convinced I would cheerfully acquiesce.

He then proceeded to read a chapter from the Bible; after which he took his leave with the same affectionate kindness with which he had greeted me, having repeated his desire that I should consider everything in his house as altogether at my disposal. It is needless to say that I was much pleased with my uncle—it was impossible to avoid being so; and I could not help saying to myself, if such a man as this is not safe from the assaults of slander, who is? I felt much happier than I had done since my father's death, and enjoyed that night the first refreshing sleep which had visited me since that event.

My curiosity respecting my male cousin did not long remain unsatisfied—he appeared the next day at dinner. His manners, though not so coarse as I had expected, were exceedingly disagreeable; there was an assurance and a forwardness for which I was not prepared; there was less of the vulgarity of manner, and almost more of that of the mind, than I had anticipated. I felt quite uncomfortable in his presence; there was just that confidence in his look and tone which would read encouragement even in mere toleration; and I felt more disgusted and annoyed at the coarse and extravagant compliments which he was pleased from time to time to pay me, than perhaps the extent of the atrocity might fully have warranted. It was, however, one consolation that he did not often appear, being much engrossed by pursuits about which I neither knew nor cared anything; but when he did appear, his attentions, either with a view to his amusement or to some more serious advantage, were so obviously and perseveringly directed to me, that young and inexperienced as I was, even *I* could not be ignorant of his preference. I felt more provoked by this odious persecution than I can express, and discouraged him with so much vigour, that I employed even rudeness to convince him that his assiduities were unwelcome; but all in vain.

This had gone on for nearly a twelvemonth, to my infinite annoyance, when one day as I was sitting at some needlework with my companion Emily, as was my habit, in the parlour, the door opened, and my cousin Edward entered the room. There was something, I thought, odd in his manner—a kind of struggle between shame and impudence—a kind of flurry and ambiguity which made him appear, if possible, more than ordinarily disagreeable.

'Your servant, ladies,' he said, seating himself at the same time; 'sorry to spoil your *tête-à-tête*, but never mind, I'll only take Emily's place for a minute or two; and then we part for a while, fair cousin. Emily, my father wants you in the corner turret. No shilly-shally; he's in a hurry.' She hesitated. 'Be off—tramp, march!' he exclaimed, in a tone which the poor girl dared not disobey.

She left the room, and Edward followed her to the door. He stood there for a minute or two, as if reflecting what he should say, perhaps satisfying himself that no one was within hearing in the hall.

At length he turned about, having closed the door, as if carelessly, with his foot; and advancing slowly, as if in deep thought, he took his seat at the side of the table opposite to mine.

There was a brief interval of silence, after which he said:

'I imagine that you have a shrewd suspicion of the object of my early visit; but I suppose I must go into particulars. Must I?'

'I have no conception,' I replied, 'what your object may be.'

'Well, well,' said he, becoming more at his ease as he proceeded, 'it may be told in a few words. You know that it is totally impossible—quite out of the question—that an offhand young fellow like me, and a good-looking girl like yourself, could meet continually, as you and I have done, without an attachment—a liking growing up on one side or other; in short, I think I have let you know as plain as if I spoke it, that I have been in love with you almost from the first time I saw you.'

He paused; but I was too much horrified to speak. He interpreted my silence favourably.

'I can tell you,' he continued, 'I'm reckoned rather hard to please, and very hard to *hit*. I can't say when I was taken with a girl before; so you see fortune reserved me—'

Here the odious wretch wound his arm round my waist. The action at once restored me to utterance, and with the most indignant vehemence I released myself from his hold, and at the same time said:

'I have not been insensible, sir, of your most disagreeable attentions—they have long been a source of much annoyance to me; and you must be aware that I have marked my disapprobation—my disgust—as unequivocally as I possibly could, without actual indelicacy.'

I paused, almost out of breath from the rapidity with which I had spoken; and without giving him time to renew the conversation, I hastily quitted the room, leaving him in a paroxysm of rage and mortification. As I ascended the stairs, I heard him open the parlour-door with violence, and take two or three rapid strides in the direction in which I was moving. I was now much frightened, and ran the whole way until I reached my room; and having locked the door, I listened breathlessly, but heard no sound. This relieved me for the present; but so much had I been overcome by the agitation and annoyance attendant upon the scene which I had just gone through, that when my cousin Emily knocked at my door, I was weeping in strong hysterics.

You will readily conceive my distress, when you reflect upon my strong dislike to my cousin Edward, combined with my youth and extreme inexperience. Any proposal of such a nature must have agitated me; but that it should have come from the man whom of all others I most loathed and abhorred, and to whom I had, as clearly as manner could do it, expressed the state of my feelings, was almost too overwhelming to be borne. It was a calamity, too, in which I could not claim the sympathy of my cousin Emily, which had always been extended to me in my minor grievances. Still I hoped that it might not be unattended with good; for I thought that one inevitable and most welcome consequence would result from this painful *eclaircissement*, in the discontinuance of my cousin's odious persecution.

When I arose next morning, it was with the fervent hope that I might never again behold the face, or even hear the name, of my cousin Edward; but such a consummation, though devoutly to be wished, was hardly likely to occur. The painful impressions of yesterday were too vivid to be at once erased; and I could not help feeling some dim foreboding of coming annoyance and evil.

To expect on my cousin's part anything like delicacy or consideration for me, was out of the question. I saw that he had set his heart upon my property, and that he was not likely easily to forego such an acquisition—possessing what might have been considered opportunities and facilities almost to compel my compliance.

I now keenly felt the unreasonableness of my father's conduct in placing me to reside with a family of all whose members, with one exception, he was wholly ignorant, and I bitterly felt the helplessness of my situation. I determined, however, in case of my cousin's persevering in his addresses, to lay all the particulars before my uncle, although he had never in kindness or intimacy gone a step beyond our first interview, and to throw myself upon his hospitality and his sense of honour for protection against a repetition of such scenes.

My cousin's conduct may appear to have been an inadequate cause for such serious uneasiness; but my alarm was caused neither by his acts nor words, but entirely by his manner, which was strange and even intimidating to excess. At the beginning of the yesterday's interview there was a sort of bullying swagger in his air, which towards the end gave place to the brutal vehemence of an undisguised ruffian—a transition which had tempted me into a belief that he might seek even forcibly to extort from me a consent to his wishes, or by means still more horrible, of which I scarcely dared to trust myself to think, to possess himself of my property.

I was early next day summoned to attend my uncle in his private room, which lay in a corner turret of the old building; and thither I accordingly went, wondering all the way what this unusual measure might prelude. When I entered the room, he did not rise in his usual courteous way to greet me, but simply pointed to a chair opposite to his own. This boded nothing agreeable. I sat down, however, silently waiting until he should open the conversation.

'Lady Margaret,' at length he said, in a tone of greater sternness than I thought him capable of using, 'I have hitherto spoken to you as a friend, but I have not forgotten that I am also your guardian, and that my authority as such gives me a right to control your conduct. I shall put a question to you, and I expect and will demand a plain, direct answer. Have I rightly been informed that you have contemptuously rejected the suit and hand of my son Edward?'

I stammered forth with a good deal of trepidation:

'I believe—that is, I have, sir, rejected my cousin's proposals; and my coldness and discouragement might have convinced him that I had determined to do so.'

'Madam,' replied he, with suppressed, but, as it appeared to me, intense anger, 'I have lived long enough to know that *coldness* and discouragement, and such terms, form the common cant of a worthless coquette. You know to the full, as well as I, that *coldness and discouragement* may be so exhibited as to convince their object that he is neither distasteful or indifferent to the person who wears this manner. You know, too, none better, that an affected neglect, when skilfully managed, is amongst the most formidable of the engines which artful beauty can employ. I tell you, madam, that having, without one word spoken in discouragement, permitted my son's most marked attentions for a twelvemonth or more, you have no right to dismiss him with no further explanation than demurely telling him that you had always looked coldly upon him; and neither your wealth nor your *ladyship*' (there was an emphasis of scorn on the word, which would have become Sir Giles Overreach himself) 'can warrant you in treating with contempt the affectionate regard of an honest heart.'

I was too much shocked at this undisguised attempt to bully me into an acquiescence in the interested and unprincipled plan for their own aggrandisement, which I now perceived my uncle and his son to have deliberately entered into, at once to find strength or collectedness to frame an answer to what he had said. At length I replied, with some firmness:

'In all that you have just now said, sir, you have grossly misstated my conduct and motives. Your information must have been most incorrect as far as it regards my conduct towards my cousin; my manner towards him could have conveyed nothing but dislike; and if anything could have added to the strong aversion which I have long felt towards him, it would be his attempting thus to trick and frighten me into a marriage which he knows to be revolting to me, and which is sought by him only as a means for securing to himself whatever property is mine.'

As I said this, I fixed my eyes upon those of my uncle, but he was too old in the world's ways to falter beneath the gaze of more searching eyes than mine; he simply said:

'Are you acquainted with the provisions of your father's will?'

I answered in the affirmative; and he continued:

'Then you must be aware that if my son Edward were—which God forbid—the unprincipled, reckless man you pretend to think him'—(here he spoke very slowly, as if he intended that every word which escaped him should be registered in my memory, while at the same time the expression of his countenance underwent a gradual but horrible change, and the eyes which he fixed upon me became so darkly vivid, that I almost lost sight of everything else)—'if he were what you have described him, think you, girl, he could find no briefer means than wedding contracts to gain his ends? 'twas but to gripe your slender neck until the breath had stopped, and lands, and lakes, and all were his.'

I stood staring at him for many minutes after he had ceased to speak, fascinated by the terrible serpent-like gaze, until he continued with a welcome change of countenance:

'I will not speak again to you upon this topic until one month has passed. You shall have time to consider the relative advantages of the two courses which are open to you. I should be sorry to hurry you to a decision. I am satisfied with having stated my feelings upon the subject, and pointed out to you the path of duty. Remember this day month— not one word sooner.'

He then rose, and I left the room, much agitated and exhausted.

This interview, all the circumstances attending it, but most particularly the formidable expression of my uncle's countenance while he talked, though hypothetically, of *murder*, combined to arouse all my worst suspicions of him. I dreaded to look upon the face that had so recently worn the appalling livery of guilt and malignity. I regarded it with the mingled fear and loathing with which one looks upon an object which has tortured them in a nightmare.

In a few days after the interview, the particulars of which I have just related, I found a note upon my toilet-table, and on opening it I read as follows:

'My dear Lady Margaret,

'You will be perhaps surprised to see a strange face in your room to-day. I have dismissed your Irish maid, and secured a French one to wait upon you—a step rendered necessary by my proposing shortly to visit the Continent, with all my family.

'Your faithful guardian,

'Arthur T——n.'

On inquiry, I found that my faithful attendant was actually gone, and far on her way to the town of Galway; and in her stead there appeared a tall, raw-boned, ill-looking, elderly Frenchwoman, whose sullen and presuming manners seemed to imply that her vocation had never before been that of a lady's-maid. I could not help regarding her as a creature of my uncle's, and therefore to be dreaded, even had she been in no other way suspicious.

Days and weeks passed away without any, even a momentary doubt upon my part, as to the course to be pursued by me. The allotted period had at length elapsed; the day arrived on which I was to communicate my decision to my uncle. Although my resolution had never for a moment wavered, I could not shake off the dread of the approaching colloquy; and my heart sunk within me as I heard the expected summons.

I had not seen my cousin Edward since the occurrence of the grand *eclaircissement*; he must have studiously avoided me—I suppose from policy, it could not have been from delicacy. I was prepared for a terrific burst of fury from my uncle, as soon as I should make known my determination; and I not unreasonably feared that some act of violence or of intimidation would next be resorted to.

Filled with these dreary forebodings, I fearfully opened the study door, and the next minute I stood in my uncle's presence. He received me with a politeness which I dreaded, as arguing a favourable anticipation respecting the answer which I was to give; and after some slight delay, he began by saying:

'It will be a relief to both of us, I believe, to bring this conversation as soon as possible to an issue. You will excuse me, then, my dear niece, for speaking with an abruptness which, under other circumstances, would be unpardonable. You have, I am certain, given the subject of our last interview fair and serious consideration; and I trust that you are now prepared with candour to lay your answer before me. A few words will suffice—we perfectly understand one another.'

He paused, and I, though feeling that I stood upon a mine which might in an instant explode, nevertheless answered with perfect composure:

'I must now, sir, make the same reply which I did upon the last occasion, and I reiterate the declaration which I then made, that I never can nor will, while life and reason remain, consent to a union with my cousin Edward.'

This announcement wrought no apparent change in Sir Arthur, except that he became deadly, almost lividly pale. He seemed lost in dark thought for a minute, and then with a slight effort said:

'You have answered me honestly and directly; and you say your resolution is unchangeable. Well, would it had been otherwise—would it had been otherwise—but be it as it is—I am satisfied.'

He gave me his hand—it was cold and damp as death; under an assumed calmness, it was evident that he was fearfully agitated. He continued to hold my hand with an almost painful pressure, while, as if unconsciously, seeming to forget my presence, he muttered:

'Strange, strange, strange, indeed! fatuity, helpless fatuity!' there was here a long pause. 'Madness *indeed* to strain a cable that is rotten to the very heart—it must break—and then—all goes.'

There was again a pause of some minutes, after which, suddenly changing his voice and manner to one of wakeful alacrity, he exclaimed:

'Margaret, my son Edward shall plague you no more. He leaves this country on to-morrow for France—he shall speak no more upon this subject—never, never more—whatever events depended upon your answer must now take their own course; but, as for this fruitless proposal, it has been tried enough; it can be repeated no more.'

At these words he coldly suffered my hand to drop, as if to express his total abandonment of all his projected schemes of alliance; and certainly the action, with the accompanying words, produced upon my mind a more solemn and depressing effect than I believed possible to have been caused by the course which I had determined to pursue; it struck upon my heart with an awe and heaviness which *will* accompany the accomplishment of an important and irrevocable act, even though no doubt or scruple remains to make it possible that the agent should wish it undone.

'Well,' said my uncle, after a little time, 'we now cease to speak upon this topic, never to resume it again. Remember you shall have no farther uneasiness from Edward; he leaves Ireland for France on to-morrow; this will be a relief to you. May I depend upon your *honour* that no word touching the subject of this interview shall ever escape you?'

I gave him the desired assurance; he said:

'It is well—I am satisfied—we have nothing more, I believe, to say upon either side, and my presence must be a restraint upon you, I shall therefore bid you farewell.'

I then left the apartment, scarcely knowing what to think of the strange interview which had just taken place.

On the next day my uncle took occasion to tell me that Edward had actually sailed, if his intention had not been interfered with by adverse circumstances; and two days subsequently he actually produced a letter from his son, written, as it said, *on board*, and despatched while the ship was getting under weigh. This was a great satisfaction to me, and as being likely to prove so, it was no doubt communicated to me by Sir Arthur.

During all this trying period, I had found infinite consolation in the society and sympathy of my dear cousin Emily. I never in after-life formed a friendship so close, so fervent, and upon which, in all its progress, I could look back with feelings of such unalloyed pleasure, upon whose termination I must ever dwell with so deep, yet so unembittered regret. In cheerful converse with her I soon recovered my spirits considerably, and passed my time agreeably enough, although still in the strictest seclusion.

Matters went on sufficiently smooth, although I could not help sometimes feeling a momentary, but horrible uncertainty respecting my uncle's character; which was not altogether unwarranted by the circumstances of the two trying interviews whose particulars I have just detailed. The unpleasant impression which these conferences were calculated to leave upon my mind, was fast wearing away, when there occurred a circumstance, slight indeed in itself, but calculated irresistibly to awaken all my worst suspicions, and to overwhelm me again with anxiety and terror.

I had one day left the house with my cousin Emily, in order to take a ramble of considerable length, for the purpose of sketching some favourite views, and we had walked about half a mile when I perceived that we had forgotten our drawing materials, the absence of which would have defeated the object of our walk. Laughing at our own thoughtlessness, we returned to the house, and leaving Emily without, I ran upstairs to procure the drawing-books and pencils, which lay in my bedroom.

As I ran up the stairs I was met by the tall, ill-looking Frenchwoman, evidently a good deal flurried.

'Que veut, madame?' said she, with a more decided effort to be polite than I had ever known her make before.

'No, no—no matter,' said I, hastily running by her in the direction of my room.

'Madame,' cried she, in a high key, 'restez ici, s'il vous plait; votre chambre n'est pas faite—your room is not ready for your reception yet.'

I continued to move on without heeding her. She was some way behind me, and feeling that she could not otherwise prevent my entrance, for I was now upon the very lobby, she made a desperate attempt to seize hold of my person: she succeeded in grasping the end of my shawl, which she drew from my shoulders; but slipping at the same time upon the polished oak floor, she fell at full length upon the boards.

A little frightened as well as angry at the rudeness of this strange woman, I hastily pushed open the door of my room, at which I now stood, in order to escape from her; but great was my amazement on entering to find the apartment preoccupied.

The window was open, and beside it stood two male figures; they appeared to be examining the fastenings of the casement, and their backs were turned towards the door. One of them was my uncle; they both turned on my entrance, as if startled. The stranger was booted and cloaked, and wore a heavy broad-leafed hat over his brows. He turned but for a moment, and averted his face; but I had seen enough to convince me that he was no other than my cousin Edward. My uncle had some iron instrument in his hand, which he hastily concealed behind his back; and coming towards me, said something as if in an explanatory tone; but I was too much shocked and confounded to understand what it might be. He said something about '*repairs—window-frames—cold, and safety.*'

I did not wait, however, to ask or to receive explanations, but hastily left the room. As I went down the stairs I thought I heard the voice of the Frenchwoman in all the shrill volubility of excuse, which was met, however, by suppressed but vehement imprecations, or what seemed to me to be such, in which the voice of my cousin Edward distinctly mingled.

I joined my cousin Emily quite out of breath. I need not say that my head was too full of other things to think much of drawing for that day. I imparted to her frankly the cause of my alarms, but at the same time as gently as I could; and with tears she promised vigilance, and devotion, and love. I never had reason for a moment to repent the unreserved confidence which I then reposed in her. She was no less surprised than I at the unexpected appearance of Edward, whose departure for France neither of us had for a moment doubted, but which was now proved by his actual presence to be nothing more than an imposture, practised, I feared, for no good end.

The situation in which I had found my uncle had removed completely all my doubts as to his designs. I magnified suspicions into certainties, and dreaded night after night that I should be murdered in my bed. The nervousness produced by sleepless nights and days of anxious fears increased the horrors of my situation to such a degree, that I at length wrote a letter to a Mr. Jefferies, an old and faithful friend of my father's, and perfectly acquainted with all his affairs, praying him, for God's sake, to relieve me from my present terrible situation, and communicating without reserve the nature and grounds of my suspicions.

This letter I kept sealed and directed for two or three days always about my person, for discovery would have been ruinous, in expectation of an opportunity which might be safely trusted, whereby to have it placed in the post-office. As neither Emily nor I were permitted to pass beyond the precincts of the demesne itself, which was surrounded by high walls formed of dry stone, the difficulty of procuring such an opportunity was greatly enhanced.

At this time Emily had a short conversation with her father, which she reported to me instantly.

After some indifferent matter, he had asked her whether she and I were upon good terms, and whether I was unreserved in my disposition. She answered in the affirmative; and he then inquired whether I had been much surprised to find him in my chamber on the other day. She answered that I had been both surprised and amused.

'And what did she think of George Wilson's appearance?'

'Who?' inquired she.

'Oh, the architect,' he answered, 'who is to contract for the repairs of the house; he is accounted a handsome fellow.'

'She could not see his face,' said Emily, 'and she was in such a hurry to escape that she scarcely noticed him.'

Sir Arthur appeared satisfied, and the conversation ended.

This slight conversation, repeated accurately to me by Emily, had the effect of confirming, if indeed anything was required to do so, all that I had before believed as to Edward's actual presence; and I naturally became, if possible, more anxious than ever to despatch the letter to Mr. Jefferies. An opportunity at length occurred.

As Emily and I were walking one day near the gate of the demesne, a lad from the village happened to be passing down the avenue from the house; the spot was secluded, and as this person was not connected by service with those whose observation I dreaded, I committed the letter to his keeping, with strict injunctions that he should put it without delay into the receiver of the town post-office; at the same time I added a suitable gratuity, and the man having made many protestations of punctuality, was soon out of sight.

He was hardly gone when I began to doubt my discretion in having trusted this person; but I had no better or safer means of despatching the letter, and I was not warranted in suspecting him of such wanton dishonesty as an inclination to tamper with it; but I could not be quite satisfied of its safety until I had received an answer, which could not arrive for a few days. Before I did, however, an event occurred which a little surprised me.

I was sitting in my bedroom early in the day, reading by myself, when I heard a knock at the door.

'Come in,' said I; and my uncle entered the room.

'Will you excuse me?' said he. 'I sought you in the parlour, and thence I have come here. I desired to say a word with you. I trust that you have hitherto found my conduct to you such as that of a guardian towards his ward should be.'

I dared not withhold my consent.

'And,' he continued, 'I trust that you have not found me harsh or unjust, and that you have perceived, my dear niece, that I have sought to make this poor place as agreeable to you as may be.'

I assented again; and he put his hand in his pocket, whence he drew a folded paper, and dashing it upon the table with startling emphasis, he said:

'Did you write that letter?'

The sudden and fearful alteration of his voice, manner, and face, but, more than all, the unexpected production of my letter to Mr. Jefferies, which I at once recognised, so confounded and terrified me, that I felt almost choking.

I could not utter a word.

'Did you write that letter?' he repeated with slow and intense emphasis. 'You did, liar and hypocrite! You dared to write this foul and infamous libel; but it shall be your last. Men will universally believe you mad, if I choose to call for an inquiry. I can make you appear so. The suspicions expressed in this letter are the hallucinations and alarms of moping lunacy. I have defeated your first attempt, madam; and by the holy God, if ever you make another, chains, straw, darkness, and the keeper's whip shall be your lasting portion!'

With these astounding words he left the room, leaving me almost fainting.

I was now almost reduced to despair; my last cast had failed; I had no course left but that of eloping secretly from the castle, and placing myself under the protection of the nearest magistrate. I felt if this were not done, and speedily, that I should be *murdered*.

No one, from mere description, can have an idea of the unmitigated horror of my situation—a helpless, weak, inexperienced girl, placed under the power and wholly at the mercy of evil men, and feeling that she had it not in her power to escape for a moment from the malignant influences under which she was probably fated to fall; and with a consciousness that if violence, if murder were designed, her dying shriek would be lost in void space; no human being would be near to aid her, no human interposition could deliver her.

I had seen Edward but once during his visit, and as I did not meet with him again, I began to think that he must have taken his departure—a conviction which was to a certain degree satisfactory, as I regarded his absence as indicating the removal of immediate danger.

Emily also arrived circuitously at the same conclusion, and not without good grounds, for she managed indirectly to learn that Edward's black horse had actually been for a day and part of a night in the castle stables, just at the time of her brother's supposed visit. The horse had gone, and, as she argued, the rider must have departed with it.

This point being so far settled, I felt a little less uncomfortable: when being one day alone in my bedroom, I happened to look out from the window, and, to my unutterable horror, I beheld, peering through an opposite casement, my cousin Edward's face. Had I seen the evil one himself in bodily shape, I could not have experienced a more sickening revulsion.

I was too much appalled to move at once from the window, but I did so soon enough to avoid his eye. He was looking fixedly into the narrow quadrangle upon which the window opened. I shrank back unperceived, to pass the rest of the day in terror and despair. I went to my room early that night, but I was too miserable to sleep.

At about twelve o'clock, feeling very nervous, I determined to call my cousin Emily, who slept, you will remember, in the next room, which communicated with mine by a second door. By this private entrance I found my way into her chamber, and without difficulty persuaded her to return to my room and sleep with me. We accordingly lay down together, she undressed, and I with my clothes on, for I was every moment walking up and down the room, and felt too nervous and miserable to think of rest or comfort.

Emily was soon fast asleep, and I lay awake, fervently longing for the first pale gleam of morning, reckoning every stroke of the old clock with an impatience which made every hour appear like six.

It must have been about one o'clock when I thought I heard a slight noise at the partition-door between Emily's room and mine, as if caused by somebody's turning the key in the lock. I held my breath, and the same sound was repeated at the second door of my room—that which opened upon the lobby—the sound was here distinctly caused by the revolution of the bolt in the lock, and it was followed by a slight pressure upon the door itself, as if to ascertain the security of the lock.

The person, whoever it might be, was probably satisfied, for I heard the old boards of the lobby creak and strain, as if under the weight of somebody moving cautiously over them. My sense of hearing became unnaturally, almost painfully acute. I suppose the imagination added distinctness to sounds vague in themselves. I thought that I could actually hear the breathing of the person who was slowly returning down the lobby. At the head of the staircase there appeared to occur a pause; and I could distinctly hear two or three sentences hastily whispered; the steps then descended the stairs with apparently less caution. I now ventured to walk quickly and lightly to the lobby-door, and attempted to open it; it was indeed fast locked upon the outside, as was also the other.

I now felt that the dreadful hour was come; but one desperate expedient remained—it was to awaken Emily, and by our united strength to attempt to force the partition-door, which was slighter than the other, and through this to pass to the lower part of the house, whence it might be possible to escape to the grounds, and forth to the village.

I returned to the bedside and shook Emily, but in vain. Nothing that I could do availed to produce from her more than a few incoherent words—it was a death-like sleep. She had certainly drank of some narcotic, as had I probably also, spite of all the caution with which I had examined everything presented to us to eat or drink.

I now attempted, with as little noise as possible, to force first one door, then the other—but all in vain. I believe no strength could have effected my object, for both doors opened inwards. I therefore collected whatever movables I could carry thither, and piled them against the doors, so as to assist me in whatever attempts I should make to resist the entrance of those without. I then returned to the bed and endeavoured again, but fruitlessly, to awaken my cousin. It was not sleep, it was torpor, lethargy, death. I knelt down and prayed with an agony of earnestness; and then seating myself upon the bed, I awaited my fate with a kind of terrible tranquillity.

I heard a faint clanking sound from the narrow court which I have already mentioned, as if caused by the scraping of some iron instrument against stones or rubbish. I at first determined not to disturb the calmness which I now felt, by uselessly watching the proceedings of those who sought my life; but as the sounds continued, the horrible curiosity which I felt overcame every other emotion, and I determined, at all hazards, to gratify it. I therefore crawled upon my knees to the window, so as to let the smallest portion of my head appear above the sill.

The moon was shining with an uncertain radiance upon the antique grey buildings, and obliquely upon the narrow court beneath, one side of which was therefore clearly illuminated, while the other was lost in obscurity, the sharp outlines of the old gables, with their nodding clusters of ivy, being at first alone visible.

Whoever or whatever occasioned the noise which had excited my curiosity, was concealed under the shadow of the dark side of the quadrangle. I placed my hand over my eyes to shade them from the moonlight, which was so bright as to be almost dazzling, and, peering into the darkness, I first dimly, but afterwards gradually, almost with full distinctness, beheld the form of a man engaged in digging what appeared to be a rude hole close under the wall. Some implements, probably a shovel and pickaxe, lay beside him, and to these he every now and then applied himself as the nature of the ground required. He pursued his task rapidly, and with as little noise as possible.

'So,' thought I, as, shovelful after shovelful, the dislodged rubbish mounted into a heap, 'they are digging the grave in which, before two hours pass, I must lie, a cold, mangled corpse. I am *theirs*—I cannot escape.'

I felt as if my reason was leaving me. I started to my feet, and in mere despair I applied myself again to each of the two doors alternately. I strained every nerve and sinew, but I might as well have attempted, with my single strength, to force the building itself from its foundation. I threw myself madly upon the ground, and clasped my hands over my eyes as if to shut out the horrible images which crowded upon me.

The paroxysm passed away. I prayed once more, with the bitter, agonised fervour of one who feels that the hour of death is present and inevitable. When I arose, I went once more to the window and looked out, just in time to see a shadowy figure glide stealthily along the wall. The task was finished. The catastrophe of the tragedy must soon be accomplished.

I determined now to defend my life to the last; and that I might be able to do so with some effect, I searched the room for something which might serve as a weapon; but either through accident, or from an anticipation of such a possibility, everything which might have been made available for such a purpose had been carefully removed. I must then die tamely and without an effort to defend myself.

A thought suddenly struck me—might it not be possible to escape through the door, which the assassin must open in order to enter the room? I resolved to make the attempt. I felt assured that the door through which ingress to the room would be effected, was that which opened upon the lobby. It was the more direct way, besides being, for obvious reasons, less liable to interruption than the other. I resolved, then, to place myself behind a projection of the wall, whose shadow would serve fully to conceal me, and when the door should be opened, and before they should have discovered the identity of the occupant of the bed, to creep noiselessly from the room, and then to trust to Providence for escape.

In order to facilitate this scheme, I removed all the lumber which I had heaped against the door; and I had nearly completed my arrangements, when I perceived the room suddenly darkened by the close approach of some shadowy object to the window. On turning my eyes in that direction, I observed at the top of the casement, as if suspended from above, first the feet, then the legs, then the body, and at length the whole figure of a man present himself. It was Edward T———n.

He appeared to be guiding his descent so as to bring his feet upon the centre of the stone block which occupied the lower part of the window; and, having secured his footing upon this, he kneeled down and began to gaze into the room. As the moon was gleaming into the chamber, and the bed-curtains were drawn, he was able to distinguish the bed itself and its contents. He appeared satisfied with his scrutiny, for he looked up and made a sign with his hand, upon which the rope by which his descent had been effected was slackened from above, and he proceeded to disengage it from his waist; this accomplished, he applied his hands to the window-frame, which must have been ingeniously contrived for the purpose, for, with apparently no resistance, the whole frame, containing casement and all, slipped from its position in the wall, and was by him lowered into the room.

The cold night wind waved the bed-curtains, and he paused for a moment—all was still again—and he stepped in upon the floor of the room. He held in his hand what appeared to be a steel instrument, shaped something like a hammer, but larger and sharper at the extremities. This he held rather behind him, while, with three long, tiptoe strides, he brought himself to the bedside.

I felt that the discovery must now be made, and held my breath in momentary expectation of the execration in which he would vent his surprise and disappointment. I closed my eyes—there was a pause, but it was a short one. I heard two dull blows, given in rapid succession: a quivering sigh, and the long-drawn, heavy breathing of the sleeper was for ever suspended. I unclosed my eyes, and saw the murderer fling the quilt across the head of his victim: he then, with the instrument of death still in his hand, proceeded to the lobby-door, upon which he tapped sharply twice or thrice. A quick step was then heard approaching, and a voice whispered something from without. Edward answered, with a kind of chuckle, 'Her ladyship is past complaining; unlock the door, in the devil's name, unless you're afraid to come in, and help me to lift the body out of the window.'

The key was turned in the lock—the door opened—and my uncle entered the room.

I have told you already that I had placed myself under the shade of a projection of the wall, close to the door. I had instinctively shrunk down, cowering towards the ground on the entrance of Edward through the window. When my uncle entered the room he and his son both stood so very close to me that his hand was every moment upon the point of touching my face. I held my breath, and remained motionless as death.

'You had no interruption from the next room?' said my uncle.

'No,' was the brief reply.

'Secure the jewels, Ned; the French harpy must not lay her claws upon them. You're a steady hand, by G——! not much blood—eh?'

'Not twenty drops,' replied his son, 'and those on the quilt.'

'I'm glad it's over,' whispered my uncle again. 'We must lift the—the *thing* through the window, and lay the rubbish over it.'

They then turned to the bedside, and, winding the bed-clothes round the body, carried it between them slowly to the window, and, exchanging a few brief words with some one below, they shoved it over the window-sill, and I heard it fall heavily on the ground underneath.

'I'll take the jewels,' said my uncle; 'there are two caskets in the lower drawer.'

He proceeded, with an accuracy which, had I been more at ease, would have furnished me with matter of astonishment, to lay his hand upon the very spot where my jewels lay; and having possessed himself of them, he called to his son:

'Is the rope made fast above?'

'I'm not a fool—to be sure it is,' replied he.

They then lowered themselves from the window. I now rose lightly and cautiously, scarcely daring to breathe, from my place of concealment, and was creeping towards the door, when I heard my cousin's voice, in a sharp whisper, exclaim: 'Scramble up again! G——d d——n you, you've forgot to lock the room-door!' and I perceived, by the straining of the rope which hung from above, that the mandate was instantly obeyed.

Not a second was to be lost. I passed through the door, which was only closed, and moved as rapidly as I could, consistently with stillness, along the lobby. Before I had gone many yards, I heard the door through which I had just passed double-locked on the inside. I glided down the stairs in terror, lest, at every corner, I should meet the murderer or one of his accomplices.

I reached the hall, and listened for a moment to ascertain whether all was silent around; no sound was audible. The parlour windows opened on the park, and through one of them I might, I thought, easily effect my escape. Accordingly, I hastily entered; but, to my consternation, a candle was burning in the room, and by its light I saw a figure seated at the dinner-table, upon which lay glasses, bottles, and the other accompaniments of a drinking-party. Two or three chairs were placed about the table irregularly, as if hastily abandoned by their occupants.

A single glance satisfied me that the figure was that of my French attendant. She was fast asleep, having probably drank deeply. There was something malignant and ghastly in the calmness of this bad woman's features, dimly illuminated as they were by the flickering blaze of the candle. A knife lay upon the table, and the terrible thought struck me—'Should I kill this sleeping accomplice in the guilt of the murderer, and thus secure my retreat?'

Nothing could be easier—it was but to draw the blade across her throat—the work of a second. An instant's pause, however, corrected me. 'No,' thought I, 'the God who has conducted me thus far through the valley of the shadow of death, will not abandon me now. I will fall into their hands, or I will escape hence, but it shall be free from the stain of blood. His will be done.'

I felt a confidence arising from this reflection, an assurance of protection which I cannot describe. There was no other means of escape, so I advanced, with a firm step and collected mind, to the window. I noiselessly withdrew the bars and unclosed the shutters—I pushed open the casement, and, without waiting to look behind me, I ran with my utmost speed, scarcely feeling the ground under me, down the avenue, taking care to keep upon the grass which bordered it.

I did not for a moment slack my speed, and I had now gained the centre point between the park-gate and the mansion-house. Here the avenue made a wider circuit, and in order to avoid delay, I directed my way across the smooth sward round which the pathway wound, intending, at the opposite side of the flat, at a point which I distinguished by a group of old birch-trees, to enter again upon the beaten track, which was from thence tolerably direct to the gate.

I had, with my utmost speed, got about half way across this broad flat, when the rapid treading of a horse's hoofs struck upon my ear. My heart swelled in my bosom as though I would smother. The clattering of galloping hoofs approached—I was pursued—they were now upon the sward on which I was running—there was not a bush or a bramble to shelter me—and, as if to render escape altogether desperate, the moon, which had hitherto been obscured, at this moment shone forth with a broad clear light, which made every object distinctly visible.

The sounds were now close behind me. I felt my knees bending under me, with the sensation which torments one in dreams. I reeled—I stumbled—I fell—and at the same instant the cause of my alarm wheeled past me at full gallop. It was one of the young fillies which pastured loose about the park, whose frolics had thus all but maddened me with terror. I scrambled to my feet, and rushed on with weak but rapid steps, my sportive companion still galloping round and round me with many a frisk and fling, until, at length, more dead than alive, I reached the avenue-gate and crossed the stile, I scarce knew how.

I ran through the village, in which all was silent as the grave, until my progress was arrested by the hoarse voice of a sentinel, who cried: 'Who goes there?' I felt that I was now safe. I turned in the direction of the voice, and fell fainting at the soldier's feet. When I came to myself, I was sitting in a miserable hovel, surrounded by strange faces, all bespeaking curiosity and compassion.

Many soldiers were in it also: indeed, as I afterwards found, it was employed as a guard-room by a detachment of troops quartered for that night in the town. In a few words I informed their officer of the circumstances which had occurred, describing also the appearance of the persons engaged in the murder; and he, without loss of time, proceeded to the mansion-house of Carrickleigh, taking with him a party of his men. But the villains had discovered their mistake, and had effected their escape before the arrival of the military.

The Frenchwoman was, however, arrested in the neighbourhood upon the next day. She was tried and condemned upon the ensuing assizes; and previous to her execution, confessed that '*she had a hand in making Hugh Tisdall's bed.*' She had been a housekeeper in the castle at the time, and a kind of *chère amie* of my uncle's. She was, in reality, able to speak English like a native, but had exclusively used the French language, I suppose to facilitate her disguise. She died the same hardened wretch which she had lived, confessing her crimes only, as she alleged, that her doing so might involve Sir Arthur T——n, the great author of her guilt and misery, and whom she now regarded with unmitigated detestation.

With the particulars of Sir Arthur's and his son's escape, as far as they are known, you are acquainted. You are also in possession of their after fate—the terrible, the tremendous retribution which, after long delays of many years, finally overtook and crushed them. Wonderful and inscrutable are the dealings of God with His creatures.

Deep and fervent as must always be my gratitude to heaven for my deliverance, effected by a chain of providential occurrences, the failing of a single link of which must have ensured my destruction, I was long before I could look back upon it with other feelings than those of bitterness, almost of agony.

The only being that had ever really loved me, my nearest and dearest friend, ever ready to sympathise, to counsel, and to assist—the gayest, the gentlest, the warmest heart—the only creature on earth that cared for me—*her* life had been the price of my deliverance; and I then uttered the wish, which no event of my long and sorrowful life has taught me to recall, that she had been spared, and that, in her stead, *I* were mouldering in the grave, forgotten and at rest.

—1839—

A CHAPTER IN THE HISTORY OF A TYRONE FAMILY

Being a Tenth Extract from the Legacy of the late Francis Purcell, P.P. of Drumcoolagh

INTRODUCTION

In the following narrative, I have endeavoured to give as nearly as possible the *ipsissima verba* of the valued friend from whom I received it, conscious that any aberration from *her* mode of telling the tale of her own life would at once impair its accuracy and its effect. Would that, with her words, I could also bring before you her animated gesture, her expressive countenance, the solemn and thrilling air and accent with which she related the dark passages in her strange, story; and, above all, that I could communicate the impressive consciousness that the narrator had seen with her own eyes, and personally acted in the scenes which she described; these accompaniments, taken with the additional circumstance that she who told the tale was one far too deeply and sadly impressed with religious principle to misrepresent or fabricate what she repeated as fact, gave to the tale a depth of interest which the events recorded could hardly, themselves, have produced.

I became acquainted with the lady from whose lips I heard this narrative nearly twenty years since, and the story struck my fancy so much that I committed it to paper while it was still fresh in my mind; and should its perusal afford you entertainment for a listless half hour, my labour shall not have been bestowed in vain.

I find that I have taken the story down as she told it, in the first person, and perhaps this is as it should be.

She began as follows:

My maiden name was Richardson,* the designation of a family of some distinction in the county of Tyrone. I was the younger of two daughters, and we were the only children. There was a difference in our ages of nearly six years, so that I did not, in my childhood, enjoy that close companionship which sisterhood, in other circumstances, necessarily involves; and while I was still a child, my sister was married.

The person upon whom she bestowed her hand was a Mr. Carew, a gentleman of property and consideration in the north of England.

I remember well the eventful day of the wedding; the thronging carriages, the noisy menials, the loud laughter, the merry faces, and the gay dresses. Such sights were then new to me, and harmonised ill with the sorrowful feelings with which I regarded the event which was to separate me, as it turned out, for ever from a sister whose tenderness

---

* I have carefully altered the names as they appear in the original MSS., for the reader will see that some of the circumstances recorded are not of a kind to reflect honour upon those involved in them; and as many are still living, in every way honoured and honourable, who stand in close relation to the principal actors in this drama, the reader will see the necessity of the course which we have adopted.

alone had hitherto more than supplied all that I wanted in my mother's affection.

The day soon arrived which was to remove the happy couple from Ashtown House. The carriage stood at the hall-door, and my poor sister kissed me again and again, telling me that I should see her soon.

The carriage drove away, and I gazed after it until my eyes filled with tears, and, returning slowly to my chamber, I wept more bitterly and, so to speak, more desolately, than ever I had done before.

My father had never seemed to love or to take an interest in me. He had desired a son, and I think he never thoroughly forgave me my unfortunate sex.

My having come into the world at all as his child he regarded as a kind of fraudulent intrusion, and as his antipathy to me had its origin in an imperfection of mine, too radical for removal, I never even hoped to stand high in his good graces.

My mother was, I dare say, as fond of me as she was of anyone; but she was a woman of a masculine and a worldly cast of mind. She had no tenderness or sympathy for the weaknesses, or even for the affections, of woman's nature, and her demeanour towards me was peremptory, and often even harsh.

It is not to be supposed, then, that I found in the society of my parents much to supply the loss of my sister. About a year after her marriage, we received letters from Mr. Carew, containing accounts of my sister's health, which, though not actually alarming, were calculated to make us seriously uneasy. The symptoms most dwelt upon were loss of appetite and cough.

The letters concluded by intimating that he would avail himself of my father and mother's repeated invitation to spend some time at Ashtown, particularly as the physician who had been consulted as to my sister's health had strongly advised a removal to her native air.

There were added repeated assurances that nothing serious was apprehended, as it was supposed that a deranged state of the liver was the only source of the symptoms which at first had seemed to intimate consumption.

In accordance with this announcement, my sister and Mr. Carew arrived in Dublin, where one of my father's carriages awaited them, in readiness to start upon whatever day or hour they might choose for their departure.

It was arranged that Mr. Carew was, as soon as the day upon which they were to leave Dublin was definitely fixed, to write to my father, who intended that the two last stages should be performed by his own horses, upon whose speed and safety far more reliance might be placed than upon those of the ordinary post-horses, which were at that time, almost without exception, of the very worst order. The journey, one of about ninety miles, was to be divided; the larger portion being reserved for the second day.

On Sunday a letter reached us, stating that the party would leave Dublin on Monday, and, in due course, reach Ashtown upon Tuesday evening.

Tuesday came: the evening closed in, and yet no carriage; darkness came on, and still no sign of our expected visitors.

Hour after hour passed away, and it was now past twelve; the night was remarkably calm, scarce a breath stirring, so that any sound, such as that produced by the rapid movement of a vehicle, would have been audible at a considerable distance. For some such sound I was feverishly listening.

It was, however, my father's rule to close the house at nightfall, and the window-shutters being fastened, I was unable to reconnoitre the avenue as I would have wished. It was nearly one o'clock, and we began almost to despair of seeing them upon that night, when I thought I distinguished the sound of wheels, but so remote and faint as to make me at first very uncertain. The noise approached; it became louder and clearer; it stopped for a moment.

I now heard the shrill screaming of the rusty iron, as the avenue-gate revolved on its hinges; again came the sound of wheels in rapid motion.

'It is they,' said I, starting up; 'the carriage is in the avenue.'

We all stood for a few moments breathlessly listening. On thundered the vehicle with the speed of a whirlwind; crack went the whip, and clatter went the wheels, as it rattled over the uneven pavement of the court. A general and furious barking from all the dogs about the house, hailed its arrival.

We hurried to the hall in time to hear the steps let down with the sharp clanging noise peculiar to the operation, and the hum of voices exerted in the bustle of arrival. The hall-door was now thrown open, and we all stepped forth to greet our visitors.

The court was perfectly empty; the moon was shining broadly and brightly upon all around; nothing was to be seen but the tall trees with their long spectral shadows, now wet with the dews of midnight.

We stood gazing from right to left, as if suddenly awakened from a dream; the dogs walked suspiciously, growling and snuffing about the court, and by totally and suddenly ceasing their former loud barking, expressing the predominance of fear.

We stared one upon another in perplexity and dismay, and I think I never beheld more pale faces assembled. By my father's direction, we looked about to find anything which might indicate or account for the noise which we had heard; but no such thing was to be seen—even the mire which lay upon the avenue was undisturbed. We returned to the house, more panic-struck than I can describe.

On the next day, we learned by a messenger, who had ridden hard the greater part of the night, that my sister was dead. On Sunday evening, she had retired to bed rather unwell, and, on Monday, her indisposition declared itself unequivocally to be malignant fever. She became hourly worse, and, on Tuesday night, a little after midnight, she expired.*

I mention this circumstance, because it was one upon which a thousand wild and fantastical reports were founded, though one would have thought that the truth scarcely required to be improved upon; and again, because it produced a strong and lasting effect upon my spirits, and indeed, I am inclined to think, upon my character.

I was, for several years after this occurrence, long after the violence of my grief subsided, so wretchedly low-spirited and nervous, that I could scarcely be said to live; and during this time, habits of

---

* The residuary legatee of the late Frances Purcell, who has the honour of selecting such of his lamented old friend's manuscripts as may appear fit for publication, in order that the lore which they contain may reach the world before scepticism and utility have robbed our species of the precious gift of credulity, and scornfully kicked before them, or trampled into annihilation those harmless fragments of picturesque superstition which it is our object to preserve, has been subjected to the charge of dealing too largely in the marvellous; and it has been half insinuated that such is his love for *diablerie*, that he is content to wander a mile out of his way, in order to meet a fiend or a goblin, and thus to sacrifice all regard for truth and accuracy to the idle hope of affrighting the imagination, and thus pandering to the bad taste of his reader. He begs leave, then, to take this opportunity of asserting his perfect innocence of all the crimes laid to his charge, and to assure his reader that he never *pandered to his bad taste*, nor went one inch out of his way to introduce witch, fairy, devil, ghost, or any other of the grim fraternity of the redoubted Raw-head-and-bloody-bones. His province, touching these tales, has been attended with no difficulty and little responsibility; indeed, he is accountable for nothing more than an alteration in the names of persons mentioned therein, when such a step seemed necessary, and for an occasional note, whenever he conceived it possible, innocently, to edge in a word. These tales have been *written down*, as the heading of each announces, by the Rev. Francis Purcell, P.P., of Drumcoolagh; and in all the instances, which are many, in which the present writer has had an opportunity of comparing the manuscript of his departed friend with the actual traditions which are current amongst the families whose fortunes they pretend to illustrate, he has uniformly found that whatever of supernatural occurred in the story, so far from having been exaggerated by him, had been rather softened down, and, wherever it could be attempted, accounted for.

indecision, arising out of a listless acquiescence in the will of others, a fear of encountering even the slightest opposition, and a disposition to shrink from what are commonly called amusements, grew upon me so strongly, that I have scarcely even yet altogether overcome them.

We saw nothing more of Mr. Carew. He returned to England as soon as the melancholy rites attendant upon the event which I have just mentioned were performed; and not being altogether inconsolable, he married again within two years; after which, owing to the remoteness of our relative situations, and other circumstances, we gradually lost sight of him.

I was now an only child; and, as my elder sister had died without issue, it was evident that, in the ordinary course of things, my father's property, which was altogether in his power, would go to me; and the consequence was, that before I was fourteen, Ashtown House was besieged by a host of suitors. However, whether it was that I was too young, or that none of the aspirants to my hand stood sufficiently high in rank or wealth, I was suffered by both parents to do exactly as I pleased; and well was it for me, as I afterwards found, that fortune, or rather Providence, had so ordained it, that I had not suffered my affections to become in any degree engaged, for my mother would never have suffered any *silly fancy* of mine, as she was in the habit of styling an attachment, to stand in the way of her ambitious views— views which she was determined to carry into effect, in defiance of every obstacle, and in order to accomplish which she would not have hesitated to sacrifice anything so unreasonable and contemptible as a girlish passion.

When I reached the age of sixteen, my mother's plans began to develop themselves; and, at her suggestion, we moved to Dublin to sojourn for the winter, in order that no time might be lost in disposing of me to the best advantage.

I had been too long accustomed to consider myself as of no importance whatever, to believe for a moment that I was in reality the cause of all the bustle and preparation which surrounded me, and being thus relieved from the pain which a consciousness of my real situation would have inflicted, I journeyed towards the capital with a feeling of total indifference.

My father's wealth and connection had established him in the best society, and, consequently, upon our arrival in the metropolis we commanded whatever enjoyment or advantages its gaieties afforded.

The tumult and novelty of the scenes in which I was involved did not fail considerably to amuse me, and my mind gradually recovered its tone, which was naturally cheerful.

It was almost immediately known and reported that I was an heiress, and of course my attractions were pretty generally acknowledged.

Among the many gentlemen whom it was my fortune to please, one, ere long, established himself in my mother's good graces, to the exclusion of all less important aspirants. However, I had not understood or even remarked his attentions, nor in the slightest degree suspected his or my mother's plans respecting me, when I was made aware of them rather abruptly by my mother herself.

We had attended a splendid ball, given by Lord M——, at his residence in Stephen's Green, and I was, with the assistance of my waiting-maid, employed in rapidly divesting myself of the rich ornaments which, in profuseness and value, could scarcely have found their equals in any private family in Ireland.

I had thrown myself into a lounging-chair beside the fire, listless and exhausted, after the fatigues of the evening, when I was aroused from the reverie into which I had fallen by the sound of footsteps approaching my chamber, and my mother entered.

'Fanny, my dear,' said she, in her softest tone, 'I wish to say a word or two with you before I go to rest. You are not fatigued, love, I hope?'

'No, no, madam, I thank you,' said I, rising at the same time from my seat, with the formal respect so little practised now.

'Sit down, my dear,' said she, placing herself upon a chair beside me; 'I must chat with you for a quarter of an hour or so. Saunders' (to the maid) 'you may leave the room; do not close the room-door, but shut that of the lobby.'

This precaution against curious ears having been taken as directed, my mother proceeded.

'You have observed, I should suppose, my dearest Fanny—indeed, you *must* have observed Lord Glenfallen's marked attentions to you?'

'I assure you, madam—' I began.

'Well, well, that is all right,' interrupted my mother; 'of course you must be modest upon the matter; but listen to me for a few moments, my love, and I will prove to your satisfaction that your modesty is quite unnecessary in this case. You have done better than we could have hoped, at least so very soon. Lord Glenfallen is in love with you. I give you joy of your conquest;' and saying this, my mother kissed my forehead.

'In love with me!' I exclaimed, in unfeigned astonishment.

'Yes, in love with you,' repeated my mother; 'devotedly, distractedly in love with you. Why, my dear, what is there wonderful in it? Look in the glass, and look at these,' she continued, pointing with a smile to the jewels which I had just removed from my person, and which now lay a glittering heap upon the table.

'May there not,' said I, hesitating between confusion and real alarm—'is it not possible that some mistake may be at the bottom of all this?'

'Mistake, dearest! none,' said my mother. 'None; none in the world. Judge for yourself; read this, my love.' And she placed in my hand a letter, addressed to herself, the seal of which was broken. I read it through with no small surprise. After some very fine complimentary flourishes upon my beauty and perfections, as also upon the antiquity and high reputation of our family, it went on to make a formal proposal of marriage, to be communicated or not to me at present, as my mother should deem expedient; and the letter wound up by a request that the writer might be permitted, upon our return to Ashtown House, which was soon to take place, as the spring was now tolerably advanced, to visit us for a few days, in case his suit was approved.

'Well, well, my dear,' said my mother, impatiently; 'do you know who Lord Glenfallen is?'

'I do, madam,' said I rather timidly, for I dreaded an altercation with my mother.

'Well, dear, and what frightens you?' continued she. 'Are you afraid of a title? What has he done to alarm you? he is neither old nor ugly.'

I was silent, though I might have said, 'He is neither young nor handsome.'

'My dear Fanny,' continued my mother, 'in sober seriousness you have been most fortunate in engaging the affections of a nobleman such as Lord Glenfallen, young and wealthy, with first-rate—yes, acknowledged *first-rate* abilities, and of a family whose influence is not exceeded by that of any in Ireland. Of course you see the offer in the same light that I do—indeed I think you *must*.'

This was uttered in no very dubious tone. I was so much astonished by the suddenness of the whole communication that I literally did not know what to say.

'You are not in love?' said my mother, turning sharply, and fixing her dark eyes upon me with severe scrutiny.

'No, madam,' said I, promptly; horrified, as what young lady would not have been, at such a query.

'I'm glad to hear it,' said my mother, drily. 'Once, nearly twenty years ago, a friend of mine consulted me as to how he should deal with a daughter who had made what they call a love-match—beggared herself, and disgraced her family; and I said, without hesitation, take no care for her, but cast her off. Such punishment I awarded for an offence committed against the reputation of a family not my own; and what I advised respecting the child of another, with full as small compunction I would *do* with mine. I cannot conceive anything more unreasonable or intolerable than that the fortune and the character of a family should be marred by the idle caprices of a girl.'

She spoke this with great severity, and paused as if she expected some observation from me.

I, however, said nothing.

'But I need not explain to you, my dear Fanny,' she continued, 'my views upon this subject; you have always known them well, and I have never yet had reason to believe you likely, voluntarily, to offend me, or to abuse or neglect any of those advantages which reason and duty tell you should be improved. Come hither, my dear; kiss me, and do not look so frightened. Well, now, about this letter, you need not answer it yet; of course you must be allowed time to make up your mind. In the meantime I will write to his lordship to give him my permission to visit us at Ashtown. Good-night, my love.'

And thus ended one of the most disagreeable, not to say astounding, conversations I had ever had. It would not be easy to describe exactly what were my feelings towards Lord Glenfallen;—whatever might have been my mother's suspicions, my heart was perfectly disengaged—and hitherto, although I had not been made in the slightest degree acquainted with his real views, I had liked him very much, as an agreeable, well-informed man, whom I was always glad to meet in society. He had served in the navy in early life, and the polish which his manners received in his after intercourse with courts and cities had not served to obliterate that frankness of manner which belongs proverbially to the sailor.

Whether this apparent candour went deeper than the outward bearing, I was yet to learn. However, there was no doubt that, as far as I had seen of Lord Glenfallen, he was, though perhaps not so young as might have been desired in a lover, a singularly pleasing man; and whatever feeling unfavourable to him had found its way into my mind, arose altogether from the dread, not an unreasonable one, that constraint might be practised upon my inclinations. I reflected, however, that Lord Glenfallen was a wealthy man, and one highly thought of; and although I could never expect to love him in the romantic sense of the term, yet I had no doubt but that, all things considered, I might be more happy with him than I could hope to be at home.

When next I met him it was with no small embarrassment, his tact and good breeding, however, soon reassured me, and effectually prevented my awkwardness being remarked upon. And I had the satisfaction of leaving Dublin for the country with the full conviction that nobody, not even those most intimate with me, even suspected the fact of Lord Glenfallen's having made me a formal proposal.

This was to me a very serious subject of self-gratulation, for, besides my instinctive dread of becoming the topic of the speculations of gossip, I felt that if the situation which I occupied in relation to him were made publicly known, I should stand committed in a manner which would scarcely leave me the power of retraction.

The period at which Lord Glenfallen had arranged to visit Ashtown House was now fast approaching, and it became my mother's wish to form me thoroughly to her will, and to obtain my consent to the proposed marriage before his arrival, so that all things might proceed smoothly, without apparent opposition or objection upon my part.

Whatever objections, therefore, I had entertained were to be subdued; whatever disposition to resistance I had exhibited or had been supposed to feel, were to be completely eradicated before he made his appearance; and my mother addressed herself to the task with a decision and energy against which even the barriers, which her imagination had created, could hardly have stood.

If she had, however, expected any determined opposition from me, she was agreeably disappointed. My heart was perfectly free, and all my feelings of liking and preference were in favour of Lord Glenfallen; and I well knew that in case I refused to dispose of myself as I was desired, my mother had alike the power and the will to render my existence as utterly miserable as even the most ill-assorted marriage could possibly have done.

You will remember, my good friend, that I was very young and very completely under the control of my parents, both of whom, my mother particularly, were unscrupulously determined in matters of this kind, and willing, when voluntary obedience on the part of those within their power was withheld, to compel a forced acquiescence by an unsparing use of all the engines of the most stern and rigorous domestic discipline.

All these combined, not unnaturally, induced me to resolve upon yielding at once, and without useless opposition, to what appeared almost to be my fate.

The appointed time was come, and my now accepted suitor arrived; he was in high spirits, and, if possible, more entertaining than ever.

I was not, however, quite in the mood to enjoy his sprightliness; but whatever I wanted in gaiety was amply made up in the triumphant and gracious good-humour of my mother, whose smiles of benevolence and exultation were showered around as bountifully as the summer sunshine.

I will not weary you with unnecessary prolixity. Let it suffice to say, that I was married to Lord Glenfallen with all the attendant pomp and circumstance of wealth, rank, and grandeur. According to the usage of the times, now humanely reformed, the ceremony was made, until long past midnight, the season of wild, uproarious, and promiscuous feasting and revelry.

Of all this I have a painfully vivid recollection, and particularly of the little annoyances inflicted upon me by the dull and coarse jokes of the wits and wags who abound in all such places, and upon all such occasions.

I was not sorry when, after a few days, Lord Glenfallen's carriage appeared at the door to convey us both from Ashtown; for any change would have been a relief from the irksomeness of ceremonial and formality which the visits received in honour of my newly-acquired titles hourly entailed upon me.

It was arranged that we were to proceed to Cahergillagh, one of the Glenfallen estates, lying, however, in a southern county, so that, owing to the difficulty of the roads at the time, a tedious journey of three days intervened.

I set forth with my noble companion, followed by the regrets of some, and by the envy of many; though God knows I little deserved the latter. The three days of travel were now almost spent, when, passing the brow of a wild heathy hill, the domain of Cahergillagh opened suddenly upon our view.

It formed a striking and a beautiful scene. A lake of considerable extent stretching away towards the west, and reflecting from its broad, smooth waters, the rich glow of the setting sun, was overhung by steep hills, covered by a rich mantle of velvet sward, broken here and there by the grey front of some old rock, and exhibiting on their shelving sides, their slopes and hollows, every variety of light and shade; a thick wood of dwarf oak, birch, and hazel skirted these hills, and clothed the shores of the lake, running out in rich luxuriance upon every promontory, and spreading upward considerably upon the side of the hills.

'There lies the enchanted castle,' said Lord Glenfallen, pointing towards a considerable level space intervening between two of the picturesque hills, which rose dimly around the lake.

This little plain was chiefly occupied by the same low, wild wood which covered the other parts of the domain; but towards the centre a mass of taller and statelier forest trees stood darkly grouped together, and among them stood an ancient square tower, with many buildings of a humbler character, forming together the manor-house, or, as it was more usually called, the Court of Cahergillagh.

As we approached the level upon which the mansion stood, the winding road gave us many glimpses of the time-worn castle and its surrounding buildings; and seen as it was through the long vistas of the fine old trees, and with the rich glow of evening upon it, I have seldom beheld an object more picturesquely striking.

I was glad to perceive, too, that here and there the blue curling smoke ascended from stacks of chimneys now hidden by the rich, dark ivy which, in a great measure, covered the building. Other indications of comfort made themselves manifest as we approached; and indeed, though the place was evidently one of considerable antiquity, it had nothing whatever of the gloom of decay about it.

'You must not, my love,' said Lord Glenfallen, 'imagine this place worse than it is. I have no taste for antiquity—at least I should not choose a house to reside in because it is old. Indeed I do not recollect that I was even so romantic as to overcome my aversion to rats and rheumatism, those faithful attendants upon your noble relics of feudalism; and I much prefer a snug, modern, unmysterious bedroom, with well-aired sheets, to the waving tapestry, mildewed cushions, and all the other interesting appliances of romance. However, though I cannot promise you all the discomfort generally belonging to an old castle, you will find legends and ghostly lore enough to claim your respect; and if old Martha be still to the fore, as I trust she is, you will soon have a supernatural and appropriate anecdote for every closet and corner of the mansion; but here we are—so, without more ado, welcome to Cahergillagh!'

We now entered the hall of the castle, and while the domestics were employed in conveying our trunks and other luggage which we had brought with us for immediate use to the apartments which Lord Glenfallen had selected for himself and me, I went with him into a spacious sitting-room, wainscoted with finely polished black oak, and hung round with the portraits of various worthies of the Glenfallen family.

This room looked out upon an extensive level covered with the softest green sward, and irregularly bounded by the wild wood I have before mentioned, through the leafy arcade formed by whose boughs and trunks the level beams of the setting sun were pouring. In the distance a group of dairymaids were plying their task, which they accompanied throughout with snatches of Irish songs which, mellowed by the distance, floated not unpleasingly to the ear; and beside them sat or lay, with all the grave importance of conscious protection, six or seven large dogs of various kinds. Farther in the distance, and through the cloisters of the arching wood, two or three ragged urchins were employed in driving such stray kine as had wandered farther than the rest to join their fellows.

As I looked upon this scene which I have described, a feeling of tranquillity and happiness came upon me, which I have never experienced in so strong a degree; and so strange to me was the sensation that my eyes filled with tears.

Lord Glenfallen mistook the cause of my emotion, and taking me kindly and tenderly by the hand, he said:

'Do not suppose, my love, that it is my intention to *settle* here. Whenever you desire to leave this, you have only to let me know your wish, and it shall be complied with; so I must entreat of you not to suffer any circumstances which I can control to give you one moment's uneasiness. But here is old Martha; you must be introduced to her, one of the heirlooms of our family.'

A hale, good-humoured, erect old woman was Martha, and an agreeable contrast to the grim, decrepid hag which my fancy had conjured up, as the depository of all the horrible tales in which I doubted not this old place was most fruitful.

She welcomed me and her master with a profusion of gratulations, alternately kissing our hands and apologising for the liberty, until at length Lord Glenfallen put an end to this somewhat fatiguing ceremonial by requesting her to conduct me to my chamber if it were prepared for my reception.

I followed Martha up an old-fashioned oak staircase into a long, dim passage, at the end of which lay the door which communicated with the apartments which had been selected for our use; here the old woman stopped, and respectfully requested me to proceed.

I accordingly opened the door, and was about to enter, when something like a mass of black tapestry, as it appeared, disturbed by my sudden approach, fell from above the door, so as completely to screen the aperture; the startling unexpectedness of the occurrence, and the rustling noise which the drapery made in its descent, caused me involuntarily to step two or three paces backwards. I turned, smiling and half-ashamed, to the old servant, and said:

'You see what a coward I am.'

The woman looked puzzled, and, without saying any more, I was about to draw aside the curtain and enter the room, when, upon turning to do so, I was surprised to find that nothing whatever interposed to obstruct the passage.

I went into the room, followed by the servant-woman, and was amazed to find that it, like the one below, was wainscoted, and that nothing like drapery was to be found near the door.

'Where is it?' said I; 'what has become of it?'

'What does your ladyship wish to know?' said the old woman.

'Where is the black curtain that fell across the door, when I attempted first to come to my chamber?' answered I.

'The cross of Christ about us!' said the old woman, turning suddenly pale.

'What is the matter, my good friend?' said I; 'you seem frightened.'

'Oh no, no, your ladyship,' said the old woman, endeavouring to conceal her agitation; but in vain, for tottering towards a chair, she sank into it, looking so deadly pale and horror-struck that I thought every moment she would faint.

'Merciful God, keep us from harm and danger!' muttered she at length.

'What can have terrified you so?' said I, beginning to fear that she had seen something more than had met my eye. 'You appear ill, my poor woman!'

'Nothing, nothing, my lady,' said she, rising. 'I beg your ladyship's pardon for making so bold. May the great God defend us from misfortune!'

'Martha,' said I, 'something *has* frightened you very much, and I insist on knowing what it is; your keeping me in the dark upon the subject will make me much more uneasy than anything you could tell me. I desire you, therefore, to let me know what agitates you; I command you to tell me.'

'Your ladyship said you saw a black curtain falling across the door when you were coming into the room,' said the old woman.

'I did,' said I; 'but though the whole thing appears somewhat strange, I cannot see anything in the matter to agitate you so excessively.'

'It's for no good you saw that, my lady,' said the crone; 'something terrible is coming. It's a sign, my lady—a sign that never fails.'

'Explain, explain what you mean, my good woman,' said I, in spite of myself, catching more than I could account for, of her superstitious terror.

'Whenever something—something *bad* is going to happen to the Glenfallen family, some one that belongs to them sees a black handkerchief or curtain just waved or falling before their faces. I saw it myself,' continued she, lowering her voice, 'when I was only a little girl, and I'll never forget it. I often heard of it before, though I never saw it till then, nor since, praised be God. But I was going into Lady Jane's room to waken her in the morning; and sure enough when I got first to the bed and began to draw the curtain, something dark was waved across the division, but only for a moment; and when I saw rightly into the bed, there was she lying cold and dead, God be merciful to me! So, my lady, there is small blame to me to be daunted when any one of the family sees it; for it's many's the story I heard of it, though I saw it but once.'

I was not of a superstitious turn of mind, yet I could not resist a feeling of awe very nearly allied to the fear which my companion had so unreservedly expressed; and when you consider my situation, the loneliness, antiquity, and gloom of the place, you will allow that the weakness was not without excuse.

In spite of old Martha's boding predictions, however, time flowed on in an unruffled course. One little incident however, though trifling in itself, I must relate, as it serves to make what follows more intelligible.

Upon the day after my arrival, Lord Glenfallen of course desired to make me acquainted with the house and domain; and accordingly we set forth upon our ramble. When returning, he became for some time silent and moody, a state so unusual with him as considerably to excite my surprise.

I endeavoured by observations and questions to arouse him—but in vain. At length, as we approached the house, he said, as if speaking to himself:

"Twere madness—madness—madness,' repeating the words bitterly—'sure and speedy ruin.'

There was here a long pause; and at length, turning sharply towards me, in a tone very unlike that in which he had hitherto addressed me, he said:

'Do you think it possible that a woman can keep a secret?'

'I am sure,' said I, 'that women are very much belied upon the score of talkativeness, and that I may answer your question with the same directness with which you put it—I reply that I *do* think a woman can keep a secret.'

'But I do not,' said he, drily.

We walked on in silence for a time. I was much astonished at his unwonted abruptness—I had almost said rudeness.

After a considerable pause he seemed to recollect himself, and with an effort resuming his sprightly manner, he said:

'Well, well, the next thing to keeping a secret well is, not to desire to possess one—talkativeness and curiosity generally go together. Now I shall make test of you, in the first place, respecting the latter of these qualities. I shall be your *Bluebeard*—tush, why do I trifle thus? Listen to me, my dear Fanny; I speak now in solemn earnest. What I desire is intimately, inseparably, connected with your happiness and honour as well as my own; and your compliance with my request will not be difficult. It will impose upon you a very trifling restraint during your sojourn here, which certain events which have occurred since our arrival have determined me shall not be a long one. You must promise me, upon your sacred honour, that you will visit *only* that part of the castle which can be reached from the front entrance, leaving the back entrance and the part of the building commanded immediately by it to the menials, as also the small garden whose high wall you see yonder; and never at any time seek to pry or peep into them, nor to open the door which communicates from the front part of the house through the corridor with the back. I do not urge this in jest or in caprice, but from a solemn conviction that danger and misery will be the certain consequences of your not observing what I prescribe. I cannot explain myself further at present. Promise me, then, these things, as you hope for peace here, and for mercy hereafter.'

I did make the promise as desired, and he appeared relieved; his manner recovered all its gaiety and elasticity: but the recollection of the strange scene which I have just described dwelt painfully upon my mind.

More than a month passed away without any occurrence worth recording; but I was not destined to leave Cahergillagh without further adventure. One day, intending to enjoy the pleasant sunshine in a ramble through the woods, I ran up to my room to procure my bonnet and shawl. Upon entering the chamber, I was surprised and somewhat startled to find it occupied. Beside the fireplace, and nearly opposite the door, seated in a large, old-fashioned elbow-chair, was placed the figure of a lady. She appeared to be nearer fifty than forty, and was dressed suitably to her age, in a handsome suit of flowered silk; she had a profusion of trinkets and jewellery about her person, and many rings upon her fingers. But although very rich, her dress was not gaudy or in ill taste. But what was remarkable in the lady was, that although her features were handsome, and upon the whole pleasing, the pupil of each eye was dimmed with the whiteness of cataract, and she was evidently stone-blind. I was for some seconds so surprised at this unaccountable apparition, that I could not find words to address her.

'Madam,' said I, 'there must be some mistake here—this is my bed-chamber.'

'Marry come up,' said the lady, sharply; '*your* chamber! Where is Lord Glenfallen?'

'He is below, madam,' replied I; 'and I am convinced he will be not a little surprised to find you here.'

'I do not think he will,' said she; 'with your good leave, talk of what you know something about. Tell him I want him. Why does the minx dilly-dally so?'

In spite of the awe which this grim lady inspired, there was something in her air of confident superiority which, when I considered our relative situations, was not a little irritating.

'Do you know, madam, to whom you speak?' said I.

'I neither know nor care,' said she; 'but I presume that you are some one about the house, so again I desire you, if you wish to continue here, to bring your master hither forthwith.'

'I must tell you, madam,' said I, 'that I am Lady Glenfallen.'

'What's that?' said the stranger, rapidly.

'I say, madam,' I repeated, approaching her that I might be more distinctly heard, 'that I am Lady Glenfallen.'

'It's a lie, you trull!' cried she, in an accent which made me start, and at the same time, springing forward, she seized me in her grasp, and shook me violently, repeating, 'It's a lie—it's a lie!' with a rapidity and vehemence which swelled every vein of her face. The violence of her action, and the fury which convulsed her face, effectually terrified me, and disengaging myself from her grasp, I screamed as loud as I could for help. The blind woman continued to pour out a torrent of abuse upon me, foaming at the mouth with rage, and impotently shaking her clenched fists towards me.

I heard Lord Glenfallen's step upon the stairs, and I instantly ran out; as I passed him I perceived that he was deadly pale, and just caught the words: 'I hope that demon has not hurt you?'

I made some answer, I forget what, and he entered the chamber, the door of which he locked upon the inside. What passed within I know not; but I heard the voices of the two speakers raised in loud and angry altercation.

I thought I heard the shrill accents of the woman repeat the words, 'Let her look to herself;' but I could not be quite sure. This short sentence, however, was, to my alarmed imagination, pregnant with fearful meaning.

The storm at length subsided, though not until after a conference of more than two long hours. Lord Glenfallen then returned, pale and agitated.

'That unfortunate woman,' said he, 'is out of her mind. I daresay she treated you to some of her ravings; but you need not dread any further interruption from her: I have brought her so far to reason. She did not hurt you, I trust.'

'No, no,' said I; 'but she terrified me beyond measure.'

'Well,' said he, 'she is likely to behave better for the future; and I dare swear that neither you nor she would desire, after what has passed, to meet again.'

This occurrence, so startling and unpleasant, so involved in mystery, and giving rise to so many painful surmises, afforded me no very agreeable food for rumination.

All attempts on my part to arrive at the truth were baffled; Lord Glenfallen evaded all my inquiries, and at length peremptorily forbid any further allusion to the matter. I was thus obliged to rest satisfied with what I had actually seen, and to trust to time to resolve the perplexities in which the whole transaction had involved me.

Lord Glenfallen's temper and spirits gradually underwent a complete and most painful change; he became silent and abstracted, his manner to me was abrupt and often harsh, some grievous anxiety seemed ever present to his mind; and under its influence his spirits sunk and his temper became soured.

I soon perceived that his gaiety was rather that which the stir and excitement of society produce, than the result of a healthy habit of mind; every day confirmed me in the opinion, that the considerate good-nature which I had so much admired in him was little more than a mere manner; and to my infinite grief and surprise, the gay, kind, open-hearted nobleman who had for months followed and flattered me, was rapidly assuming the form of a gloomy, morose, and singularly selfish man. This was a bitter discovery, and I strove to conceal it from myself as long as I could; but the truth was not to be denied, and I was forced to believe that Lord Glenfallen no longer loved me, and that he was at little pains to conceal the alteration in his sentiments.

One morning after breakfast, Lord Glenfallen had been for some time walking silently up and down the room, buried in his moody reflections, when pausing suddenly, and turning towards me, he exclaimed:

'I have it—I have it! We must go abroad, and stay there too; and if that does not answer, why—why, we must try some more effectual expedient. Lady Glenfallen, I have become involved in heavy embarrassments. A wife, you know, must share the fortunes of her husband, for better for worse; but I will waive my right if you prefer remaining here—here at Cahergillagh. For I would not have you seen elsewhere without the state to which your rank entitles you; besides, it would break your poor mother's heart,' he added, with sneering gravity. 'So make up your mind—Cahergillagh or France. I will start if possible in a week, so determine between this and then.'

He left the room, and in a few moments I saw him ride past the window, followed by a mounted servant. He had directed a domestic to inform me that he should not be back until the next day.

I was in very great doubt as to what course of conduct I should pursue, as to accompanying him in the continental tour so suddenly determined upon. I felt that it would be a hazard too great to encounter; for at Cahergillagh I had always the consciousness to sustain me, that if his temper at any time led him into violent or unwarrantable treatment of me, I had a remedy within reach, in the protection and support of my own family, from all useful and effective communication with whom, if once in France, I should be entirely debarred.

As to remaining at Cahergillagh in solitude, and, for aught I knew, exposed to hidden dangers, it appeared to me scarcely less objectionable than the former proposition; and yet I feared that with one or other I must comply, unless I was prepared to come to an actual breach with Lord Glenfallen. Full of these unpleasing doubts and perplexities, I retired to rest.

I was wakened, after having slept uneasily for some hours, by some person shaking me rudely by the shoulder; a small lamp burned in my room, and by its light, to my horror and amazement, I discovered that my visitant was the self-same blind old lady who had so terrified me a few weeks before.

I started up in the bed, with a view to ring the bell, and alarm the domestics; but she instantly anticipated me by saying:

'Do not be frightened, silly girl! If I had wished to harm you I could have done it while you were sleeping; I need not have wakened you. Listen to me, now, attentively and fearlessly, for what I have to say interests you to the full as much as it does me. Tell me here, in the presence of God, did Lord Glenfallen marry you—*actually marry* you? Speak the truth, woman.'

'As surely as I live and speak,' I replied, 'did Lord Glenfallen marry me, in presence of more than a hundred witnesses.'

'Well,' continued she, 'he should have told you *then*, before you married him, that he had a wife living, which wife I am. I feel you tremble—tush! do not be frightened. I do not mean to harm you. Mark me now—you are *not* his wife. When I make my story known you will be so neither in the eye of God nor of man. You must leave this house upon to-morrow. Let the world know that your husband has another wife living; go you into retirement, and leave him to justice, which will surely overtake him. If you remain in this house after to-morrow you will reap the bitter fruits of your sin.'

So saying, she quitted the room, leaving me very little disposed to sleep.

Here was food for my very worst and most terrible suspicions; still there was not enough to remove all doubt. I had no proof of the truth of this woman's statement.

Taken by itself, there was nothing to induce me to attach weight to it; but when I viewed it in connection with the extraordinary mystery of some of Lord Glenfallen's proceedings, his strange anxiety to exclude me from certain portions of the mansion, doubtless lest I should encounter this person—the strong influence, nay, command which she possessed over him, a circumstance clearly established by the very fact of her residing in the very place where, of all others, he should least have desired to find her—her thus acting, and continuing to act in direct contradiction to his wishes; when, I say, I viewed her disclosure in connection with all these circumstances, I could not help feeling that there was at least a fearful verisimilitude in the allegations which she had made.

Still I was not satisfied, nor nearly so. Young minds have a reluctance almost insurmountable to believing, upon anything short of unquestionable proof, the existence of premeditated guilt in anyone whom they have ever trusted; and in support of this feeling I was assured that if the assertion of Lord Glenfallen, which nothing in this woman's manner had led me to disbelieve, were true, namely that her mind was unsound, the whole fabric of my doubts and fears must fall to the ground.

I determined to state to Lord Glenfallen freely and accurately the substance of the communication which I had just heard, and in his words and looks to seek for its proof or refutation. Full of these thoughts, I remained wakeful and excited all night, every moment fancying that I heard the step or saw the figure of my recent visitor, towards whom I felt a species of horror and dread which I can hardly describe.

There was something in her face, though her features had evidently been handsome, and were not, at first sight, unpleasing, which, upon a nearer inspection, seemed to indicate the habitual prevalence and indulgence of evil passions, and a power of expressing mere animal anger, with an intenseness that I have seldom seen equalled, and to which an almost unearthly effect was given by the convulsive quivering of the sightless eyes.

You may easily suppose that it was no very pleasing reflection to me to consider that, whenever caprice might induce her to return, I was within the reach of this violent and, for aught I knew, insane woman, who had, upon that very night, spoken to me in a tone of menace, of which her mere words, divested of the manner and look with which she uttered them, can convey but a faint idea.

Will you believe me when I tell you that I was actually afraid to leave my bed in order to secure the door, lest I should again encounter the dreadful object lurking in some corner or peeping from behind the window-curtains, so very a child was I in my fears.

The morning came, and with it Lord Glenfallen. I knew not, and indeed I cared not, where he might have been; my thoughts were wholly engrossed by the terrible fears and suspicions which my last night's conference had suggested to me. He was, as usual, gloomy and abstracted, and I feared in no very fitting mood to hear what I had to say with patience, whether the charges were true or false.

I was, however, determined not to suffer the opportunity to pass, or Lord Glenfallen to leave the room, until, at all hazards, I had unburdened my mind.

'My lord,' said I, after a long silence, summoning up all my firmness—'my lord, I wish to say a few words to you upon a matter of very great importance, of very deep concernment to you and to me.'

I fixed my eyes upon him to discern, if possible, whether the announcement caused him any uneasiness; but no symptom of any such feeling was perceptible.

'Well, my dear,' said he, 'this is no doubt a very grave preface, and portends, I have no doubt, something extraordinary. Pray let us have it without more ado.'

He took a chair, and seated himself nearly opposite to me.

'My lord,' said I, 'I have seen the person who alarmed me so much a short time since, the blind lady, again, upon last night.' His face, upon which my eyes were fixed, turned pale; he hesitated for a moment, and then said:

'And did you, pray, madam, so totally forget or spurn my express command, as to enter that portion of the house from which your promise, I might say your oath, excluded you?—answer me that!' he added fiercely.

'My lord,' said I, 'I have neither forgotten your *commands*, since such they were, nor disobeyed them. I was, last night, wakened from my sleep, as I lay in my own chamber, and accosted by the person whom I have mentioned. How she found access to the room I cannot pretend to say.'

'Ha! this must be looked to,' said he, half reflectively; 'and pray,' added he, quickly, while in turn he fixed his eyes upon me, 'what did this person say? since some comment upon her communication forms, no doubt, the sequel to your preface.'

'Your lordship is not mistaken,' said I; 'her statement was so extraordinary that I could not think of withholding it from you. She told me, my lord, that you had a wife living at the time you married me, and that she was that wife.'

Lord Glenfallen became ashy pale, almost livid; he made two or three efforts to clear his voice to speak, but in vain, and turning suddenly from me, he walked to the window. The horror and dismay which, in the olden time, overwhelmed the woman of Endor when her spells unexpectedly conjured the dead into her presence, were but types of what I felt when thus presented with what appeared to be almost unequivocal evidence of the guilt whose existence I had before so strongly doubted.

There was a silence of some moments, during which it were hard to conjecture whether I or my companion suffered most.

Lord Glenfallen soon recovered his self-command; he returned to the table, again sat down and said:

'What you have told me has so astonished me, has unfolded such a tissue of motiveless guilt, and in a quarter from which I had so little reason to look for ingratitude or treachery, that your announcement almost deprived me of speech; the person in question, however, has one excuse, her mind is, as I told you before, unsettled. You should have remembered that, and hesitated to receive as unexceptionable evidence against the honour of your husband, the ravings of a lunatic. I now tell you that this is the last time I shall speak to you upon this subject, and, in the presence of the God who is to judge me, and as I hope for mercy in the day of judgment, I swear that the charge thus brought against me is utterly false, unfounded, and ridiculous; I defy the world in any point to taint my honour; and, as I have never taken the opinion of madmen touching your character or morals, I think it but fair to require that you will evince a like tenderness for me; and now, once for all, never again dare to repeat to me your insulting suspicions, or the clumsy and infamous calumnies of fools. I shall instantly let the worthy lady who contrived this somewhat original device, understand fully my opinion upon the matter. Good morning;' and with these words he left me again in doubt, and involved in all horrors of the most agonising suspense.

I had reason to think that Lord Glenfallen wreaked his vengeance upon the author of the strange story which I had heard, with a violence which was not satisfied with mere words, for old Martha, with whom I was a great favourite, while attending me in my room, told me that she feared her master had ill-used the poor blind Dutch woman, for that she had heard her scream as if the very life were leaving her, but added a request that I should not speak of what she had told me to any one, particularly to the master.

'How do you know that she is a Dutch woman?' inquired I, anxious to learn anything whatever that might throw a light upon the history of this person, who seemed to have resolved to mix herself up in my fortunes.

'Why, my lady,' answered Martha, 'the master often calls her the Dutch hag, and other names you would not like to hear, and I am sure she is neither English nor Irish; for, whenever they talk together, they speak some queer foreign lingo, and fast enough, I'll be bound. But I ought not to talk about her at all; it might be as much as my place is worth to mention her—only you saw her first yourself, so there can be no great harm in speaking of her now.'

'How long has this lady been here?' continued I.

'She came early on the morning after your ladyship's arrival,' answered she; 'but do not ask me any more, for the master would think nothing of turning me out of doors for daring to speak of her at all, much less to *you*, my lady.'

I did not like to press the poor woman further, for her reluctance to speak on this topic was evident and strong.

You will readily believe that upon the very slight grounds which my information afforded, contradicted as it was by the solemn oath of my husband, and derived from what was, at best, a very questionable source, I could not take any very decisive measure whatever; and as to the menace of the strange woman who had thus unaccountably twice intruded herself into my chamber, although, at the moment, it occasioned me some uneasiness, it was not, even in my eyes, sufficiently formidable to induce my departure from Cahergillagh.

A few nights after the scene which I have just mentioned, Lord Glenfallen having, as usual, early retired to his study, I was left alone in the parlour to amuse myself as best I might.

It was not strange that my thoughts should often recur to the agitating scenes in which I had recently taken a part.

The subject of my reflections, the solitude, the silence, and the lateness of the hour, as also the depression of spirits to which I had of late been a constant prey, tended to produce that nervous excitement which places us wholly at the mercy of the imagination.

In order to calm my spirits I was endeavouring to direct my thoughts into some more pleasing channel, when I heard, or thought I heard, uttered, within a few yards of me, in an odd, half-sneering tone, the words,

'There is blood upon your ladyship's throat.'

So vivid was the impression that I started to my feet, and involuntarily placed my hand upon my neck.

I looked around the room for the speaker, but in vain.

I went then to the room-door, which I opened, and peered into the passage, nearly faint with horror lest some leering, shapeless thing should greet me upon the threshold.

When I had gazed long enough to assure myself that no strange object was within sight,

'I have been too much of a rake lately; I am racking out my nerves,' said I, speaking aloud, with a view to reassure myself.

I rang the bell, and, attended by old Martha, I retired to settle for the night.

While the servant was—as was her custom—arranging the lamp which I have already stated always burned during the night in my chamber, I was employed in undressing, and, in doing so, I had recourse to a large looking-glass which occupied a considerable portion of the wall in which it was fixed, rising from the ground to a height of about six feet—this mirror filled the space of a large panel in the wainscoting opposite the foot of the bed.

I had hardly been before it for the lapse of a minute when something like a black pall was slowly waved between me and it.

'Oh, God! there it is,' I exclaimed, wildly. 'I have seen it again, Martha—the black cloth.'

'God be merciful to us, then!' answered she, tremulously crossing herself. 'Some misfortune is over us.'

'No, no, Martha,' said I, almost instantly recovering my collectedness; for, although of a nervous temperament, I had never been superstitious. 'I do not believe in omens. You know I saw, or fancied I saw, this thing before, and nothing followed.'

'The Dutch lady came the next morning,' replied she.

'But surely her coming scarcely deserved such a dreadful warning,' I replied.

'She is a strange woman, my lady,' said Martha; 'and she is not *gone* yet—mark my words.'

'Well, well, Martha,' said I, 'I have not wit enough to change your opinions, nor inclination to alter mine; so I will talk no more of the matter. Good-night,' and so I was left to my reflections.

After lying for about an hour awake, I at length fell into a kind of doze; but my imagination was still busy, for I was startled from this unrefreshing sleep by fancying that I heard a voice close to my face exclaim as before:

'There is blood upon your ladyship's throat.'

The words were instantly followed by a loud burst of laughter.

Quaking with horror, I awakened, and heard my husband enter the room. Even this was a relief.

Scared as I was, however, by the tricks which my imagination had played me, I preferred remaining silent, and pretending to sleep, to attempting to engage my husband in conversation, for I well knew that his mood was such, that his words would not, in all probability, convey anything that had not better be unsaid and unheard.

Lord Glenfallen went into his dressing-room, which lay upon the right-hand side of the bed. The door lying open, I could see him by himself, at full length upon a sofa, and, in about half an hour, I became aware, by his deep and regularly drawn respiration, that he was fast asleep.

When slumber refuses to visit one, there is something peculiarly irritating, not to the temper, but to the nerves, in the consciousness that some one is in your immediate presence, actually enjoying the boon which you are seeking in vain; at least, I have always found it so, and never more than upon the present occasion.

A thousand annoying imaginations harassed and excited me; every object which I looked upon, though ever so familiar, seemed to have acquired a strange phantom-like character, the varying shadows thrown by the flickering of the lamplight, seemed shaping themselves into grotesque and unearthly forms, and whenever my eyes wandered to the sleeping figure of my husband, his features appeared to undergo the strangest and most demoniacal contortions.

Hour after hour was told by the old clock, and each succeeding one found me, if possible, less inclined to sleep than its predecessor.

It was now considerably past three; my eyes, in their involuntary wanderings, happened to alight upon the large mirror which was, as I have said, fixed in the wall opposite the foot of the bed. A view of it was commanded from where I lay, through the curtains. As I gazed fixedly upon it, I thought I perceived the broad sheet of glass shifting its position in relation to the bed; I riveted my eyes upon it with intense scrutiny; it was no deception, the mirror, as if acting of its own impulse, moved slowly aside, and disclosed a dark aperture in the wall, nearly as large as an ordinary door; a figure evidently stood in this, but the light was too dim to define it accurately.

It stepped cautiously into the chamber, and with so little noise, that had I not actually seen it, I do not think I should have been aware of its presence. It was arrayed in a kind of woollen night-dress, and a white handkerchief or cloth was bound tightly about the head; I had no difficulty, spite of the strangeness of the attire, in recognising the blind woman whom I so much dreaded.

She stooped down, bringing her head nearly to the ground, and in that attitude she remained motionless for some moments, no doubt in order to ascertain if any suspicious sound were stirring.

She was apparently satisfied by her observations, for she immediately recommenced her silent progress towards a ponderous mahogany dressing-table of my husband's. When she had reached it, she paused again, and appeared to listen attentively for some minutes; she then noiselessly opened one of the drawers, from which, having groped for some time, she took something, which I soon perceived to be a case of razors. She opened it, and tried the edge of each of the two instruments upon the skin of her hand; she quickly selected one, which she fixed firmly in her grasp. She now stooped down as before, and having listened for a time, she, with the hand that was disengaged, groped her way into the dressing-room where Lord Glenfallen lay fast asleep.

I was fixed as if in the tremendous spell of a nightmare. I could not stir even a finger; I could not lift my voice; I could not even breathe; and though I expected every moment to see the sleeping man murdered, I could not even close my eyes to shut out the horrible spectacle, which I had not the power to avert.

I saw the woman approach the sleeping figure, she laid the unoccupied hand lightly along his clothes, and having thus ascertained his identity, she, after a brief interval, turned back and again entered my chamber; here she bent down again to listen.

I had now not a doubt but that the razor was intended for my throat; yet the terrific fascination which had locked all my powers so long, still continued to bind me fast.

I felt that my life depended upon the slightest ordinary exertion, and yet I could not stir one joint from the position in which I lay, nor even make noise enough to waken Lord Glenfallen.

The murderous woman now, with long, silent steps, approached the bed; my very heart seemed turning to ice; her left hand, that which was disengaged, was upon the pillow; she gradually slid it forward towards my head, and in an instant, with the speed of lightning, it was clutched in my hair, while, with the other hand, she dashed the razor at my throat.

A slight inaccuracy saved me from instant death; the blow fell short, the point of the razor grazing my throat. In a moment, I know not how,

I found myself at the other side of the bed, uttering shriek after shriek; the wretch was, however, determined if possible to murder me.

Scrambling along by the curtains, she rushed round the bed towards me; I seized the handle of the door to make my escape. It was, however, fastened. At all events, I could not open it. From the mere instinct of recoiling terror, I shrunk back into a corner. She was now within a yard of me. Her hand was upon my face.

I closed my eyes fast, expecting never to open them again, when a blow, inflicted from behind by a strong arm, stretched the monster senseless at my feet. At the same moment the door opened, and several domestics, alarmed by my cries, entered the apartment.

I do not recollect what followed, for I fainted. One swoon succeeded another, so long and death-like, that my life was considered very doubtful.

At about ten o'clock, however, I sunk into a deep and refreshing sleep, from which I was awakened at about two, that I might swear my deposition before a magistrate, who attended for that purpose.

I accordingly did so, as did also Lord Glenfallen, and the woman was fully committed to stand her trial at the ensuing assizes.

I shall never forget the scene which the examination of the blind woman and of the other parties afforded.

She was brought into the room in the custody of two servants. She wore a kind of flannel wrapper which had not been changed since the night before. It was torn and soiled, and here and there smeared with blood, which had flowed in large quantities from a wound in her head. The white handkerchief had fallen off in the scuffle, and her grizzled hair fell in masses about her wild and deadly pale countenance.

She appeared perfectly composed, however, and the only regret she expressed throughout, was at not having succeeded in her attempt, the object of which she did not pretend to conceal.

On being asked her name, she called herself the Countess Glenfallen, and refused to give any other title.

'The woman's name is Flora Van-Kemp,' said Lord Glenfallen.

'It *was*, it *was*, you perjured traitor and cheat!' screamed the woman; and then there followed a volley of words in some foreign language. 'Is there a magistrate here?' she resumed; 'I am Lord Glenfallen's wife—I'll prove it—write down my words. I am willing to be hanged or burned, so *he* meets his deserts. I did try to kill that doll of his; but it was he who put it into my head to do it—two wives were too many; I was to murder her, or she was to hang me; listen to all I have to say.'

Here Lord Glenfallen interrupted.

'I think, sir,' said he, addressing the magistrate, 'that we had better proceed to business; this unhappy woman's furious recriminations but waste our time. If she refuses to answer your questions, you had better, I presume, take my depositions.'

'And are you going to swear away my life, you black-perjured murderer?' shrieked the woman. 'Sir, sir, sir, you must hear me,' she continued, addressing the magistrate; 'I can convict him—he bid me murder that girl, and then, when I failed, he came behind me, and struck me down, and now he wants to swear away my life. Take down all I say.'

'If it is your intention,' said the magistrate, 'to confess the crime with which you stand charged, you may, upon producing sufficient evidence, criminate whom you please.'

'Evidence!—I have no evidence but myself,' said the woman. 'I will swear it all—write down my testimony—write it down, I say—we shall hang side by side, my brave lord—all your own handy-work, my gentle husband.'

This was followed by a low, insolent, and sneering laugh, which, from one in her situation, was sufficiently horrible.

'I will not at present hear anything,' replied he, 'but distinct answers to the questions which I shall put to you upon this matter.'

'Then you shall hear nothing,' replied she sullenly, and no inducement or intimidation could bring her to speak again.

Lord Glenfallen's deposition and mine were then given, as also those of the servants who had entered the room at the moment of my rescue.

The magistrate then intimated that she was committed, and must proceed directly to gaol, whither she was brought in a carriage of Lord Glenfallen's, for his lordship was naturally by no means indifferent to the effect which her vehement accusations against himself might produce, if uttered before every chance hearer whom she might meet with between Cahergillagh and the place of confinement whither she was despatched.

During the time which intervened between the committal and the trial of the prisoner, Lord Glenfallen seemed to suffer agonies of mind which baffle all description; he hardly ever slept, and when he did, his slumbers seemed but the instruments of new tortures, and his waking hours were, if possible, exceeded in intensity of terrors by the dreams which disturbed his sleep.

Lord Glenfallen rested, if to lie in the mere attitude of repose were to do so, in his dressing-room, and thus I had an opportunity of witnessing, far oftener than I wished it, the fearful workings of his mind. His agony often broke out into such fearful paroxysms that delirium and total loss of reason appeared to be impending. He frequently spoke of flying from the country, and bringing with him all the witnesses of the appalling scene upon which the prosecution was founded; then, again, he would fiercely lament that the blow which he had inflicted had not ended all.

The assizes arrived, however, and upon the day appointed Lord Glenfallen and I attended in order to give our evidence.

The cause was called on, and the prisoner appeared at the bar.

Great curiosity and interest were felt respecting the trial, so that the court was crowded to excess.

The prisoner, however, without appearing to take the trouble of listening to the indictment, pleaded guilty, and no representations on the part of the court availed to induce her to retract her plea.

After much time had been wasted in a fruitless attempt to prevail upon her to reconsider her words, the court proceeded, according to the usual form, to pass sentence.

This having been done, the prisoner was about to be removed, when she said, in a low, distinct voice:

'A word—a word, my lord!—Is Lord Glenfallen here in the court?'

On being told that he was, she raised her voice to a tone of loud menace, and continued:

'Hardress, Earl of Glenfallen, I accuse you here in this court of justice of two crimes,—first, that you married a second wife, while the first was living; and again, that you prompted me to the murder, for attempting which I am to die. Secure him—chain him—bring him here.'

There was a laugh through the court at these words, which were naturally treated by the judge as a violent extemporary recrimination, and the woman was desired to be silent.

'You won't take him, then?' she said; 'you won't try him? You'll let him go free?'

It was intimated by the court that he would certainly be allowed 'to go free,' and she was ordered again to be removed.

Before, however, the mandate was executed, she threw her arms wildly into the air, and uttered one piercing shriek so full of preternatural rage and despair, that it might fitly have ushered a soul into those realms where hope can come no more.

The sound still rang in my ears, months after the voice that had uttered it was for ever silent.

The wretched woman was executed in accordance with the sentence which had been pronounced.

For some time after this event, Lord Glenfallen appeared, if possible, to suffer more than he had done before, and altogether his language, which often amounted to half confessions of the guilt imputed to him, and all the circumstances connected with the late occurrences, formed a mass of evidence so convincing that I wrote to my father, detailing the grounds of my fears, and imploring him to come to Cahergillagh without delay, in order to remove me from my husband's control, previously to taking legal steps for a final separation.

Circumstanced as I was, my existence was little short of intolerable, for, besides the fearful suspicions which attached to my husband, I plainly perceived that if Lord Glenfallen were not relieved, and that speedily, insanity must supervene. I therefore expected my father's arrival, or at least a letter to announce it, with indescribable impatience.

About a week after the execution had taken place, Lord Glenfallen one morning met me with an unusually sprightly air.

'Fanny,' said he, 'I have it now for the first time in my power to explain to your satisfaction everything which has hitherto appeared suspicious or mysterious in my conduct. After breakfast come with me to my study, and I shall, I hope, make all things clear.'

This invitation afforded me more real pleasure than I had experienced for months. Something had certainly occurred to tranquillise my husband's mind in no ordinary degree, and I thought it by no means impossible that he would, in the proposed interview, prove himself the most injured and innocent of men.

Full of this hope, I repaired to his study at the appointed hour. He was writing busily when I entered the room, and just raising his eyes, he requested me to be seated.

I took a chair as he desired, and remained silently awaiting his leisure, while he finished, folded, directed, and sealed his letter. Laying it then upon the table with the address downward, he said,

'My dearest Fanny, I know I must have appeared very strange to you and very unkind—often even cruel. Before the end of this week I will show you the necessity of my conduct—how impossible it was that I should have seemed otherwise. I am conscious that many acts of mine must have inevitably given rise to painful suspicions—suspicions which, indeed, upon one occasion, you very properly communicated to me. I have got two letters from a quarter which commands respect, containing information as to the course by which I may be enabled to prove the negative of all the crimes which even the most credulous suspicion could lay to my charge. I expected a third by this morning's post, containing documents which will set the matter for ever at rest, but owing, no doubt, to some neglect, or, perhaps, to some difficulty in collecting the papers, some inevitable delay, it has not come to hand this morning, according to my expectation. I was finishing one to the very same quarter when you came in, and if a sound rousing be worth anything, I think I shall have a special messenger before two days have passed. I have been anxiously considering with myself, as to whether I had better imperfectly clear up your doubts by submitting to your inspection the two letters which I have already received, or wait till I can triumphantly vindicate myself by the production of the documents which I have already mentioned, and I have, I think, not unnaturally decided upon the latter course. However, there is a person in the next room whose testimony is not without its value—excuse me for one moment.'

So saying, he arose and went to the door of a closet which opened from the study; this he unlocked, and half opening the door, he said,

'It is only I,' and then slipped into the room and carefully closed and locked the door behind him.

I immediately heard his voice in animated conversation. My curiosity upon the subject of the letter was naturally great, so, smothering any little scruples which I might have felt, I resolved to look at the address of the letter which lay, as my husband had left it, with its face upon the table. I accordingly drew it over to me and turned up the direction.

For two or three moments I could scarce believe my eyes, but there could be no mistake—in large characters were traced the words, 'To the Archangel Gabriel in Heaven.'

I had scarcely returned the letter to its original position, and in some degree recovered the shock which this unequivocal proof of insanity produced, when the closet door was unlocked, and Lord Glenfallen re-entered the study, carefully closing and locking the door again upon the outside.

'Whom have you there?' inquired I, making a strong effort to appear calm.

'Perhaps,' said he, musingly, 'you might have some objection to seeing her, at least for a time.'

'Who is it?' repeated I.

'Why,' said he, 'I see no use in hiding it—the blind Dutchwoman. I have been with her the whole morning. She is very anxious to get out of that closet; but you know she is odd, she is scarcely to be trusted.'

A heavy gust of wind shook the door at this moment with a sound as if something more substantial were pushing against it.

'Ha, ha, ha!—do you hear her?' said he, with an obstreperous burst of laughter.

The wind died away in a long howl, and Lord Glenfallen, suddenly checking his merriment, shrugged his shoulders, and muttered:

'Poor devil, she has been hardly used.'

'We had better not tease her at present with questions,' said I, in as unconcerned a tone as I could assume, although I felt every moment as if I should faint.

'Humph! may be so,' said he. 'Well, come back in an hour or two, or when you please, and you will find us here.'

He again unlocked the door, and entered with the same precautions which he had adopted before, locking the door upon the inside; and as I hurried from the room, I heard his voice again exerted as if in eager parley.

I can hardly describe my emotions; my hopes had been raised to the highest, and now, in an instant, all was gone—the dreadful consummation was accomplished—the fearful retribution had fallen upon the guilty man—the mind was destroyed—the power to repent was gone.

The agony of the hours which followed what I would still call my *awful* interview with Lord Glenfallen, I cannot describe; my solitude was, however, broken in upon by Martha, who came to inform me of the arrival of a gentleman, who expected me in the parlour.

I accordingly descended, and, to my great joy, found my father seated by the fire.

This expedition upon his part was easily accounted for: my communications had touched the honour of the family. I speedily informed him of the dreadful malady which had fallen upon the wretched man.

My father suggested the necessity of placing some person to watch him, to prevent his injuring himself or others.

I rang the bell, and desired that one Edward Cooke, an attached servant of the family, should be sent to me.

I told him distinctly and briefly the nature of the service required of him, and, attended by him, my father and I proceeded at once to the study. The door of the inner room was still closed, and everything in the outer chamber remained in the same order in which I had left it.

We then advanced to the closet-door, at which we knocked, but without receiving any answer.

We next tried to open the door, but in vain—it was locked upon the inside. We knocked more loudly, but in vain.

Seriously alarmed, I desired the servant to force the door, which was, after several violent efforts, accomplished, and we entered the closet.

Lord Glenfallen was lying on his face upon a sofa.

'Hush!' said I, 'he is asleep.' We paused for a moment.

'He is too still for that,' said my father.

We all of us felt a strong reluctance to approach the figure.

'Edward,' said I, 'try whether your master sleeps.'

The servant approached the sofa where Lord Glenfallen lay. He leant his ear towards the head of the recumbent figure, to ascertain whether the sound of breathing was audible. He turned towards us, and said:

'My lady, you had better not wait here; I am sure he is dead!'

'Let me see the face,' said I, terribly agitated; 'you *may* be mistaken.'

The man then, in obedience to my command, turned the body round, and, gracious God! what a sight met my view. He was, indeed, perfectly dead.

The whole breast of the shirt, with its lace frill, was drenched with gore, as was the couch underneath the spot where he lay.

The head hung back, as it seemed, almost severed from the body by a frightful gash, which yawned across the throat. The instrument which had inflicted it was found under his body.

All, then, was over; I was never to learn the history in whose termination I had been so deeply and so tragically involved.

The severe discipline which my mind had undergone was not bestowed in vain. I directed my thoughts and my hopes to that place where there is no more sin, nor danger, nor sorrow.

Thus ends a brief tale whose prominent incidents many will recognise as having marked the history of a distinguished family; and though it refers to a somewhat distant date, we shall be found not to have taken, upon that account, any liberties with the facts, but in our statement of all the incidents to have rigorously and faithfully adhered to the truth.

—1839/1851—

SCHALKEN THE PAINTER

'For he is not a man as I am that we should come together; neither is there any that might lay his hand upon us both. Let him, therefore, take his rod away from me, and let not his fear terrify me.'

THERE exists, at this moment, in good preservation, a remarkable work of Schalken's. The curious management of its lights constitutes, as usual in his pieces, the chief apparent merit of the picture. I say *apparent*, for in its subject and not in its handling, however exquisite, consists its real value. The picture represents the interior of what might be a chamber in some antique religious building; and its foreground is occupied by a female figure, in a species of white robe, part of which is arranged so as to form a veil. The dress, however, is not that of any religious order. In her hand she bears a lamp, by which alone her figure and face are illuminated; and her features wear such an arch smile as well becomes a pretty woman when practising some prankish roguery; in the background, and, excepting where the dim red light of an expiring fire serves to define the form, in total shadow, stands the figure of a man dressed in the old Flemish fashion, in an attitude of alarm, his hand being placed on the hilt of his sword, which he appears to be in the act of drawing.

There are some pictures which impress one, I know not how, with a conviction that they represent not the mere ideal shapes and combinations which have floated through the imagination of the artist, but scenes, faces, and situations which have actually existed. There is in that strange picture something that stamps it as the representation of reality.

And such in truth it is, for it faithfully records a remarkable and mysterious occurrence, and perpetuates, in the face of the female figure, which occupies the most prominent place in the design, an accurate portrait of Rose Velderkaust, the niece of Gerard Douw, the first, and, I believe, the only love of Godfrey Schalken. My great grandfather knew the painter well; from Schalken himself he learned the fearful story of the painting, and from him too he ultimately received the picture itself as a bequest. The story and the picture have become heirlooms in my family, and having described the latter, I shall, if you please, attempt to relate the tradition which has descended with the canvass.

There are few forms on which the mantle of romance hangs more ungracefully than upon that of the uncouth Schalken—the boorish but most cunning worker in oils, whose pieces delight the critics of our day almost as much as his manners disgusted the refined of his own; and yet this man, so rude, so dogged, so slovenly in the midst of his celebrity, had, in his obscure, but happier days, played the hero in a wild romance of mystery and passion.

When Schalken studied under the renowned Gerard Douw, he was a very young man; and in spite of his phlegmatic temperament, he at once fell over head and ears in love with the beautiful niece of his wealthy master. Rose Velderkaust was still younger than he, having not yet attained her seventeenth year, and if tradition speaks truth, she possessed all the soft and dimpling charms of the fair, light-haired, Flemish maidens. The young painter loved honestly and fervently. His frank adoration was rewarded. He declared his love, and extracted a faltering confession in return. He was the happiest and proudest painter in all Christendom. But there was somewhat to dash his elation; he was poor and undistinguished. He dared not ask old Gerard for the hand of his sweet ward. He must first win a reputation and a competence.

There were, therefore, many dread uncertainties and cold delays before him; he had to fight his way against sore odds. But he had won the heart of dear Rose Velderkaust, and that was half the battle. It is needless to say his exertions were redoubled, and his lasting celebrity proves that his industry was not unrewarded by success.

These ardent labours, and worse still, the hopes that elevated and beguiled them, were, however, destined to experience a sudden interruption—of a character so mysterious as to baffle all inquiry, and to throw over the events themselves a shadow of preternatural horror.

Schalken had one evening outstayed all his fellow-pupils, and still pursued his work in the deserted room. As the daylight was fast failing, he laid aside his colours, and applied himself to the completion of a sketch on which he had expended extraordinary pains. It was a religious composition, and represented the temptations of a pot-bellied Saint Anthony. The young artist, however destitute of elevation, had, nevertheless, discernment enough to be dissatisfied with his own work, and many were the patient erasures and improvements which saint and devil underwent, yet all in vain. The large, old-fashioned room was silent, and, with the exception of himself, quite emptied of its usual inmates. An hour had thus passed away, nearly two, without any improved result. Daylight had already declined, and twilight was deepening into the darkness of night. The patience of the young painter was exhausted, and he stood before his unfinished production, angry and mortified, one hand buried in the folds of his long hair, and the other holding the piece of charcoal which had so ill-performed its office, and which he now rubbed, without much regard to the sable streaks it produced, with irritable pressure upon his ample Flemish inexpressibles.

'Curse the subject!' said the young man, aloud; 'curse the picture, the devils, the saint—'

At this moment a short, sudden sniff, uttered close beside him, made the artist turn sharply round, and he now, for the first time, became aware that his labours had been overlooked by a stranger.

Within about a yard and half, and rather behind him, there stood the figure of an elderly man, in a cloak and a broad-brimmed, conical hat; in his hand, which was protected with a heavy gauntlet-shaped glove, he carried a long ebony walking-stick, surmounted with what appeared, as it glittered dimly in the twilight, to be a massive head of gold, and upon his breast, through the folds of the cloak, there shone the links of a rich chain of the same metal. The room was so obscure that nothing further of the appearance of the figure could be ascertained, and the heavy flap of his hat threw his features into profound shadow. It would not have been easy to conjecture the age of the intruder; but a quantity of dark hair escaping from beneath this sombre hat, as well as his firm and upright carriage, seemed to indicate that his years could not yet exceed threescore, or thereabouts. There was an air of gravity and importance about the garb of this person, and something indescribably odd, I might say awful, in the perfect, stone-like stillness of the figure, that effectually checked the testy comment which had at once risen to the lips of the irritated artist. He therefore, as soon as he had sufficiently recovered his surprise, asked the stranger, civilly, to be seated, and desired to know if he had any message to leave for his master.

'Tell Gerard Douw,' said the unknown, without altering his attitude in the smallest degree, 'that Minheer Vanderhausen, of Rotterdam, desires to speak with him on to-morrow evening at this hour, and if he please, in this room, upon matters of weight; that is all.'

The stranger, having finished this message, turned abruptly, and, with a quick, but silent step, quitted the room, before Schalken had time to say a word in reply. The young man felt a curiosity to see in what direction the burgher of Rotterdam would turn, on quitting the *studio*, and for that purpose he went directly to the window which commanded the door. A lobby of considerable extent intervened between the inner door of the painter's room and the street entrance, so that Schalken occupied the post of observation, as he conjectured, before the old man could possibly have reached the street. He watched in vain, however. There was no other mode of exit. Had the queer old man vanished, or was he lurking about the recesses of the lobby for some sinister purpose? This last suggestion filled the mind of Schalken with a vague uneasiness, which was so unaccountably intense as to make him alike afraid to remain in the room alone, and reluctant to pass through the lobby. However, with an effort apparently very disproportioned to the occasion, he summoned resolution to leave the room, and having locked the door, and thrust the key into his pocket, without looking to the right or left, he traversed the passage which had so recently, perhaps still, contained the person of his mysterious visitant, scarcely venturing to breathe till he had arrived in the open street.

'Minheer Vanderhausen!' said Gerard Douw within himself, as the appointed hour approached, 'Minheer Vanderhausen, of Rotterdam! I never heard of the man till yesterday. What can he want of me? A portrait, perhaps, to be painted; or a poor relation to be apprenticed; or a collection to be valued; or—pshaw! there's no one in Rotterdam to leave me a legacy. Well, whatever the business may be, we shall soon know it all.'

It was now the close of day, and again every easel, except that of Schalken, was deserted. Gerard Douw was pacing the apartment with the restless step of impatient expectation, sometimes pausing to glance over the work of one of his absent pupils, but more frequently placing himself at the window, from whence he might observe the passengers who threaded the obscure by-street in which his studio was placed.

'Said you not, Godfrey,' exclaimed Douw, after a long and fruitless gaze from his post of observation, and turning to Schalken, 'that the hour he appointed was about seven by the clock of the Stadhouse?'

'It had just told seven when I first saw him, sir,' answered the student.

'The hour is close at hand, then,' said the master, consulting a horologe as large and as round as an orange. 'Minheer Vanderhausen, from Rotterdam—is it not so?'

'Such was the name.'

'And an elderly man, richly clad?' pursued Douw, musingly.

'As well as I might see,' replied his pupil; 'he could not be young, nor yet very old, neither; and his dress was rich and grave, as might become a citizen of wealth and consideration.'

At this moment the sonorous boom of the Stadhouse clock told, stroke after stroke, the hour of seven; the eyes of both master and student were directed to the door; and it was not until the last peal of the old bell had ceased to vibrate, that Douw exclaimed—

'So, so; we shall have his worship presently, that is, if he means to keep his hour; if not, you may wait for him, Godfrey, if you court his acquaintance. But what, after all, if it should prove but a mummery, got up by Vankarp, or some such wag. I wish you had run all risks, and cudgelled the old burgomaster soundly. I'd wager a dozen of Rhenish his worship would have unmasked, and pleaded old acquaintance in a trice.'

'Here he comes, sir,' said Schalken, in a low, monitory tone; and instantly, upon turning towards the door, Gerard Douw observed the same figure which had, on the day before, so unexpectedly greeted his pupil Schalken.

There was something in the air of the figure which at once satisfied the painter that there was no masquerading in the case, and that he really stood in the presence of a man of worship; and so, without hesitation, he doffed his cap, and, courteously saluting the stranger, requested him to be seated. The visitor waved his hand slightly, as if in acknowledgment of the courtesy, but remained standing.

'I have the honour to see Minheer Vanderhausen of Rotterdam?' said Gerard Douw.

'The same,' was the laconic reply of his visitor.

'I understand your worship desires to speak with me,' continued Douw, 'and I am here by appointment to wait your commands.'

'Is that a man of trust?' said Vanderhausen, turning towards Schalken, who stood at a little distance behind his master.

'Certainly,' replied Gerard.

'Then let him take this box, and get the nearest jeweller or goldsmith to value its contents, and let him return hither with a certificate of the valuation.'

At the same time, he placed a small case about nine inches square in the hands of Gerard Douw, who was as much amazed at its weight as at the strange abruptness with which it was handed to him. In accordance with the wishes of the stranger, he delivered it into the hands of Schalken, and repeating his directions, despatched him upon the mission.

Schalken disposed his precious charge securely beneath the folds of his cloak, and rapidly traversing two or three narrow streets, he stopped at a corner house, the lower part of which was then occupied by the shop of a Jewish goldsmith. He entered the shop, and calling the little Hebrew into the obscurity of its back recesses, he proceeded to lay before him Vanderhausen's casket. On being examined by the light of a lamp, it appeared entirely cased with lead, the outer surface of which was much scraped and soiled, and nearly white with age. This having been partially removed, there appeared beneath a box of some hard wood, which also they forced open, and after the removal of two or three folds of linen, they discovered its contents to be a mass of golden ingots, closely packed, and, as the Jew declared, of the most perfect quality. Every ingot underwent the scrutiny of the little Jew, who seemed to feel an epicurean delight in touching and testing these morsels of the glorious metal; and each one of them was replaced in its berth with the exclamation: '*Meinn Gott*, how very perfect! not one grain of alloy—beautiful, beautiful!' The task was at length finished, and the Jew certified under his hand the value of the ingots submitted to his examination, to amount to many thousand rix-dollars. With the desired document in his pocket, and the rich box of gold carefully pressed under his arm, and concealed by his cloak, he retraced his way, and entering the studio, found his master and the stranger in close conference. Schalken had no sooner left the room, in order to execute the commission he had taken in charge, than Vanderhausen addressed Gerard Douw in the following terms:—

'I cannot tarry with you to-night more than a few minutes, and so I shall shortly tell you the matter upon which I come. You visited the town of Rotterdam some four months ago, and then I saw in the Church of St. Lawrence your niece, Rose Velderkaust. I desire to marry her; and if I satisfy you that I am wealthier than any other husband you can dream of for her, I expect that you will forward my suit with your authority. If you approve my proposal, you must close with it here and now, for I cannot wait for calculations and delays.'

Gerard Douw was hugely astonished at the nature of Minheer Vanderhausen's communication, but he did not venture to express his surprise; for besides the motives supplied by prudence and politeness, the painter experienced a sort of chill and oppression, like that which is said to supervene when one is placed in unconscious proximity with the object of a natural antipathy—an undefined but overpowering sensation, while standing in the presence of the eccentric stranger, which made him very unwilling to say anything which might reasonably offend him.

'I have no doubt,' said Gerard, after two or three prefatory hems, 'that the alliance which you propose would prove alike advantageous and honourable to my niece; but you must be aware that she has a will of her own, and may not acquiesce in what *we* may design for her advantage.'

'Do not seek to deceive me, sir painter,' said Vanderhausen; 'you are her guardian—she is your ward; she is mine if *you* like to make her so.'

The man of Rotterdam moved forward a little as he spoke, and Gerard Douw, he scarce knew why, inwardly prayed for the speedy return of Schalken.

'I desire,' said the mysterious gentleman, 'to place in your hands at once an evidence of my wealth, and a security for my liberal dealing with your niece. The lad will return in a minute or two with a sum in value five times the fortune which she has a right to expect from her husband. This shall lie in your hands, together with her dowry, and you may apply the united sum as suits her interest best; it shall be all exclusively hers while she lives: is that liberal?'

Douw assented, and inwardly acknowledged that fortune had been extraordinarily kind to his niece; the stranger, he thought, must be both wealthy and generous, and such an offer was not to be despised, though made by a humourist, and one of no very prepossessing presence. Rose had no very high pretensions, for she had but a modest dowry, which she owed entirely to the generosity of her uncle; neither had she any right to raise exceptions on the score of birth, for her own origin was far from splendid; and as to other objections, Gerard resolved, and, indeed, by the usages of the time, was warranted in resolving, not to listen to them for a moment.

'Sir,' said he, addressing the stranger, 'your offer is liberal, and whatever hesitation I may feel in closing with it immediately, arises solely from my not having the honour of knowing anything of your family or station. Upon these points you can, of course, satisfy me without difficulty?'

'As to my respectability,' said the stranger, drily, 'you must take that for granted at present; pester me with no inquiries; you can discover nothing more about me than I choose to make known. You shall have sufficient security for my respectability—my word, if you are honourable; if you are sordid, my gold.'

'A testy old gentleman,' thought Douw, 'he will have his own way; but, all things considered, I am not justified in declining his offer. I will not pledge myself unnecessarily, however.'

'You will not pledge yourself unnecessarily,' said Vanderhausen, strangely uttering the very words which had just floated through the mind of his companion; 'but you will do so if it *is* necessary, I presume; and I will show you that I consider it indispensable. If the gold I mean to leave in your hands satisfy you, and if you don't wish my proposal to be at once withdrawn, you must, before I leave this room, write your name to this engagement.'

Having thus spoken, he placed a paper in the hands of the master, the contents of which expressed an engagement entered into by Gerard Douw, to give to Wilken Vanderhausen of Rotterdam, in marriage, Rose Velderkaust, and soforth, within one week of the date thereof. While the painter was employed in reading this covenant, by the light of a twinkling oil lamp in the far wall of the room, Schalken, as we have stated, entered the studio, and having delivered the box and the valuation of the Jew, into the hands of the stranger, he was about to retire, when Vanderhausen called to him to wait; and, presenting the case and the certificate to Gerard Douw, he paused in silence until he had satisfied himself, by an inspection of both, respecting the value of the pledge left in his hands. At length he said—

'Are you content?'

The painter said he would fain have another day to consider.

'Not an hour,' said the suitor, apathetically.

'Well then,' said Douw, with a sore effort, 'I *am* content, it is a bargain.'

'Then sign,' said Vanderhausen, 'for I am weary.'

At the same time he produced a small case of writing materials, and Gerard signed the important document.

'Let this youth witness the covenant,' said the old man; and Godfrey Schalken unconsciously attested the instrument which for ever bereft him of his dear Rose Velderkaust.

The compact being thus completed, the strange visitor folded the paper, and stowed it safely in an inner pocket.

'I will visit you to-morrow night at nine o'clock, at your own house, Gerard Douw, and will see the object of our contract;' and so saying, Wilken Vanderhausen moved stiffly, but rapidly, out of the room.

Schalken, eager to resolve his doubts, had placed himself by the window, in order to watch the street entrance; but the experiment served only to support his suspicions, for the old man did not issue from the door. This was *very* strange—odd, nay fearful. He and his master returned together, and talked but little on the way, for each had his own subjects of reflection, of anxiety, and of hope. Schalken, however, did not know the ruin which menaced his dearest projects.

Gerard Douw knew nothing of the attachment which had sprung up between his pupil and his niece; and even if he had, it is doubtful whether he would have regarded its existence as any serious obstruction to the wishes of Minheer Vanderhausen. Marriages were then and there matters of traffic and calculation; and it would have appeared as absurd in the eyes of the guardian to make a mutual attachment an essential element in a contract of the sort, as it would have been to draw up his bonds and receipts in the language of romance.

The painter, however, did not communicate to his niece the important step which he had taken in her behalf, a forbearance caused not by any anticipated opposition on her part, but solely by a ludicrous consciousness that if she were to ask him for a description of her destined bridegroom, he would be forced to confess that he had not once seen his face, and if called upon, would find it absolutely impossible to identify him. Upon the next day, Gerard Douw, after dinner, called his niece to him, and having scanned her person with an air of satisfaction, he took her hand, and looking upon her pretty innocent face with a smile of kindness, he said:—

'Rose, my girl, that face of yours will make your fortune.' Rose blushed and smiled. 'Such faces and such tempers seldom go together, and when they do, the combination is a love-charm such as few heads or hearts can resist; trust me, you will soon be a bride, girl. But this is trifling, and I am pressed for time; so make ready the large room by eight o'clock to-night, and give directions for supper at nine. I expect a friend; and observe me, child, do you trick yourself out handsomely. I will not have him think us poor or sluttish.'

With these words he left her, and took his way to the room in which his pupils worked.

When the evening closed in, Gerard called Schalken, who was about to take his departure to his own obscure and comfortless lodgings, and asked him to come home and sup with Rose and Vanderhausen. The invitation was, of course, accepted, and Gerard Douw and his pupil soon found themselves in the handsome and, even then, antique chamber, which had been prepared for the reception of the stranger. A cheerful wood fire blazed in the hearth, a little at one side of which an old-fashioned table, which shone in the fire-light like burnished gold, was awaiting the supper, for which preparations were going forward; and ranged with exact regularity, stood the tall-backed chairs, whose ungracefulness was more than compensated by their comfort. The little party, consisting of Rose, her uncle, and the artist, awaited the arrival of the expected visitor with considerable impatience. Nine o'clock at length came, and with it a summons at the street door, which being speedily answered, was followed by a slow and emphatic tread upon the staircase; the steps moved heavily across the lobby, the door of the room in which the party we have described were assembled slowly opened, and there entered a figure which startled, almost appalled, the phlegmatic Dutchmen, and nearly made Rose scream with terror. It was the form, and arrayed in the garb of Minheer Vanderhausen; the air, the gait, the height were the same, but the features had never been seen by any of the party before. The stranger stopped at the door of the room, and displayed his form and face completely. He wore a dark-coloured cloth cloak, which was short and full, not falling quite to his knees; his legs were cased in dark purple silk stockings, and his shoes were adorned with roses of the same colour. The opening of the cloak in front showed the under-suit to consist of some very dark, perhaps sable material, and his hands were enclosed in a pair of heavy leather gloves, which ran up considerably above the wrist, in the manner of a gauntlet. In one hand he carried his walking-stick and his hat, which he had removed, and the other hung heavily by his side. A quantity of grizzled hair descended in long folds from his head, and rested upon the plaits of a stiff ruff, which effectually concealed his neck. So far all was well; but the face!—all the flesh of the face was coloured with the bluish leaden hue which is sometimes induced by metallic medicines, administered in excessive quantities; the eyes showed an undue proportion of muddy white, and had a certain indefinable character of insanity; the hue of the lips bearing the usual relation to that of the face, was, consequently, nearly black; and the entire character of the countenance was sensual, malignant, and even satanic. It was remarkable that the worshipful stranger suffered as little as possible of his flesh to appear, and that during his visit he did not once remove his gloves. Having stood for some moments at the door, Gerard Douw at length found breath and collectedness to bid him welcome, and with a mute inclination of the head, the stranger stepped forward into the room. There was something indescribably odd, even horrible, about all his motions, something undefinable, that was unnatural, unhuman; it was as if the limbs were guided and directed by a spirit unused to the management of bodily machinery. The stranger spoke hardly at all during his visit, which did not exceed half an hour; and the host himself could scarcely muster courage enough to utter the few necessary salutations and courtesies; and, indeed, such was the nervous terror which the presence of Vanderhausen inspired, that very little would have made all his entertainers fly in downright panic from the room. They had not so far lost all self-possession, however, as to fail to observe two strange peculiarities of their visitor. During his stay his eyelids did not once close, or, indeed, move in the slightest degree; and farther, there was a death-like stillness in his whole person, owing to the absence of the heaving motion of the chest, caused by the process of respiration. These two peculiarities, though when told they may appear trifling, produced a very striking and unpleasant effect when seen and observed. Vanderhausen at length relieved the painter of Leyden of his inauspicious presence; and with no trifling sense of relief the little party heard the street door close after him.

'Dear uncle,' said Rose, 'what a frightful man! I would not see him again for the wealth of the States.'

'Tush, foolish girl,' said Douw, whose sensations were anything but comfortable. 'A man may be as ugly as the devil, and yet, if his heart and actions are good, he is worth all the pretty-faced perfumed puppies that walk the Mall. Rose, my girl, it is very true he has not thy pretty face, but I know him to be wealthy and liberal; and were he ten times more ugly, these two virtues would be enough to counterbalance all his deformity, and if not sufficient actually to alter the shape and hue of his features, at least enough to prevent one's thinking them so much amiss.'

'Do you know uncle,' said Rose, 'when I saw him standing at the door, I could not get it out of my head that I saw the old painted wooden figure that used to frighten me so much in the Church of St. Laurence at Rotterdam.'

Gerard laughed, though he could not help inwardly acknowledging the justness of the comparison. He was resolved, however, as far as he could, to check his niece's disposition to dilate upon the ugliness of her intended bridegroom, although he was not a little pleased, as well as puzzled, to observe that she appeared totally exempt from that mysterious dread of the stranger which, he could not disguise it from himself, most painfully affected him, as also his pupil Godfrey Schalken.

Early on the next day there arrived, from various quarters of the town, presents of silks, velvets, jewellery, and soforth, for Rose; and also a packet directed to Gerard Douw, which, on being opened, was found to contain a contract of marriage, formally drawn up between

Wilken Vanderhausen of the *Boom-quay*, in Rotterdam, and Rose Velderkaust of Leyden, niece to Gerard Douw, master in the art of painting, also of the same city; and containing engagements on the part of Vanderhausen to make settlements upon his bride, far more splendid than he had before led her guardian to believe likely, and which were to be secured to her use in the most unexceptionable manner possible—the money being placed in the hand of Gerard Douw himself.

I have no sentimental scenes to describe, no cruelty of guardians, no magnanimity of wards, no agonies, or transports of lovers. The record I have to make is one of sordidness, levity, and heartlessness. In less than a week after the first interview which we have just described, the contract of marriage was fulfilled, and Schalken saw the prize which he would have risked existence to secure, carried off in solemn pomp by his repulsive rival. For two or three days he absented himself from the school; he then returned and worked, if with less cheerfulness, with far more dogged resolution than before: the stimulus of love had given place to that of ambition. Months passed away, and, contrary to his expectation, and, indeed, to the direct promise of the parties, Gerard Douw heard nothing of his niece or her worshipful spouse. The interest of the money, which was to have been demanded in quarterly sums, lay unclaimed in his hands.

He began to grow extremely uneasy. Minheer Vanderhausen's direction in Rotterdam he was fully possessed of; after some irresolution he finally determined to journey thither—a trifling undertaking, and easily accomplished—and thus to satisfy himself of the safety and comfort of his ward, for whom he entertained an honest and strong affection. His search was in vain, however; no one in Rotterdam had ever heard of Minheer Vanderhausen. Gerard Douw left not a house in the Boom-quay untried, but all in vain. No one could give him any information whatever touching the object of his inquiry, and he was obliged to return to Leyden, nothing wiser, and far more anxious, than when he left it.

On his arrival he hastened to the establishment from which Vanderhausen had hired the lumbering, though, considering the times, most luxurious vehicle, which the bridal party had employed to convey them to Rotterdam. From the driver of this machine he learned, that having proceeded by slow stages, they had late in the evening approached Rotterdam; but that before they entered the city, and while yet nearly a mile from it, a small party of men, soberly clad, and after the old fashion, with peaked beards and moustaches, standing in the centre of the road, obstructed the further progress of the carriage. The driver reined in his horses, much fearing, from the obscurity of the hour, and the loneliness of the road, that some mischief was intended. His fears were, however, somewhat allayed by his observing that these strange men carried a large litter, of an antique shape, and which they immediately set down upon the pavement, whereupon the bridegroom, having opened the coach door from within, descended, and having assisted his bride to do likewise, led her, weeping bitterly and wringing her hands, to the litter, which they both entered. It was then raised by the men who surrounded it, and speedily carried towards the city, and before it had proceeded very far, the darkness concealed it from the view of the Dutch coachman. In the inside of the vehicle he found a purse, whose contents more than thrice paid the hire of the carriage and man. He saw and could tell nothing more of Minheer Vanderhausen and his beautiful lady.

This mystery was a source of profound anxiety, and even of grief, to Gerard Douw. There was evidently fraud in the dealing of Vanderhausen with him, though for what purpose committed he could not imagine. He greatly doubted how far it was possible for a man possessing such a countenance to be in reality anything but a villain, and every day that passed without his hearing from or of his niece, instead of inducing him to forget his fears, on the contrary tended more and more to aggravate them. The loss of her cheerful society tended also to depress his spirits; and in order to dispel the gloom which often stole upon his mind after his daily occupations were over, he was wont frequently to ask Schalken to accompany him home, and share his otherwise solitary supper.

One evening, the painter and his pupil were sitting by the fire, having accomplished a comfortable meal, and had yielded to the silent and delicious melancholy of digestion, when their ruminations were disturbed by a loud sound at the street door, as if occasioned by some person rushing and scrambling vehemently against it. A domestic had run without delay to ascertain the cause of the disturbance, and they heard him twice or thrice interrogate the applicant for admission, but without eliciting any other answer but a sustained reiteration of the sounds. They heard him then open the hall-door, and immediately there followed a light and rapid tread upon the staircase. Schalken advanced towards the door. It opened before he reached it, and Rose rushed into the room. She looked wild, fierce, and haggard with terror and exhaustion, but her dress surprised them as much even as her unexpected appearance. It consisted of a kind of white woollen wrapper, made close about the neck, and descending to the very ground. It was much deranged and travel-soiled. The poor creature had hardly entered the chamber when she fell senseless on the floor. With some difficulty they succeeded in reviving her, and on recovering her senses she instantly exclaimed, in a tone of terror rather than mere impatience—

'Wine! wine!—quickly, or I'm lost!'

Astonished and almost scared at the strange agitation in which the call was made, they at once administered to her wishes, and she drank some wine with a haste and eagerness which surprised them. She had hardly swallowed it, when she exclaimed, with the same urgency—

'Food, for God's sake, food, at once, or I perish!'

A large fragment of a roast joint was upon the table, and Schalken immediately began to cut some, but he was anticipated; for no sooner did she see it than she caught it, a more than mortal image of famine, and with her hands, and even with her teeth, she tore off the flesh, and swallowed it. When the paroxysm of hunger had been a little appeased, she appeared on a sudden overcome with shame, or it may have been that other more agitating thoughts overpowered and scared her, for she began to weep bitterly, and to wring her hands.

'Oh, send for a minister of God,' said she; 'I am not safe till he comes: send for him speedily!'

Gerard Douw despatched a messenger instantly, and prevailed on his niece to allow him to surrender his bed-chamber to her use. He also persuaded her to retire there at once to rest: her consent was extorted upon the condition that they would not leave her for a moment.

'Oh, that the holy man were here!' she said: 'he can deliver me: the dead and the living can never be one: God has forbidden it!'

With these mysterious words, she surrendered herself to their guidance, and they proceeded to the chamber which Gerard Douw had assigned to her use.

'Do not, do not leave me for a moment!' she said; 'I am lost for ever if you do.'

Gerard Douw's chamber was approached through a spacious apartment, which they were now about to enter. He and Schalken each carried a candle, so that a sufficiency of light was cast upon all surrounding objects. They were now entering the large chamber, which, as I have said, communicated with Douw's apartment, when Rose suddenly stopped, and, in a whisper which thrilled them both with horror, she said—

'Oh, God! he is here! he is here! See, see!—there he goes!'

She pointed towards the door of the inner room, and Schalken thought he saw a shadowy and ill-defined form gliding into that apartment. He drew his sword, and, raising the candle so as to throw its light with increased distinctness upon the objects in the room, he entered the chamber into which the shadow had glided. No figure was there—nothing but the furniture which belonged to the room; and yet he could not be deceived as to the fact that something had moved before them into the chamber. A sickening dread came upon him, and the cold perspiration broke out in heavy drops upon his forehead: nor was he more composed when he heard the increased urgency and agony of entreaty with which Rose implored them not to leave her for a moment.

'I saw him,' said she; 'he's here. I cannot be deceived; I know him; he's by me; he is with me; he's in the room. Then, for God's sake, as you would save me, do not stir from beside me.'

They at length prevailed upon her to lie down upon the bed, where she continued to urge them to stay by her. She frequently uttered incoherent sentences, repeating again and again, 'The dead and the living cannot be one: God has forbidden it!' And then again, 'Rest to the wakeful—sleep to the sleep-walkers!' These and such mysterious and broken sentences she continued to utter until the clergyman arrived. Gerard Douw began to fear, naturally enough, that terror or ill-treatment had unsettled the poor girl's intellect; and he half suspected, from the suddenness of her appearance, the unseasonableness of the hour, and, above all, from the wildness and terror of her manner, that she had made her escape from some place of confinement for lunatics, and was in imminent fear of pursuit. He resolved to summon medical advice as soon as the mind of his niece had been in some measure set at rest by the offices of the clergyman whose attendance she had so earnestly desired; and until this object had been attained, he did not venture to put any questions to her which might possibly, by reviving painful or horrible recollections, increase her agitation. The clergyman soon arrived—a man of ascetic countenance and venerable age—one whom Gerard Douw respected much, forasmuch as he was a veteran polemic, though one perhaps more dreaded as a combatant than beloved as a Christian—of pure morality, subtle brain, and frozen heart. He entered the chamber which communicated with that in which Rose reclined, and immediately on his arrival she requested him to pray for her, as for one who lay in the hands of Satan, and who could hope for deliverance only from heaven.

That you may distinctly understand all the circumstances of the event which I am going to describe, it is necessary to state the relative position of the parties who were engaged in it. The old clergyman and Schalken were in the ante-room of which I have already spoken; Rose lay in the inner chamber, the door of which was open; and by the side of the bed, at her urgent desire, stood her guardian; a candle burned in the bed-chamber, and three were lighted in the outer apartment. The old man now cleared his voice, as if about to commence, but before he had time to begin, a sudden gust of air blew out the candle which served to illuminate the room in which the poor girl lay, and she, with hurried alarm, exclaimed—

'Godfrey, bring in another candle; the darkness is unsafe.'

Gerard Douw, forgetting for the moment her repeated injunctions, in the immediate impulse, stepped from the bed-chamber into the other, in order to supply what she desired.

'Oh God! do not go, dear uncle,' shrieked the unhappy girl—and at the same time she sprung from the bed, and darted after him, in order, by her grasp, to detain him. But the warning came too late, for scarcely had he passed the threshold, and hardly had his niece had time to utter the startling exclamation, when the door which divided the two rooms closed violently after him, as if swung to by a strong blast of wind. Schalken and he both rushed to the door, but their united and desperate efforts could not avail so much as to shake it. Shriek after shriek burst from the inner chamber, with all the piercing loudness of despairing terror. Schalken and Douw strained every nerve to force open the door; but all in vain. There was no sound of struggling from within, but the screams seemed to increase in loudness, and at the same time they heard the bolts of the latticed window withdrawn, and the window itself grated upon the sill as if thrown open. One *last* shriek, so long, and piercing, and agonised, as to be scarcely human, swelled from the room, and suddenly there followed a death-like silence. A light step was heard crossing the floor, as if from the bed to the window; and almost at the same instant the door gave way, and, yielding to the pressure of the external applicants, they were nearly precipitated into the room. It was empty. The window was open, and Schalken sprung to a chair, and gazed out upon the street and canal below. There was no one there; but he saw, or thought he saw, the waters of the broad canal beneath settling ring after ring in heavy circles, as if a moment before disturbed by the submersion of some ponderous body.

No trace of Rose was ever after found, nor was anything certain respecting her mysterious wooer discovered or even suspected—no clue whereby to trace the intricacies of the labyrinth, and to arrive at its solution, presented itself. But an incident occurred, which, though it will not be received by our rational readers in lieu of evidence, produced, nevertheless, a strong and a lasting impression upon the mind of Schalken. Many years after the events which we have detailed, Schalken, then residing far away, received an intimation of his father's death, and of his intended burial upon a fixed day in the church of Rotterdam. It was necessary that a very considerable journey should be performed by the funeral procession, which, as it will readily be believed, was not very numerously attended. Schalken with difficulty arrived in Rotterdam late in the day upon which the funeral was appointed to take place. It had not then arrived. Evening closed in, and still it did not appear.

Schalken strolled down to the church; he found it open; notice of the approach of the funeral had been given, and the vault in which the body was to be laid had been opened. The sexton, on seeing a well-dressed gentleman, whose object was to attend the expected obsequies, pacing the aisle of the church, hospitably invited him to share with him the comforts of a blazing fire, which, as was his custom in winter time upon such occasions, he had kindled in the hearth of a chamber in which he was accustomed to await the arrival of such grisly guests, and which communicated, by a flight of steps, with the vault below. In this chamber, Schalken and his entertainer seated themselves; and the sexton, after some fruitless attempts to engage his guest in conversation, was obliged to apply himself to his tobacco-pipe and can, to solace his solitude. In spite of his grief and cares, the fatigues of a rapid journey of nearly forty hours gradually overcame the mind and body of Godfrey Schalken, and he sank into a deep sleep, from which he was awakened by some one's shaking him gently by the shoulder. He first thought that the old sexton had called him, but *he* was no longer in the room. He roused himself, and as soon as he could clearly see what was around him, he perceived a female form, clothed in a kind of light robe of white, part of which was so disposed as to form a veil, and in her hand she carried a lamp. She was moving rather away from him, in the direction of the flight of steps which conducted towards the vaults. Schalken felt a vague alarm at the sight of this figure, and at the same time an irresistible impulse to follow its guidance. He followed it towards the vaults, but when it reached the head of the stairs, he paused; the figure paused also, and, turning gently round, displayed, by the light of the lamp it carried, the face and features of his first love,

Rose Velderkaust. There was nothing horrible, or even sad, in the countenance. On the contrary, it wore the same arch smile which used to enchant the artist long before in his happy days. A feeling of awe and of interest, too intense to be resisted, prompted him to follow the spectre, if spectre it were. She descended the stairs—he followed—and, turning to the left, through a narrow passage, she led him, to his infinite surprise, into what appeared to be an old-fashioned Dutch apartment, such as the pictures of Gerard Douw have served to immortalise. Abundance of costly antique furniture was disposed about the room, and in one corner stood a four-post bed, with heavy black cloth curtains around it; the figure frequently turned towards him with the same arch smile; and when she came to the side of the bed, she drew the curtains, and, by the light of the lamp, which she held towards its contents, she disclosed to the horror-stricken painter, sitting bolt upright in the bed, the livid and demoniac form of Vanderhausen. Schalken had hardly seen him, when he fell senseless upon the floor, where he lay until discovered, on the next morning, by persons employed in closing the passages into the vaults. He was lying in a cell of considerable size, which had not been disturbed for a long time, and he had fallen beside a large coffin, which was supported upon small stone pillars, a security against the attacks of vermin.

To his dying day Schalken was satisfied of the reality of the vision which he had witnessed, and he has left behind him a curious evidence of the impression which it wrought upon his fancy, in a painting executed shortly after the event I have narrated, and which is valuable not only as exhibiting the peculiarities which have made Schalken's pictures sought after, but even more so as presenting a portrait of his early love, Rose Velderkaust, whose mysterious fate must always remain matter of speculation.

— 1861 —

ULTOR DE LACY:
A LEGEND OF CAPPERCULLEN

CHAPTER I

The Jacobite's Legacy

IN my youth I heard a great many Irish family traditions, more or less of a supernatural character, some of them very peculiar, and all, to a child at least, highly interesting. One of these I will now relate, though the translation to cold type from oral narrative, with all the aids of animated human voice and countenance, and the appropriate *mise en scène* of the old-fashioned parlour fireside and its listening circle of excited faces, and, outside, the wintry blast and the moan of leafless boughs, with the occasional rattle of the clumsy old window-frame behind shutter and curtain, as the blast swept by, is at best a trying one.

About midway up the romantic glen of Cappercullen, near the point where the counties of Limerick, Clare, and Tipperary converge, upon the then sequestered and forest-bound range of the Slieve-Felim hills, there stood, in the reigns of the two earliest Georges, the picturesque and massive remains of one of the finest of the Anglo-Irish castles of Munster—perhaps of Ireland.

It crowned the precipitous edge of the wooded glen, itself half-buried among the wild forest that covered that long and solitary range. There was no human habitation within a circle of many miles, except the half-dozen hovels and the small thatched chapel composing the little village of Murroa, which lay at the foot of the glen among the straggling skirts of the noble forest.

Its remoteness and difficulty of access saved it from demolition. It was worth nobody's while to pull down and remove the ponderous and clumsy oak, much less the masonry or flagged roofing of the pile. Whatever would pay the cost of removal had been long since carried away. The rest was abandoned to time—the destroyer.

The hereditary owners of this noble building and of a wide territory in the contiguous counties I have named, were English—the De Lacys—long naturalised in Ireland. They had acquired at least this portion of their estate in the reign of Henry VIII., and held it, with some vicissitudes, down to the establishment of the revolution in Ireland, when they suffered attainder, and, like other great families of that period, underwent a final eclipse.

The De Lacy of that day retired to France, and held a brief command in the Irish Brigade, interrupted by sickness. He retired, became a poor hanger-on of the Court of St. Germains, and died early in the eighteenth century—as well as I remember, 1705—leaving an only son, hardly twelve years old, called by the strange but significant name of Ultor.

At this point commences the marvellous ingredient of my tale.

When his father was dying, he had him to his bedside, with no one by except his confessor; and having told him, first, that on reaching the age of twenty-one, he was to lay claim to a certain small estate in the county of Clare, in Ireland, in right of his mother—the title-deeds of which he gave him—and next, having enjoined him not to marry before the age of thirty, on the ground that earlier marriages destroyed the spirit and the power of enterprise, and would incapacitate him from the accomplishment of his destiny—the restoration of his family—he then went on to open to the child a matter which so terrified him that he cried lamentably, trembling all over, clinging to the priest's gown with one hand and to his father's cold wrist with the other, and imploring him, with screams of horror, to desist from his communication.

But the priest, impressed, no doubt, himself, with its necessity, compelled him to listen. And then his father showed him a small picture, from which also the child turned with shrieks, until similarly constrained to look. They did not let him go until he had carefully conned the features, and was able to tell them, from memory, the colour of the eyes and hair, and the fashion and hues of the dress. Then his father gave him a black box containing this portrait, which was a full-length miniature, about nine inches long, painted very finely in oils, as smooth as enamel, and folded above it a sheet of paper, written over in a careful and very legible hand.

The deeds and this black box constituted the most important legacy bequeathed to his only child by the ruined Jacobite, and he deposited them in the hands of the priest, in trust, till his boy, Ultor, should have attained to an age to understand their value, and to keep them securely.

When this scene was ended, the dying exile's mind, I suppose, was relieved, for he spoke cheerily, and said he believed he would recover; and they soothed the crying child, and his father kissed him, and gave him a little silver coin to buy fruit with; and so they sent him off with another boy for a walk, and when he came back his father was dead.

He remained in France under the care of this ecclesiastic until he had attained the age of twenty-one, when he repaired to Ireland, and his title being unaffected by his father's attainder, he easily made good his claim to the small estate in the county of Clare.

There he settled, making a dismal and solitary tour now and then of the vast territories which had once been his father's, and nursing those gloomy and impatient thoughts which befitted the enterprises to which he was devoted.

Occasionally he visited Paris, that common centre of English, Irish, and Scottish disaffection; and there, when a little past thirty, he married the daughter of another ruined Irish house. His bride returned with him to the melancholy seclusion of their Munster residence, where she bore him in succession two daughters—Alice, the elder, dark-eyed and dark-haired, grave and sensible—Una, four years younger, with large blue eyes and long and beautiful golden hair.

Their poor mother was, I believe, naturally a light-hearted, sociable, high-spirited little creature; and her gay and childish nature pined in the isolation and gloom of her lot. At all events she died young, and the children were left to the sole care of their melancholy and embittered father. In process of time the girls grew up, tradition says, beautiful. The elder was designed for a convent, the younger her father hoped to mate as nobly as her high blood and splendid beauty seemed to promise, if only the great game on which he had resolved to stake all succeeded.

CHAPTER II

The Fairies in the Castle

The Rebellion of '45 came, and Ultor de Lacy was one of the few Irishmen implicated treasonably in that daring and romantic insurrection. Of course there were warrants out against him, but he was not to be found. The young ladies, indeed, remained as heretofore in their father's lonely house in Clare; but whether he had crossed the water or was still in Ireland was for some time unknown, even to them. In due course he was attainted, and his little estate forfeited. It was a miserable catastrophe—a tremendous and beggarly waking up from a life-long dream of returning principality.

In due course the officers of the crown came down to take possession, and it behoved the young ladies to flit. Happily for them the ecclesiastic I have mentioned was not quite so confident as their father, of his winning back the magnificent patrimony of his ancestors; and by his advice the daughters had been secured twenty pounds a year each, under the marriage settlement of their parents, which was all that stood between this proud house and literal destitution.

Late one evening, as some little boys from the village were returning from a ramble through the dark and devious glen of Cappercullen, with their pockets laden with nuts and 'frahans,' to their amazement and even terror they saw a light streaming redly from the narrow window of one of the towers overhanging the precipice among the ivy and the lofty branches, across the glen, already dim in the shadows of the deepening night.

'Look—look—look—'tis the Phooka's tower!' was the general cry, in the vernacular Irish, and a universal scamper commenced.

The bed of the glen, strewn with great fragments of rock, among which rose the tall stems of ancient trees, and overgrown with a tangled copse, was at the best no favourable ground for a run. Now it was dark; and, terrible work breaking through brambles and hazels, and tumbling over rocks. Little Shaeen Mull Ryan, the last of the panic rout, screaming to his mates to wait for him—saw a whitish figure emerge from the thicket at the base of the stone flight of steps that descended the side of the glen, close by the castle-wall, intercepting his flight, and a discordant male voice shrieked—

'I have you!'

At the same time the boy, with a cry of terror, tripped and tumbled; and felt himself roughly caught by the arm, and hauled to his feet with a shake.

A wild yell from the child, and a volley of terror and entreaty followed.

'Who is it, Larry; what's the matter?' cried a voice, high in air, from the turret window. The words floated down through the trees, clear and sweet as the low notes of a flute.

'Only a child, my lady; a boy.'

'Is he hurt?'

'Are you hurted?' demanded the whitish man, who held him fast, and repeated the question in Irish; but the child only kept blubbering and crying for mercy, with his hands clasped, and trying to drop on his knees.

Larry's strong old hand held him up. He *was* hurt, and bleeding from over his eye.

'Just a trifle hurted, my lady!'

'Bring him up here.'

Shaeen Mull Ryan gave himself over. He was among 'the good people,' who he knew would keep him prisoner for ever and a day. There was no good in resisting. He grew bewildered, and yielded himself passively to his fate, and emerged from the glen on the platform above; his captor's knotted old hand still on his arm, and looked round on the tall mysterious trees, and the grey front of the castle, revealed in the imperfect moonlight, as upon the scenery of a dream.

The old man who, with thin wiry legs, walked by his side, in a dingy white coat, and blue facings, and great pewter buttons, with his silver grey hair escaping from under his battered three-cocked hat; and his shrewd puckered resolute face, in which the boy could read no promise of sympathy, showing so white and phantom-like in the moonlight, was, as he thought, the incarnate ideal of a fairy.

This figure led him in silence under the great arched gateway, and across the grass-grown court, to the door in the far angle of the building; and so, in the dark, round and round, up a stone screw stair, and with a short turn into a large room, with a fire of turf and wood, burning on its long unused hearth, over which hung a pot, and about it an old woman with a great wooden spoon was busy. An iron candlestick supported their solitary candle; and about the floor of the room, as well as on the table and chairs, lay a litter of all sorts of things; piles of old faded hangings, boxes, trunks, clothes, pewter-plates, and cups; and I know not what more.

But what instantly engaged the fearful gaze of the boy were the figures of two ladies; red drugget cloaks they had on, like the peasant girls of Munster and Connaught, and the rest of their dress was pretty much in keeping. But they had the grand air, the refined expression and beauty, and above all, the serene air of command that belong to people of a higher rank.

The elder, with black hair and full brown eyes, sat writing at the deal table on which the candle stood, and raised her dark gaze to the boy as he came in. The other, with her hood thrown back, beautiful and *riant*, with a flood of wavy golden hair, and great blue eyes, and with something kind, and arch, and strange in her countenance, struck him as the most wonderful beauty he could have imagined.

They questioned the man in a language strange to the child. It was not English, for he had a smattering of that, and the man's story seemed to amuse them. The two young ladies exchanged a glance, and smiled mysteriously. He was more convinced than ever that he was among the good people. The younger stepped gaily forward and said—

'Do you know who *I* am, my little man? Well, I'm the fairy Una, and this is my palace; and that fairy you see there (pointing to the dark lady, who was looking out something in a box), is my sister and family physician, the Lady Graveairs; and these (glancing at the old man and woman), are some of my courtiers; and I'm considering now what I shall do with *you*, whether I shall send you to-night to Lough Guir, riding on a rush, to make my compliments to the Earl of Desmond in his enchanted castle; or, straight to your bed, two thousand miles under ground, among the gnomes; or to prison in that little corner of the moon you see through the window—with the man-in-the-moon for your gaoler, for thrice three hundred years and a day! There, don't cry. You only see how serious a thing it is for you, little boys, to come so near my castle. Now, for this once, I'll let you go. But, henceforward, any boys I, or my people, may find within half a mile round my castle, shall belong to me for life, and never behold their home or their people more.'

And she sang a little air and chased mystically half a dozen steps before him, holding out her cloak with her pretty fingers, and curtseying very low, to his indescribable alarm.

Then, with a little laugh, she said—

'My little man, we must mend your head.'

And so they washed his scratch, and the elder one applied a plaister to it. And she of the great blue eyes took out of her pocket a little French box of bon-bons and emptied it into his hand, and she said—

'You need not be afraid to eat these—they are very good—and I'll send my fairy, Blanc-et-bleu, to set you free. Take him (she addressed Larry), and let him go, with a solemn charge.'

The elder, with a grave and affectionate smile, said, looking on the fairy—

'Brave, dear, wild Una! nothing can ever quell your gaiety of heart.'

And Una kissed her merrily on the cheek.

So the oak door of the room again opened, and Shaeen, with his conductor, descended the stair. He walked with the scared boy in grim silence near half way down the wild hill-side toward Murroa, and then he stopped, and said in Irish—

'You never saw the fairies before, my fine fellow, and 'tisn't often those who once set eyes on us return to tell it. Whoever comes nearer, night or day, than this stone,' and he tapped it with the end of his cane, 'will never see his home again, for we'll keep him till the day of judgment; good-night, little gossoon—and away with you.'

So these young ladies, Alice and Una, with two old servants, by their father's direction, had taken up their abode in a portion of that side of the old castle which overhung the glen; and with the furniture and hangings they had removed from their late residence, and with the aid of glass in the casements and some other indispensable repairs, and a thorough airing, they made the rooms they had selected just habitable, as a rude and temporary shelter.

CHAPTER III

The Priest's Adventures in the Glen

At first, of course, they saw or heard little of their father. In general, however, they knew that his plan was to procure some employment in France, and to remove them there. Their present strange abode was only an adventure and an episode, and they believed that any day they might receive instructions to commence their journey.

After a little while the pursuit relaxed. The government, I believe, did not care, provided he did not obtrude himself, what became of him, or where he concealed himself. At all events, the local authorities showed no disposition to hunt him down. The young ladies' charges on the little forfeited property were paid without any dispute, and no vexatious inquiries were raised as to what had become of the furniture and other personal property which had been carried away from the forfeited house.

The haunted reputation of the castle—for in those days, in matters of the marvellous, the oldest were children—secured the little family in the seclusion they coveted. Once, or sometimes twice a week, old Laurence, with a shaggy little pony, made a secret expedition to the city of Limerick, starting before dawn, and returning under the cover of the night, with his purchases. There was beside an occasional sly moonlit visit from the old parish priest, and a midnight mass in the old castle for the little outlawed congregation.

As the alarm and inquiry subsided, their father made them, now and then, a brief and stealthy visit. At first these were but of a night's duration, and with great precaution; but gradually they were extended and less guarded. Still he was, as the phrase is in Munster, 'on his keeping.' He had firearms always by his bed, and had arranged places of concealment in the castle in the event of a surprise. But no attempt nor any disposition to molest him appearing, he grew more at ease, if not more cheerful.

It came, at last, that he would sometimes stay so long as two whole months at a time, and then depart as suddenly and mysteriously as he came. I suppose he had always some promising plot on hand, and his head full of ingenious treason, and lived on the sickly and exciting dietary of hope deferred.

Was there a poetical justice in this, that the little *ménage* thus secretly established, in the solitary and time-worn pile, should have themselves experienced, but from causes not so easily explicable, those very supernatural perturbations which they had themselves essayed to inspire?

The interruption of the old priest's secret visits was the earliest consequence of the mysterious interference which now began to display itself. One night, having left his cob in care of his old sacristan in the little village, he trudged on foot along the winding pathway, among the grey rocks and ferns that threaded the glen, intending a ghostly visit to the fair recluses of the castle, and he lost his way in this strange fashion.

There was moonlight, indeed, but it was little more than quarter-moon, and a long train of funereal clouds were sailing slowly across the sky—so that, faint and wan as it was, the light seldom shone full out, and was often hidden for a minute or two altogether. When he reached the point in the glen where the castle-stairs were wont to be, he could see nothing of them, and above, no trace of the castle-towers. So, puzzled somewhat, he pursued his way up the ravine, wondering how his walk had become so unusually protracted and fatiguing.

At last, sure enough, he saw the castle as plain as could be, and a lonely streak of candle-light issuing from the tower, just as usual, when his visit was expected. But he could not find the stair; and had to clamber among the rocks and copse-wood the best way he could. But when he emerged at top, there was nothing but the bare heath. Then the clouds stole over the moon again, and he moved along with hesitation and difficulty, and once more he saw the outline of the castle against the sky, quite sharp and clear. But this time it proved to be a great battlemented mass of cloud on the horizon. In a few minutes more he was quite close, all of a sudden, to the great front, rising grey and dim in the feeble light, and not till he could have struck it with his good oak 'wattle' did he discover it to be only one of those wild, grey frontages of living rock that rise here and there in picturesque tiers along the slopes of those solitary mountains. And so, till dawn, pursuing this mirage of the castle, through pools and among ravines, he wore out a night of miserable misadventure and fatigue.

Another night, riding up the glen, so far as the level way at bottom would allow, and intending to make his nag fast at his customary tree, he hears on a sudden a horrid shriek at top of the steep rocks above his head, and something—a gigantic human form, it seemed—came tumbling and bounding headlong down through the rocks, and fell with a fearful impetus just before his horse's hoofs and there lay like a huge palpitating carcass. The horse was scared, as, indeed, was his rider, too, and more so when this apparently lifeless thing sprang up to his legs, and throwing his arms apart to bar their further progress, advanced his white and gigantic face towards them. Then the horse started about, with a snort of terror, nearly unseating the priest, and broke away into a furious and uncontrollable gallop.

I need not recount all the strange and various misadventures which the honest priest sustained in his endeavours to visit the castle, and its isolated tenants. They were enough to wear out his resolution, and frighten him into submission. And so at last these spiritual visits quite ceased; and fearing to awaken inquiry and suspicion, he thought it only prudent to abstain from attempting them in the daytime.

So the young ladies of the castle were more alone than ever. Their father, whose visits were frequently of long duration, had of late ceased altogether to speak of their contemplated departure for France, grew angry at any allusion to it, and they feared, had abandoned the plan altogether.

CHAPTER IV

The Light in the Bell Tower

Shortly after the discontinuance of the priest's visits, old Laurence, one night, to his surprise, saw light issuing from a window in the Bell Tower. It was at first only a tremulous red ray, visible only for a few minutes, which seemed to pass from the room, through whose window it escaped upon the courtyard of the castle, and so to lose itself. This tower and casement were in the angle of the building, exactly confronting that in which the little outlawed family had taken up their quarters.

The whole family were troubled at the appearance of this dull red ray from the chamber in the Bell Tower. Nobody knew what to make of it. But Laurence, who had campaigned in Italy with his old master, the young ladies' grandfather—'the heavens be his bed this night!'—was resolved to see it out, and took his great horse-pistols with him, and ascended to the corridor leading to the tower. But his search was vain.

This light left a sense of great uneasiness among the inmates, and most certainly it was not pleasant to suspect the establishment of an independent and possibly dangerous lodger or even colony, within the walls of the same old building.

The light very soon appeared again, steadier and somewhat brighter, in the same chamber. Again old Laurence buckled on his armour, swearing ominously to himself, and this time bent in earnest upon conflict. The young ladies watched in thrilling suspense from the great window in *their* stronghold, looking diagonally across the court. But as Laurence, who had entered the massive range of buildings opposite, might be supposed to be approaching the chamber from which this ill-omened glare proceeded, it steadily waned, finally disappearing altogether, just a few seconds before his voice was heard shouting from the arched window to know which way the light had gone.

This lighting up of the great chamber of the Bell Tower grew at last to be of frequent and almost continual recurrence. It was, there, long ago, in times of trouble and danger, that the De Lacys of those evil days used to sit in feudal judgment upon captive adversaries, and, as tradition alleged, often gave them no more time for shrift and prayer, than it needed to mount to the battlement of the turret over-head, from which they were forthwith hung by the necks, for a caveat and admonition to all evil disposed persons viewing the same from the country beneath.

Old Laurence observed these mysterious glimmerings with an evil and an anxious eye, and many and various were the stratagems he tried, but in vain, to surprise the audacious intruders. It is, however, I believe, a fact that no phenomenon, no matter how startling at first, if prosecuted with tolerable regularity, and unattended with any new circumstances of terror, will very long continue to excite alarm or even wonder.

So the family came to acquiesce in this mysterious light. No harm accompanied it. Old Laurence, as he smoked his lonely pipe in the grass-grown courtyard, would cast a disturbed glance at it, as it softly glowed out through the darking aperture, and mutter a prayer or an oath. But he had given over the chase as a hopeless business. And Peggy Sullivan, the old dame of all work, when, by chance, for she never willingly looked toward the haunted quarter, she caught the faint reflection of its dull effulgence with the corner of her eye, would sign herself with the cross or fumble at her beads, and deeper furrows would gather in her forehead, and her face grow ashen and perturbed. And this was not mended by the levity with which the young ladies, with whom the spectre had lost his influence, familiarity, as usual, breeding contempt, had come to talk, and even to jest, about it.

CHAPTER V

The Man with the Claret-Mark

But as the former excitement flagged, old Peggy Sullivan produced a new one; for she solemnly avowed that she had seen a thin-faced man, with an ugly red mark all over the side of his cheek, looking out of the same window, just at sunset, before the young ladies returned from their evening walk.

This sounded in their ears like an old woman's dream, but still it was an excitement, jocular in the morning, and just, perhaps, a little fearful as night overspread the vast and desolate building, but still, not wholly unpleasant. This little flicker of credulity suddenly, however, blazed up into the full light of conviction.

Old Laurence, who was not given to dreaming, and had a cool, hard head, and an eye like a hawk, saw the same figure, just about the same hour, when the last level gleam of sunset was tinting the summits of the towers and the tops of the tall trees that surrounded them.

He had just entered the court from the great gate, when he heard all at once the hard peculiar twitter of alarm which sparrows make when a cat or a hawk invades their safety, rising all round from the thick ivy that overclimbed the wall on his left, and raising his eyes listlessly, he saw, with a sort of shock, a thin, ungainly man, standing with his legs crossed, in the recess of the window from which the light was wont to issue, leaning with his elbows on the stone mullion, and looking down with a sort of sickly sneer, his hollow yellow cheeks being deeply stained on one side with what is called a 'claret mark.'

'I have you at last, you villain!' cried Larry, in a strange rage and panic: 'drop down out of that on the grass here, and give yourself up, or I'll shoot you.'

The threat was backed with an oath, and he drew from his coat pocket the long holster pistol he was wont to carry, and covered his man cleverly.

'I give you while I count ten—one-two-three-four. If you draw back, I'll fire, mind; five-six—you'd better be lively—seven-eight-nine—one chance more; will you come down? Then take it—ten!'

Bang went the pistol. The sinister stranger was hardly fifteen feet removed from him, and Larry was a dead shot. But this time he made a scandalous miss, for the shot knocked a little white dust from the stone wall a full yard at one side; and the fellow never shifted his negligent posture or qualified his sardonic smile during the procedure.

Larry was mortified and angry.

'You'll not get off this time, my tulip!' he said with a grin, exchanging the smoking weapon for the loaded pistol in reserve.

'What are you pistolling, Larry?' said a familiar voice close by his elbow, and he saw his master, accompanied by a handsome young man in a cloak.

'That villain, your honour, in the window, there.'

'Why there's nobody there, Larry,' said De Lacy, with a laugh, though that was no common indulgence with him.

As Larry gazed, the figure somehow dissolved and broke up without receding. A hanging tuft of yellow and red ivy nodded queerly in place of the face, some broken and discoloured masonry in perspective took up the outline and colouring of the arms and figure, and two imperfect red and yellow lichen streaks carried on the curved tracing of the long spindle shanks. Larry blessed himself, and drew his hand across his damp forehead, over his bewildered eyes, and could not speak for a minute. It was all some devilish trick; he could take his oath he saw every feature in the fellow's face, the lace and buttons of his cloak and doublet, and even his long finger nails and thin yellow fingers that overhung the cross-shaft of the window, where there was now nothing but a rusty stain left.

The young gentleman who had arrived with De Lacy, staid that night and shared with great apparent relish the homely fare of the family. He was a gay and gallant Frenchman, and the beauty of the younger lady, and her pleasantry and spirit, seemed to make his hours pass but too swiftly, and the moment of parting sad.

When he had departed early in the morning, Ultor De Lacy had a long talk with his elder daughter, while the younger was busy with her early dairy task, for among their retainers this *proles generosa* reckoned a 'kind' little Kerry cow.

He told her that he had visited France since he had been last at Cappercullen, and how good and gracious their sovereign had been, and how he had arranged a noble alliance for her sister Una. The young gentleman was of high blood, and though not rich, had, nevertheless, his acres and his *nom de terre*, besides a captain's rank in the army. He was, in short, the very gentleman with whom they had parted only that morning. On what special business he was now in Ireland there was no necessity that he should speak; but being here he had brought him hither to present him to his daughter, and found that the impression she had made was quite what was desirable.

'You, you know, dear Alice, are promised to a conventual life. Had it been otherwise—'

He hesitated for a moment.

'You are right, dear father,' she said, kissing his hand, 'I *am* so promised, and no earthly tie or allurement has power to draw me from that holy engagement.'

'Well,' he said, returning her caress, 'I do not mean to urge you upon that point. It must not, however, be until Una's marriage has taken place. That cannot be, for many good reasons, sooner than this time twelve months; we shall then exchange this strange and barbarous abode for Paris, where are many eligible convents, in which are entertained as sisters some of the noblest ladies of France; and there, too, in Una's marriage will be continued, though not the name, at all events the blood, the lineage, and the title which, so sure as justice ultimately governs the course of human events, will be again established, powerful and honoured in this country, the scene of their ancient glory and transitory misfortunes. Meanwhile, we must not mention this engagement to Una. Here she runs no risk of being sought or won; but the mere knowledge that her hand was absolutely pledged, might excite a capricious opposition and repining such as neither I nor you would like to see; therefore be secret.'

The same evening he took Alice with him for a ramble round the castle wall, while they talked of grave matters, and he as usual allowed her a dim and doubtful view of some of those cloud-built castles in which he habitually dwelt, and among which his jaded hopes revived.

They were walking upon a pleasant short sward of darkest green, on one side overhung by the grey castle walls, and on the other by the forest trees that here and there closely approached it, when precisely as they turned the angle of the Bell Tower, they were encountered by a person walking directly towards them. The sight of a stranger, with the exception of the one visitor introduced by her father, was in this place so absolutely unprecedented, that Alice was amazed and affrighted to such a degree that for a moment she stood stock-still.

But there was more in this apparition to excite unpleasant emotions, than the mere circumstance of its unexpectedness. The figure was very strange, being that of a tall, lean, ungainly man, dressed in a dingy suit, somewhat of a Spanish fashion, with a brown laced cloak, and faded red stockings. He had long lank legs, long arms, hands, and fingers, and a very long sickly face, with a drooping nose, and a sly, sarcastic leer, and a great purplish stain over-spreading more than half of one cheek.

As he strode past, he touched his cap with his thin, discoloured fingers, and an ugly side glance, and disappeared round the corner. The eyes of father and daughter followed him in silence.

Ultor De Lacy seemed first absolutely terror-stricken, and then suddenly inflamed with ungovernable fury. He dropped his cane on the ground, drew his rapier, and, without wasting a thought on his daughter, pursued.

He just had a glimpse of the retreating figure as it disappeared round the far angle. The plume, and the lank hair, the point of the rapier-scabbard, the flutter of the skirt of the cloak, and one red stocking and heel; and this was the last he saw of him.

When Alice reached his side, his drawn sword still in his hand, he was in a state of abject agitation.

'Thank Heaven, he's gone!' she exclaimed.

'He's gone,' echoed Ultor, with a strange glare.

'And you are safe,' she added, clasping his hand.

He sighed a great sigh.

'And you don't think he's coming back?'

'He!—who?'

'The stranger who passed us but now. Do you know him, father?'

'Yes—and—no, child—I know him not—and yet I know him too well. Would to heaven we could leave this accursed haunt to-night. Cursed be the stupid malice that first provoked this horrible feud, which no sacrifice and misery can appease, and no exorcism can quell or even suspend. The wretch has come from afar with a sure instinct to devour my last hope—to dog us into our last retreat—and to blast with his triumph the very dust and ruins of our house. What ails that stupid priest that he has given over his visits? Are *my* children to be left without mass or confession—the sacraments which *guard* as well as save—because he once loses his way in a mist, or mistakes a streak of foam in the brook for a dead man's face? D——n him!'

'See, Alice, if he won't come,' he resumed, 'you must only *write* your confession to him in full—you and Una. Laurence is trusty, and will carry it—and we'll get the bishop's—or, if need be, the Pope's leave for him to give you absolution. I'll move heaven and earth, but you *shall* have the sacraments, poor children!—and see him. I've been a wild fellow in my youth, and never pretended to sanctity; but I know there's but one safe way—and—and—keep you each a bit of this—(he opened a small silver box)—about you while you stay here—fold and sew it up reverently in a bit of the old psaltery parchment and wear it next your hearts—'tis a fragment of the consecrated wafer—and will help, with the saints' protection, to guard you from harm—and be strict in fasts, and constant in prayer—*I* can do nothing—nor devise any help. The curse has fallen, indeed, on me and mine.'

And Alice, saw, in silence, the tears of despair roll down his pale and agitated face.

This adventure was also a secret, and Una was to hear nothing of it.

CHAPTER VI

Voices

Now Una, nobody knew why, began to lose spirit, and to grow pale. Her fun and frolic were quite gone! Even her songs ceased. She was silent with her sister, and loved solitude better. She said she was well, and quite happy, and could in no wise be got to account for the lamentable change that had stolen over her. She had grown odd too, and obstinate in trifles; and strangely reserved and cold.

Alice was very unhappy in consequence. What was the cause of this estrangement—had she offended her, and how? But Una had never before borne resentment for an hour. What could have altered her entire nature so? Could it be the shadow and chill of coming insanity?

Once or twice, when her sister urged her with tears and entreaties to disclose the secret of her changed spirits and demeanour, she seemed to listen with a sort of silent wonder and suspicion, and then she looked for a moment full upon her, and seemed on the very point of revealing all. But the earnest dilated gaze stole downward to the floor, and subsided into an odd wily smile, and she began to whisper to herself, and the smile and the whisper were both a mystery to Alice.

She and Alice slept in the same bedroom—a chamber in a projecting tower—which on their arrival, when poor Una was so merry, they had hung round with old tapestry, and decorated fantastically according to their skill and frolic. One night, as they went to bed, Una said, as if speaking to herself—

'Tis my last night in this room—I shall sleep no more with Alice.'

'And what has poor Alice done, Una, to deserve your strange unkindness?'

Una looked on her curiously, and half frightened, and then the odd smile stole over her face like a gleam of moonlight.

'My poor Alice, what have you to do with it?' she whispered.

'And why do you talk of sleeping no more with me?' said Alice.

'Why? Alice dear—no why—no reason—only a knowledge that it must be so, or Una will die.'

'Die, Una darling!—what can you mean?'

'Yes, sweet Alice, die, indeed. We must all die some time, you know, or—or undergo a change; and my time is near—*very* near—unless I sleep apart from you.'

'Indeed, Una, sweetheart, I think you *are* ill, but not near death.'

'Una knows what you think, wise Alice—but she's not mad—on the contrary, she's wiser than other folks.'

'She's sadder and stranger too,' said Alice, tenderly.

'Knowledge is sorrow,' answered Una, and she looked across the room through her golden hair which she was combing—and through the window, beyond which lay the tops of the great trees, and the still foliage of the glen in the misty moonlight.

"'Tis enough, Alice dear; it must be so. The bed must move hence, or Una's bed will be low enough ere long. See, it shan't be far though, only into that small room.'

She pointed to an inner room or closet opening from that in which they lay. The walls of the building were hugely thick, and there were double doors of oak between the chambers, and Alice thought, with a sigh, how completely separated they were going to be.

However she offered no opposition. The change was made, and the girls for the first time since childhood lay in separate chambers. A few nights afterwards Alice, awoke late in the night from a dreadful dream, in which the sinister figure which she and her father had encountered in their ramble round the castle walls, bore a principal part.

When she awoke there were still in her ears the sounds which had mingled in her dream. They were the notes of a deep, ringing, bass voice rising from the glen beneath the castle walls—something between humming and singing—listlessly unequal and intermittent, like the melody of a man whiling away the hours over his work. While she was wondering at this unwonted minstrelsy, there came a silence, and—could she believe her ears?—it certainly was Una's clear low contralto—softly singing a bar or two from the window. Then once more silence—and then again the strange manly voice, faintly chaunting from the leafy abyss.

With a strange wild feeling of suspicion and terror, Alice glided to the window. The moon who sees so many things, and keeps all secrets, with her cold impenetrable smile, was high in the sky. But Alice saw the red flicker of a candle from Una's window, and, she thought, the shadow of her head against the deep side wall of its recess. Then this was gone, and there were no more sights or sounds that night.

As they sate at breakfast, the small birds were singing merrily from among the sun-tipped foliage.

'I love this music,' said Alice, unusually pale and sad; 'it comes with the pleasant light of morning. I remember, Una, when *you* used to sing, like those gay birds, in the fresh beams of the morning; that was in the old time, when Una kept no secret from poor Alice.'

'And Una knows what her sage Alice means; but there are other birds, silent all day long, and, they say, the sweetest too, that love to sing by *night* alone.'

So things went on—the elder girl pained and melancholy—the younger silent, changed, and unaccountable.

A little while after this, very late one night, on awaking, Alice heard a conversation being carried on in her sister's room. There seemed to be no disguise about it. She could not distinguish the words, indeed, the walls being some six feet thick, and two great oak doors intercepting. But Una's clear voice, and the deep bell-like tones of the unknown, made up the dialogue.

Alice sprung from her bed, threw her clothes about her, and tried to enter her sister's room; but the inner door was bolted. The voices ceased to speak as she knocked, and Una opened it, and stood before her in her night-dress, candle in hand.

'Una—Una, darling, as you hope for peace, tell me who is here?' cried frightened Alice, with her trembling arms about her neck.

Una drew back, with her large, innocent blue eyes fixed full upon her. 'Come in, Alice,' she said, coldly.

And in came Alice, with a fearful glance around. There was no hiding place there; a chair, a table, a little bedstead, and two or three pegs in the wall to hang clothes on; a narrow window, with two iron bars across; no hearth or chimney—nothing but bare walls.

Alice looked round in amazement, and her eyes glanced with painful inquiry into those of her sister's. Una smiled one of her peculiar sidelong smiles, and said—

'Strange dreams! I've been dreaming—so has Alice. She hears and sees Una's dreams, and wonders—and well she may.'

And she kissed her sister's cheek with a cold kiss, and lay down in her little bed, her slender hand under her head, and spoke no more.

Alice, not knowing what to think, went back to hers.

About this time Ultor de Lacy returned. He heard his elder daughter's strange narrative with marked uneasiness, and his agitation seemed to grow rather than subside. He enjoined her, however, not to mention it to the old servant, nor in presence of anybody she might chance to see, but only to him and to the priest, if he could be persuaded to resume his duty and return. The trial, however, such as it was, could not endure very long; matters had turned out favourably. The union of his younger daughter might be accomplished within a few months, and in eight or nine weeks they should be on their way to Paris.

A night or two after her father's arrival, Alice, in the dead of the night, heard the well-known strange deep voice speaking softly, as it seemed, close to her own window on the outside; and Una's voice, clear and tender, spoke in answer. She hurried to her own casement, and pushed it open, kneeling in the deep embrasure, and looking with a stealthy and affrighted gaze towards her sister's window. As she crossed the floor the voices subsided, and she saw a light withdrawn from within. The moonbeams slanted bright and clear on the whole side of the castle overlooking the glen, and she plainly beheld the shadow of a man projected on the wall as on a screen.

This black shadow recalled with a horrid thrill the outline and fashion of the figure in the Spanish dress. There were the cap and mantle, the rapier, the long thin limbs and sinister angularity. It was so thrown obliquely that the hands reached to the window-sill, and the feet stretched and stretched, longer and longer as she looked, toward the ground, and disappeared in the general darkness; and the rest, with a sudden flicker, shot downwards, as shadows will on the sudden movement of a light, and was lost in one gigantic leap down the castle wall.

'I do not know whether I dream or wake when I hear and see these sights; but I will ask my father to sit up with me, and we *two* surely cannot be mistaken. May the holy saints keep and guard us!' And in her terror she buried her head under the bed-clothes, and whispered her prayers for an hour.

CHAPTER VII

Una's Love

'I have been with Father Denis,' said De Lacy, next day, 'and he will come to-morrow; and, thank Heaven! you may both make your confession and hear mass, and my mind will be at rest; and you'll find poor Una happier and more like herself.'

But 'tween cup and lip there's many a slip. The priest was not destined to hear poor Una's shrift. When she bid her sister good-night she looked on her with her large, cold, wild eyes, till something of her old human affections seemed to gather there, and they slowly filled with tears, which dropped one after the other on her homely dress as she gazed in her sister's face.

Alice, delighted, sprang up, and clasped her arms about her neck. 'My own darling treasure, 'tis all over; you love your poor Alice again, and will be happier than ever.'

But while she held her in her embrace Una's eyes were turned towards the window, and her lips apart, and Alice felt instinctively that her thoughts were already far away.

'Hark!—listen!—hush!' and Una, with her delighted gaze fixed, as if she saw far away beyond the castle wall, the trees, the glen, and the night's dark curtain, held her hand raised near her ear, and waved her head slightly in time, as it seemed, to music that reached not Alice's ear, and smiled her strange pleased smile, and then the smile slowly faded away, leaving that sly suspicious light behind it which somehow scared her sister with an uncertain sense of danger; and she sang in tones so sweet and low that it seemed but a reverie of a song, recalling, as Alice fancied, the strain to which she had just listened in that strange ecstasy, the plaintive and beautiful Irish ballad, 'Shule, shule, shule, aroon,' the midnight summons of the outlawed Irish soldier to his darling to follow him.

Alice had slept little the night before. She was now overpowered with fatigue; and leaving her candle burning by her bedside, she fell into a deep sleep. From this she awoke suddenly, and completely, as will sometimes happen without any apparent cause, and she saw Una come into the room. She had a little purse of embroidery—her own work—in her hand; and she stole lightly to the bedside, with her peculiar oblique smile, and evidently thinking that her sister was asleep.

Alice was thrilled with a strange terror, and did not speak or move; and her sister, slipped her hand softly under her bolster, and withdrew it. Then Una stood for a while by the hearth, and stretched her hand up to the mantelpiece, from which she took a little bit of chalk, and Alice thought she saw her place it in the fingers of a long yellow hand that was stealthily introduced from her own chamber-door to receive it; and Una paused in the dark recess of the door, and smiled over her shoulder toward her sister, and then glided into her room, closing the doors.

Almost freezing with terror, Alice rose and glided after her, and stood in her chamber, screaming—

'Una, Una, in heaven's name what troubles you?'

But Una seemed to have been sound asleep in her bed, and raised herself with a start, and looking upon her with a peevish surprise, said—

'What does Alice seek here?'

'You were in my room, Una, dear; you seem disturbed and troubled.'

'Dreams, Alice. My dreams crossing your brain; only dreams—dreams. Get you to bed, and sleep.'

And to bed she went, but *not* to sleep. She lay awake more than an hour; and then Una emerged once more from her room. This time she was fully dressed, and had her cloak and thick shoes on, as their rattle on the floor plainly discovered. She had a little bundle tied up in a handkerchief in her hand, and her hood was drawn about her head; and thus equipped, as it seemed, for a journey, she came and stood at the foot of Alice's bed, and stared on her with a look so soulless and terrible that her senses almost forsook her. Then she turned and went back into her own chamber.

She may have returned; but Alice thought not—at least she did not see her. But she lay in great excitement and perturbation; and was terrified, about an hour later, by a knock at her chamber door—not that opening into Una's room, but upon the little passage from the stone screw staircase. She sprang from her bed; but the door was secured on the inside, and she felt relieved. The knock was repeated, and she heard some one laughing softly on the outside.

The morning came at last; that dreadful night was over. But Una! Where was Una?

Alice never saw her more. On the head of her empty bed were traced in chalk the words—Ultor de Lacy, Ultor O'Donnell. And Alice found beneath her own pillow the little purse of embroidery she had seen in Una's hand. It was her little parting token, and bore the simple legend—'Una's love!'

De Lacy's rage and horror were boundless. He charged the priest, in frantic language, with having exposed his child, by his cowardice and neglect, to the machinations of the Fiend, and raved and blasphemed like a man demented.

It is said that he procured a solemn exorcism to be performed, in the hope of disenthralling and recovering his daughter. Several times, it is alleged, she was seen by the old servants. Once on a sweet summer morning, in the window of the tower, she was perceived combing her beautiful golden tresses, and holding a little mirror in her hand; and first, when she saw herself discovered, she looked affrighted, and then smiled, her slanting, cunning smile. Sometimes, too, in the glen, by moonlight, it was said belated villagers had met her, always startled first, and then smiling, generally singing snatches of old Irish ballads, that seemed to bear a sort of dim resemblance to her melancholy fate. The apparition has long ceased. But it is said that now and again, perhaps once in two or three years, late on a summer night, you may hear—but faint and far away in the recesses of the glen—the sweet, sad notes of Una's voice, singing those plaintive melodies. This, too, of course, in time will cease, and all be forgotten.

CHAPTER VIII

Sister Agnes and the Portrait

When Ultor de Lacy died, his daughter Alice found among his effects a small box, containing a portrait such as I have described. When she looked on it, she recoiled in horror. There, in the plenitude of its sinister peculiarities, was faithfully portrayed the phantom which lived with a vivid and horrible accuracy in her remembrance. Folded in the same box was a brief narrative, stating that, 'A.D. 1601, in the month of

December, Walter de Lacy, of Cappercullen, made many prisoners at the ford of Ownhey, or Abington, of Irish and Spanish soldiers, flying from the great overthrow of the rebel powers at Kinsale, and among the number one Roderic O'Donnell, an arch traitor, and near kinsman to that other O'Donnell who led the rebels; who, claiming kindred through his mother to De Lacy, sued for his life with instant and miserable entreaty, and offered great ransom, but was by De Lacy, through great zeal for the queen, as some thought, cruelly put to death. When he went to the tower-top, where was the gallows, finding himself in extremity, and no hope of mercy, he swore that though he could work them no evil before his death, yet that he would devote himself thereafter to blast the greatness of the De Lacys, and never leave them till his work was done. He hath been seen often since, and always for that family perniciously, insomuch that it hath been the custom to show to young children of that lineage the picture of the said O'Donnell, in little, taken among his few valuables, to prevent their being misled by him unawares, so that he should not have his will, who by devilish wiles and hell-born cunning, hath steadfastly sought the ruin of that ancient house, and especially to leave that *stemma generosum* destitute of issue for the transmission of their pure blood and worshipful name.'

Old Miss Croker, of Ross House, who was near seventy in the year 1821, when she related this story to me, had seen and conversed with Alice de Lacy, a professed nun, under the name of Sister Agnes, in a religious house in King-street, in Dublin, founded by the famous Duchess of Tyrconnell, and had the narrative from her own lips. I thought the tale worth preserving, and have no more to say.

— 1868 —

SQUIRE TOBY'S WILL

MANY persons accustomed to travel the old York and London road, in the days of stage-coaches, will remember passing, in the afternoon, say, of an autumn day, in their journey to the capital, about three miles south of the town of Applebury, and a mile and a half before you reach the old Angel Inn, a large black-and-white house, as those old-fashioned cage-work habitations are termed, dilapidated and weather-stained, with broad lattice windows glimmering all over in the evening sun with little diamond panes, and thrown into relief by a dense background of ancient elms. A wide avenue, now overgrown like a churchyard with grass and weeds, and flanked by double rows of the same dark trees, old and gigantic, with here and there a gap in their solemn files, and sometimes a fallen tree lying across on the avenue, leads up to the hall-door.

Looking up its sombre and lifeless avenue from the top of the London coach, as I have often done, you are struck with so many signs of desertion and decay,—the tufted grass sprouting in the chinks of the steps and window-stones, the smokeless chimneys over which the jackdaws are wheeling, the absence of human life and all its evidence, that you conclude at once that the place is uninhabited and abandoned to decay. The name of this ancient house is Gylingden Hall. Tall hedges and old timber quickly shroud the old place from view, and about a quarter of a mile further on you pass, embowered in melancholy trees, a small and ruinous Saxon chapel, which, time out of mind, has been the burying-place of the family of Marston, and partakes of the neglect and desolation which brood over their ancient dwelling-place.

The grand melancholy of the secluded valley of Gylingden, lonely as an enchanted forest, in which the crows returning to their roosts among the trees, and the straggling deer who peep from beneath their branches, seem to hold a wild and undisturbed dominion, heightens the forlorn aspect of Gylingden Hall.

Of late years repairs have been neglected, and here and there the roof is stripped, and 'the stitch in time' has been wanting. At the side of the house exposed to the gales that sweep through the valley like a torrent through its channel, there is not a perfect window left, and the shutters but imperfectly exclude the rain. The ceilings and walls are mildewed and green with damp stains. Here and there, where the drip falls from the ceiling, the floors are rotting. On stormy nights, as the guard described, you can hear the doors clapping in the old house, as far away as old Gryston bridge, and the howl and sobbing of the wind through its empty galleries.

About seventy years ago died the old Squire, Toby Marston, famous in that part of the world for his hounds, his hospitality, and his vices. He had done kind things, and he had fought duels: he had given away money and he had horse-whipped people. He carried with him some blessings and a good many curses, and left behind him an amount of debts and charges upon the estates which appalled his two sons, who had no taste for business or accounts, and had never suspected, till that wicked, open-handed, and swearing old gentleman died, how very nearly he had run the estates into insolvency.

They met at Gylingden Hall. They had the will before them, and lawyers to interpret, and information without stint, as to the encumbrances with which the deceased had saddled them. The will was so framed as to set the two brothers instantly at deadly feud.

These brothers differed in some points; but in one material characteristic they resembled one another, and also their departed father. They never went into a quarrel by halves, and once in, they did not stick at trifles.

The elder, Scroope Marston, the more dangerous man of the two, had never been a favourite of the old Squire. He had no taste for the sports of the field and the pleasures of a rustic life. He was no athlete, and he certainly was not handsome. All this the Squire resented. The young man, who had no respect for him, and outgrew his fear of his violence as he came to manhood, retorted. This aversion, therefore, in the ill-conditioned old man grew into positive hatred. He used to wish that d——d pippin-squeezing, hump-backed rascal Scroope, out of the way of better men—meaning his younger son Charles; and in his cups would talk in a way which even the old and young fellows who followed his hounds, and drank his port, and could stand a reasonable amount of brutality, did not like.

Scroope Marston was slightly deformed, and he had the lean sallow face, piercing black eyes, and black lank hair, which sometimes accompany deformity.

'I'm no feyther o' that hog-backed creature. I'm no sire of hisn, d——n him! I'd as soon call that tongs son o' mine,' the old man used to bawl, in allusion to his son's long, lank limbs: 'Charlie's a man, but that's a jack-an-ape. He has no good-nature; there's nothing handy, nor manly, nor no one turn of a Marston in him.'

And when he was pretty drunk, the old Squire used to swear he should never 'sit at the head o' that board; nor frighten away folk from Gylingden Hall wi' his d——d hatchet-face—the black loon!'

'Handsome Charlie was the man for his money. He knew what a horse was, and could sit to his bottle; and the lasses were all clean *wad* about him. He was a Marston every inch of his six foot two.'

Handsome Charlie and he, however, had also had a row or two. The old Squire was free with his horsewhip as with his tongue, and on occasion when neither weapon was quite practicable, had been known to give a fellow 'a tap o' his knuckles.' Handsome Charlie, however, thought there was a period at which personal chastisement should cease; and one night, when the port was flowing, there was some allusion to Marion Hayward, the miller's daughter, which for some reason the old gentleman did not like. Being 'in liquor,' and having clearer ideas about pugilism than self-government, he struck out, to the surprise of all present, at Handsome Charlie. The youth threw back his head scientifically, and nothing followed but the crash of a decanter on the floor. But the old Squire's blood was up, and he bounced from his chair. Up jumped Handsome Charlie, resolved to stand no nonsense. Drunken Squire Lilbourne, intending to mediate, fell flat on the floor, and cut his ear among the glasses. Handsome Charlie caught the thump which the old Squire discharged at him upon his open hand, and catching him by the cravat, swung him with his back to the wall. They said the old man never looked so purple, nor his eyes so goggle before; and then Handsome Charlie pinioned him tight to the wall by both arms.

'Well, I say—come, don't you talk no more nonsense o' that sort, and I won't lick you,' croaked the old Squire. 'You stopped that un clever, you did. Didn't he? Come, Charlie, man, gie us your hand, I say, and sit down again, lad.' And so the battle ended; and I believe it was the last time the Squire raised his hand to Handsome Charlie.

But those days were over. Old Toby Marston lay cold and quiet enough now, under the drip of the mighty ash-tree within the Saxon ruin where so many of the old Marston race returned to dust, and were forgotten. The weather-stained top-boots and leather-breeches, the three-cornered cocked hat to which old gentlemen of that day still clung, and the well-known red waistcoat that reached below his hips, and the fierce pug face of the old Squire, were now but a picture of memory. And the brothers between whom he had planted an irreconcilable quarrel, were now in their new mourning suits, with the gloss still on, debating furiously across the table in the great oak parlour, which had so often resounded to the banter and coarse songs, the oaths and laughter of the congenial neighbours whom the old Squire of Gylingden Hall loved to assemble there.

These young gentlemen, who had grown up in Gylingden Hall, were not accustomed to bridle their tongues, nor, if need be, to hesitate about a blow. Neither had been at the old man's funeral. His death had been sudden. Having been helped to his bed in that hilarious and quarrelsome state which was induced by port and punch, he was found dead in the morning,—his head hanging over the side of the bed, and his face very black and swollen.

Now the Squire's will despoiled his eldest son of Gylingden, which had descended to the heir time out of mind. Scroope Marston was furious. His deep stern voice was heard inveighing against his dead father and living brother, and the heavy thumps on the table with which he enforced his stormy recriminations resounded through the large chamber. Then broke in Charles's rougher voice, and then came a quick alternation of short sentences, and then both voices together in growing loudness and anger, and at last, swelling the tumult, the expostulations of pacific and frightened lawyers, and at last a sudden break up of the conference. Scroope broke out of the room, his pale furious face showing whiter against his long black hair, his dark fierce eyes blazing, his hands clenched, and looking more ungainly and deformed than ever in the convulsions of his fury.

Very violent words must have passed between them; for Charlie, though he was the winning man, was almost as angry as Scroope. The elder brother was for holding possession of the house, and putting his rival to legal process to oust him. But his legal advisers were clearly against it. So, with a heart boiling over with gall, up he went to London, and found the firm who had managed his father's business fair and communicative enough. They looked into the settlements, and found that Gylingden was excepted. It was very odd, but so it was, specially excepted; so that the right of the old Squire to deal with it by his will could not be questioned.

Notwithstanding all this, Scroope, breathing vengeance and aggression, and quite willing to wreck himself provided he could run his brother down, assailed Handsome Charlie, and battered old Squire Toby's will in the Prerogative Court and also at common law, and the feud between the brothers was knit, and every month their exasperation was heightened.

Scroope was beaten, and defeat did not soften him. Charles might have forgiven hard words; but he had been himself worsted during the long campaign in some of those skirmishes, special motions, and so forth, that constitute the episodes of a legal epic like that in which the Marston brothers figured as opposing combatants; and the blight of law-costs had touched him, too, with the usual effect upon the temper of a man of embarrassed means.

Years flew, and brought no healing on their wings. On the contrary, the deep corrosion of this hatred bit deeper by time. Neither brother married. But an accident of a different kind befell the younger, Charles Marston, which abridged his enjoyments very materially.

This was a bad fall from his hunter. There were severe fractures, and there was concussion of the brain. For some time it was thought that he could not recover. He disappointed these evil auguries, however. He did recover, but changed in two essential particulars. He had received an injury in his hip, which doomed him never more to sit in the saddle. And the rollicking animal spirits which hitherto had never failed him, had now taken flight for ever.

He had been for five days in a state of coma—absolute insensibility—and when he recovered consciousness he was haunted by an indescribable anxiety.

Tom Cooper, who had been butler in the palmy days of Gylingden Hall, under old Squire Toby, still maintained his post with old-fashioned fidelity, in these days of faded splendour and frugal housekeeping. Twenty years had passed since the death of his old master. He had grown lean, and stooped, and his face, dark with the peculiar brown of age, furrowed and gnarled, and his temper, except with his master, had waxed surly.

His master had visited Bath and Buxton, and came back, as he went, lame, and halting gloomily about with the aid of a stick. When the hunter was sold, the last tradition of the old life at Gylingden disappeared. The young Squire, as he was still called, excluded by his mischance from the hunting-field, dropped into a solitary way of life, and halted slowly and solitarily about the old place, seldom raising his eyes, and with an appearance of indescribable gloom.

Old Cooper could talk freely on occasion with his master; and one day he said, as he handed him his hat and stick in the hall:

'You should rouse yourself up a bit, Master Charles!'

'It's past rousing with me, old Cooper.'

'It's just this, I'm thinking: there's something on your mind, and you won't tell no one. There's no good keeping it on your stomach. You'll be a deal lighter if you tell it. Come, now, what is it, Master Charlie?'

The Squire looked with his round grey eyes straight into Cooper's eyes. He felt that there was a sort of spell broken. It was like the old rule of the ghost who can't speak till it is spoken to. He looked earnestly into old Cooper's face for some seconds, and sighed deeply.

'It ain't the first good guess you've made in your day, old Cooper, and I'm glad you've spoke. It's bin on my mind, sure enough, ever since I had that fall. Come in here after me, and shut the door.'

The Squire pushed open the door of the oak parlour, and looked round on the pictures abstractedly. He had not been there for some time, and, seating himself on the table, he looked again for a while in Cooper's face before he spoke.

'It's not a great deal, Cooper, but it troubles me, and I would not tell it to the parson nor the doctor; for, God knows what they'd say, though there's nothing to signify in it. But you were always true to the family, and I don't mind if I tell you.'

''Tis as safe with Cooper, Master Charles, as if 'twas locked in a chest, and sunk in a well.'

'It's only this,' said Charles Marston, looking down on the end of his stick, with which he was tracing lines and circles, 'all the time I was lying like dead, as you thought, after that fall, I was with the old master.' He raised his eyes to Cooper's again as he spoke, and with an awful oath he repeated—'I was with him, Cooper!'

'He was a good man, sir, in his way,' repeated old Cooper, returning his gaze with awe. 'He was a good master to me, and a good father to you, and I hope he's happy. May God rest him!'

'Well,' said Squire Charles, 'it's only this: the whole of that time I was with him, or he was with me—I don't know which. The upshot is, we were together, and I thought I'd never get out of his hands again, and all the time he was bullying me about some one thing; and if it was to save my life, Tom Cooper, by —— from the time I waked I never could call to mind what it was; and I think I'd give that hand to know; and if you can think of anything it might be—for God's sake! don't be afraid, Tom Cooper, but speak it out, for he threatened me hard, and it was surely him.'

Here ensued a silence.

'And what did you think it might be yourself, Master Charles?' said Cooper.

'I han't thought of aught that's likely. I'll never hit on't—*never*. I thought it might happen he knew something about that d—— hump-backed villain, Scroope, that swore before Lawyer Gingham I made away with a paper of settlements—me and father; and, as I hope to be saved, Tom Cooper, there never was a bigger lie! I'd a had the law of him for them identical words, and cast him for more than he's worth; only Lawyer Gingham never goes into nothing for me since money grew scarce in Gylingden; and I can't change my lawyer, I owe him such a hatful of money. But he did, he swore he'd hang me yet for it. He said it in them identical words—he'd never rest till he *hanged* me for it, and I think it was, like enough, something about *that*, the old master was troubled; but it's enough to drive a man mad. I *can't* bring it to mind—I can't remember a word he said, only he threatened awful, and looked—Lord a mercy on us!—frightful bad.'

'There's no need he should. May the Lord a-mercy on him!' said the old butler.

'No, of course; and you're not to tell a soul, Cooper—not a living soul, mind, that I said he looked bad, nor nothing about it.'

'God forbid!' said old Cooper, shaking his head. 'But I was thinking, sir, it might ha' been about the slight that's bin so long put on him by having no stone over him, and never a scratch o' a chisel to say who he is.'

'Ay! Well, I didn't think o' that. Put on your hat, old Cooper, and come down wi' me; for I'll look after that, at any rate.'

There is a bye-path leading by a turnstile to the park, and thence to the picturesque old burying-place, which lies in a nook by the roadside, embowered in ancient trees. It was a fine autumnal sunset, and melancholy lights and long shadows spread their peculiar effects over the landscape as 'Handsome Charlie' and the old butler made their way slowly toward the place where Handsome Charlie was himself to lie at last.

'Which of the dogs made that howling all last night?' asked the Squire, when they had got on a little way.

"Twas a strange dog, Master Charlie, in front of the house; ours was all in the yard—a white dog wi' a black head, he looked to be, and he was smelling round them mounting-steps the old master, God be wi' him! set up, the time his knee was bad. When the tyke got up a' top of them, howlin' up at the windows, I'd a liked to shy something at him.'

'Hullo! Is that like him?' said the Squire, stopping short, and pointing with his stick at a dirty-white dog, with a large black head, which was scampering round them in a wide circle, half crouching with that air of uncertainty and deprecation which dogs so well know how to assume.

He whistled the dog up. He was a large, half-starved bull-dog.

'That fellow has made a long journey—thin as a whipping-post, and stained all over, and his claws worn to the stumps,' said the Squire, musingly.'He isn't a bad dog, Cooper. My poor father liked a good bulldog, and knew a cur from a good 'un.'

The dog was looking up into the Squire's face with the peculiar grim visage of his kind, and the Squire was thinking irreverently how strong a likeness it presented to the character of his father's fierce pug features when he was clutching his horsewhip and swearing at a keeper.

'If I did right I'd shoot him. He'll worry the cattle, and kill our dogs,' said the Squire. 'Hey, Cooper? I'll tell the keeper to look after him. That fellow could pull down a sheep, and he shan't live on my mutton.'

But the dog was not to be shaken off. He looked wistfully after the Squire, and after they had got a little way on, he followed timidly.

It was vain trying to drive him off. The dog ran round them in wide circles, like the infernal dog in 'Faust'; only he left no track of thin flame behind him. These manoeuvres were executed with a sort of beseeching air, which flattered and touched the object of this odd preference. So he called him up again, patted him, and then and there in a manner adopted him.

The dog now followed their steps dutifully, as if he had belonged to Handsome Charlie all his days. Cooper unlocked the little iron door, and the dog walked in close behind their heels, and followed them as they visited the roofless chapel.

The Marstons were lying under the floor of this little building in rows. There is not a vault. Each has his distinct grave enclosed in a lining of masonry. Each is surmounted by a stone kist, on the upper flag of which is enclosed his epitaph, except that of poor old Squire Toby. Over him was nothing but the grass and the line of masonry which indicate the site of the kist, whenever his family should afford him one like the rest.

'Well, it does look shabby. It's the elder brother's business; but if he won't, I'll see to it myself, and I'll take care, old boy, to cut sharp and deep in it, that the elder son having refused to lend a hand the stone was put there by the younger.'

They strolled round this little burial-ground. The sun was now below the horizon, and the red metallic glow from the clouds, still illuminated by the departed sun, mingled luridly with the twilight. When Charlie peeped again into the little chapel, he saw the ugly dog stretched upon Squire Toby's grave, looking at least twice his natural length, and performing such antics as made the young Squire stare. If you have ever seen a cat stretched on the floor, with a bunch of

Valerian, straining, writhing, rubbing its jaws in long-drawn caresses, and in the absorption of a sensual ecstasy, you have seen a phenomenon resembling that which Handsome Charlie witnessed on looking in.

The head of the brute looked so large, its body so long and thin, and its joints so ungainly and dislocated, that the Squire, with old Cooper beside him, looked on with a feeling of disgust and astonishment, which, in a moment or two more, brought the Squire's stick down upon him with a couple of heavy thumps. The beast awakened from his ecstasy, sprang to the head of the grave, and there on a sudden, thick and bandy as before, confronted the Squire, who stood at its foot, with a terrible grin, and eyes that glared with the peculiar green of canine fury.

The next moment the dog was crouching abjectly at the Squire's feet.

'Well, he's a rum 'un!' said old Cooper, looking hard at him.

'I like him,' said the Squire.

'I don't,' said Cooper.

'But he shan't come in here again,' said the Squire.

'I shouldn't wonder if he was a witch,' said old Cooper, who remembered more tales of witchcraft than are now current in that part of the world.

'He's a good dog,' said the Squire, dreamily. 'I remember the time I'd a given a handful for him—but I'll never be good for nothing again. Come along.'

And he stooped down and patted him. So up jumped the dog and looked up in his face, as if watching for some sign, ever so slight, which he might obey.

Cooper did not like a bone in that dog's skin. He could not imagine what his master saw to admire in him. He kept him all night in the gun-room, and the dog accompanied him in his halting rambles about the place. The fonder his master grew of him, the less did Cooper and the other servants like him.

'He hasn't a point of a good dog about him,' Cooper would growl. 'I think Master Charlie be blind. And old Captain (an old red parrot, who sat chained to a perch in the oak parlour, and conversed with himself, and nibbled at his claws and bit his perch all day),—old Captain, the only living thing, except one or two of us, and the Squire himself, that remembers the old master, the minute he saw the dog, screeched as if he was struck, shakin' his feathers out quite wild, and drops down, poor old soul, a-hangin' by his foot, in a fit.'

But there is no accounting for fancies, and the Squire was one of those dogged persons who persist more obstinately in their whims the more they are opposed. But Charles Marston's health suffered by his lameness. The transition from habitual and violent exercise to such a life as his privation now consigned him to, was never made without a risk to health; and a host of dyspeptic annoyances, the existence of which he had never dreamed of before, now beset him in sad earnest. Among these was the now not unfrequent troubling of his sleep with dreams and nightmares. In these his canine favourite invariably had a part and was generally a central, and sometimes a solitary figure. In these visions the dog seemed to stretch himself up the side of the Squire's bed, and in dilated proportions to sit at his feet, with a horrible likeness to the pug features of old Squire Toby, with his tricks of wagging his head and throwing up his chin; and then he would talk to him about Scroope, and tell him 'all wasn't straight,' and that he 'must make it up wi' Scroope,' that he, the old Squire, had 'served him an ill turn,' that 'time was nigh up,' and that 'fair was fair,' and he was 'troubled where he was, about Scroope.'

Then in his dream this semi-human brute would approach his face to his, crawling and crouching up his body, heavy as lead, till the face of the beast was laid on his, with the same odious caresses and stretchings and writhings which he had seen over the old Squire's grave. Then Charlie would wake up with a gasp and a howl, and start upright in the bed, bathed in a cold moisture, and fancy he saw something white sliding off the foot of the bed. Sometimes he thought it might be the curtain with white lining that slipped down, or the coverlet disturbed by his uneasy turnings; but he always fancied, at such moments, that he saw something white sliding hastily off the bed; and always when he had been visited by such dreams the dog next morning was more than usually caressing and servile, as if to obliterate, by a more than ordinary welcome, the sentiment of disgust which the horror of the night had left behind it.

The doctor half-satisfied the Squire that there was nothing in these dreams, which, in one shape or another, invariably attended forms of indigestion such as he was suffering from.

For a while, as if to corroborate this theory, the dog ceased altogether to figure in them. But at last there came a vision in which, more unpleasantly than before, he did resume his old place.

In his nightmare the room seemed all but dark; he heard what he knew to be the dog walking from the door round his bed slowly, to the side from which he always had come upon it. A portion of the room was uncarpeted, and he said he distinctly heard the peculiar tread of a dog, in which the faint clatter of the claws is audible. It was a light stealthy step, but at every tread the whole room shook heavily; he felt something place itself at the foot of his bed, and saw a pair of green eyes staring at him in the dark, from which he could not remove his own. Then he heard, as he thought, the old Squire Toby say—'The eleventh hour be passed, Charlie, and ye've done nothing—you and I 'a done Scroope a wrong!' and then came a good deal more, and then—'The time's nigh up, it's going to strike.' And with a long low growl, the thing began to creep up upon his feet; the growl continued, and he saw the reflection of the up-turned green eyes upon the bed-clothes, as it began slowly to stretch itself up his body towards his face. With a loud scream, he waked. The light, which of late the Squire was accustomed to have in his bedroom, had accidentally gone out. He was afraid to get up, or even to look about the room for some time; so sure did he feel of seeing the green eyes in the dark fixed on him from some corner. He had hardly recovered from the first agony which nightmare leaves behind it, and was beginning to collect his thoughts, when he heard the clock strike twelve. And he bethought him of the words 'the eleventh hour be passed—time's nigh up—it's going to strike!' and he almost feared that he would hear the voice reopening the subject.

Next morning the Squire came down looking ill.

'Do you know a room, old Cooper,' said he, 'they used to call King Herod's Chamber?'

'Ay, sir; the story of King Herod was on the walls o't when I was a boy.'

'There's a closet off it—is there?'

'I can't be sure o' that; but 'tisn't worth your looking at, now; the hangings was rotten, and took off the walls, before you was born; and there's nou't there but some old broken things and lumber. I seed them put there myself by poor Twinks; he was blind of an eye, and footman afterwards. You'll remember Twinks? He died here, about the time o' the great snow. There was a deal o' work to bury him, poor fellow!'

'Get the key, old Cooper; I'll look at the room,' said the Squire.

'And what the devil can you want to look at it for?' said Cooper, with the old-world privilege of a rustic butler.

'And what the devil's that to you? But I don't mind if I tell you. I don't want that dog in the gun-room, and I'll put him somewhere else; and I don't care if I put him there.'

'A bull-dog in a bedroom! Oons, sir! the folks 'ill say you're clean mad!'

'Well, let them; get you the key, and let us look at the room.'

'You'd shoot him if you did right, Master Charlie. You never heard what a noise he kept up all last night in the gun-room, walking to and fro growling like a tiger in a show; and, say what you like, the dog's not worth his feed; he hasn't a point of a dog; he's a bad dog.'

'I know a dog better than you—and he's a good dog!' said the Squire, testily.

'If you was a judge of a dog you'd hang that 'un,' said Cooper.

'I'm not a-going to hang him, so there's an end. Go you, and get the key; and don't be talking, mind, when you go down. I may change my mind.'

Now this freak of visiting King Herod's room had, in truth, a totally different object from that pretended by the Squire. The voice in his nightmare had uttered a particular direction, which haunted him, and would give him no peace until he had tested it. So far from liking that dog to-day, he was beginning to regard it with a horrible suspicion; and if old Cooper had not stirred his obstinate temper by seeming to dictate, I dare say he would have got rid of that inmate effectually before evening.

Up to the third storey, long disused, he and old Cooper mounted. At the end of a dusty gallery, the room lay. The old tapestry, from which the spacious chamber had taken its name, had long given place to modern paper, and this was mildewed, and in some places hanging from the walls. A thick mantle of dust lay over the floor. Some broken chairs and boards, thick with dust, lay, along with other lumber, piled together at one end of the room.

They entered the closet, which was quite empty. The Squire looked round, and you could hardly have said whether he was relieved or disappointed.

'No furniture here,' said the Squire, and looked through the dusty window. 'Did you say anything to me lately—I don't mean this morning—about this room, or the closet—or anything—I forget—'

'Lor' bless you! Not I. I han't been thinkin' o' this room this forty year.'

'Is there any sort of old furniture called a *buffet*—do you remember?' asked the Squire.

'A buffet? why, yes—to be sure—there was a buffet, sure enough, in this closet, now you bring it to my mind,' said Cooper. 'But it's papered over.'

'And what is it?'

'A little cupboard in the wall,' answered the old man.

'Ho—I see—and there's such a thing here, is there, under the paper? Show me whereabouts it was.'

'Well—I think it was somewhere about here,' answered he, rapping his knuckles along the wall opposite the window. 'Ay, there it is,' he added, as the hollow sound of a wooden door was returned to his knock.

The Squire pulled the loose paper from the wall, and disclosed the doors of a small press, about two feet square, fixed in the wall.

'The very thing for my buckles and pistols, and the rest of my gimcracks,' said the Squire. 'Come away, we'll leave the dog where he is. Have you the key of that little press?'

No, he had not. The old master had emptied and locked it up, and desired that it should be papered over, and that was the history of it.

Down came the Squire, and took a strong turn-screw from his gun-case; and quietly he reascended to King Herod's room, and, with little trouble, forced the door of the small press in the closet wall. There were in it some letters and cancelled leases, and also a parchment deed which he took to the window and read with much agitation. It was a supplemental deed executed about a fortnight after the others, and previously to his father's marriage, placing Gylingden under strict settlement to the elder son, in what is called 'tail male.' Handsome Charlie, in his fraternal litigation, had acquired a smattering of technical knowledge, and he perfectly well knew that the effect of this would be not only to transfer the house and lands to his brother Scroope, but to leave him at the mercy of that exasperated brother, who might recover from him personally every guinea he had ever received by way of rent, from the date of his father's death.

It was a dismal, clouded day, with something threatening in its aspect, and the darkness, where he stood, was made deeper by the top of one of the huge old trees overhanging the window.

In a state of awful confusion he attempted to think over his position. He placed the deed in his pocket, and nearly made up his mind to destroy it. A short time ago he would not have hesitated for a moment under such circumstances; but now his health and his nerves were shattered, and he was under a supernatural alarm which the strange discovery of this deed had powerfully confirmed.

In this state of profound agitation he heard a sniffing at the closet-door, and then an impatient scratch and a long low growl. He screwed his courage up, and, not knowing what to expect, threw the door open and saw the dog, not in his dream-shape, but wriggling with joy, and crouching and fawning with eager submission; and then wandering about the closet, the brute growled awfully into the corners of it, and seemed in an unappeasable agitation.

Then the dog returned and fawned and crouched again at his feet.

After the first moment was over, the sensations of abhorrence and fear began to subside, and he almost reproached himself for requiting the affection of this poor friendless brute with the antipathy which he had really done nothing to earn.

The dog pattered after him down the stairs. Oddly enough, the sight of this animal, after the first revulsion, reassured him; it was, in his eyes, so attached, so good-natured, and palpably so mere a dog.

By the hour of evening the Squire had resolved on a middle course; he would not inform his brother of his discovery, nor yet would he destroy the deed. He would never marry. He was past that time. He would leave a letter, explaining the discovery of the deed, addressed to the only surviving trustee—who had probably forgotten everything about it—and having seen out his own tenure, he would provide that all should be set right after his death. Was not that fair? at all events it quite satisfied what he called his conscience, and he thought it a devilish good compromise for his brother; and he went out, towards sunset, to take his usual walk.

Returning in the darkening twilight, the dog, as usual attending him, began to grow frisky and wild, at first scampering round him in great circles, as before, nearly at the top of his speed, his great head between his paws as he raced. Gradually more excited grew the pace and narrower his circuit, louder and fiercer his continuous growl, and the Squire stopped and grasped his stick hard, for the lurid eyes and grin of the brute threatened an attack. Turning round and round as the excited brute encircled him, and striking vainly at him with his stick, he grew at last so tired that he almost despaired of keeping him longer at bay; when on a sudden the dog stopped short and crawled up to his feet wriggling and crouching submissively.

Nothing could be more apologetic and abject; and when the Squire dealt him two heavy thumps with his stick, the dog whimpered only, and writhed and licked his feet. The Squire sat down on a prostrate tree; and his dumb companion, recovering his wonted spirits immediately, began to sniff and nuzzle among the roots. The Squire felt in his breast-pocket for the deed—it was safe; and again he pondered, in this loneliest of spots, on the question whether he should preserve it for restoration after his death to his brother, or destroy it forthwith. He began rather to lean toward the latter solution, when the long low growl of the dog not far off startled him.

He was sitting in a melancholy grove of old trees, that slants gently westward. Exactly the same odd effect of light I have before described—a faint red glow reflected downward from the upper sky, after the sun had set, now gave to the growing darkness a lurid uncertainty. This grove, which lies in a gentle hollow, owing to its circumscribed horizon on all but one side, has a peculiar character of loneliness.

He got up and peeped over a sort of barrier, accidentally formed of the trunks of felled trees laid one over the other, and saw the dog straining up the other side of it, and hideously stretched out, his ugly head looking in consequence twice the natural size. His dream was coming over him again. And now between the trunks the brute's ungainly head was thrust, and the long neck came straining through, and the body, twining after it like a huge white lizard; and as it came striving and twisting through, it growled and glared as if it would devour him.

As swiftly as his lameness would allow, the Squire hurried from this solitary spot towards the house. What thoughts exactly passed through his mind as he did so, I am sure he could not have told. But when the dog came up with him it seemed appeased, and even in high good-humour, and no longer resembled the brute that haunted his dreams.

That night, near ten o'clock, the Squire, a good deal agitated, sent for the keeper, and told him that he believed the dog was mad, and that he must shoot him. He might shoot the dog in the gun-room, where he was—a grain of shot or two in the wainscot did not matter, and the dog must not have a chance of getting out.

The Squire gave the gamekeeper his double-barrelled gun, loaded with heavy shot. He did not go with him beyond the hall. He placed his hand on the keeper's arm; the keeper said his hand trembled, and that he looked 'as white as curds.'

'Listen a bit!' said the Squire under his breath.

They heard the dog in a state of high excitement in the room—growling ominously, jumping on the window-stool and down again, and running round the room.

'You'll need to be sharp, mind—don't give him a chance—slip in edgeways, d'ye see? and give him both barrels!'

'Not the first mad dog I've knocked over, sir,' said the man, looking very serious as he cocked the gun.

As the keeper opened the door, the dog had sprung into the empty grate. He said he 'never see sich a stark, staring devil.' The beast made a twist round, as if, he thought, to jump up the chimney—'but that wasn't to be done at no price,'—and he made a yell—not like a dog—like a man caught in a mill-crank, and before he could spring at the keeper, he fired one barrel into him. The dog leaped towards him, and rolled over, receiving the second barrel in his head, as he lay snorting at the keeper's feet!

'I never seed the like; I never heard a screech like that!' said the keeper, recoiling. 'It makes a fellow feel queer.'

'Quite dead?' asked the Squire.

'Not a stir in him, sir,' said the man, pulling him along the floor by the neck.

'Throw him outside the hall-door now,' said the Squire; 'and mind you pitch him outside the gate to-night—old Cooper says he's a witch,' and the pale Squire smiled, 'so he shan't lie in Gylingden.'

Never was man more relieved than the Squire, and he slept better for a week after this than he had done for many weeks before.

It behoves us all to act promptly on our good resolutions. There is a determined gravitation towards evil, which, if left to itself, will bear down first intentions. If at one moment of superstitious fear, the Squire had made up his mind to a great sacrifice, and resolved in the matter of that deed so strangely recovered, to act honestly by his brother, that resolution very soon gave place to the compromise with fraud, which so conveniently postponed the restitution to the period when further enjoyment on his part was impossible. Then came more tidings of Scroope's violent and minatory language, with always the same burthen—that he would leave no stone unturned to show that there had existed a deed which Charles had either secreted or destroyed, and that he would never rest till he had hanged him.

This of course was wild talk. At first it had only enraged him; but, with his recent guilty knowledge and suppression, had come fear. His danger was the existence of the deed, and little by little he brought himself to a resolution to destroy it. There were many falterings and recoils before he could bring himself to commit this crime. At length, however, he did it, and got rid of the custody of that which at any time might become the instrument of disgrace and ruin. There was relief in this, but also the new and terrible sense of actual guilt.

He had got pretty well rid of his supernatural qualms. It was a different kind of trouble that agitated him now.

But this night, he imagined, he was awakened by a violent shaking of his bed. He could see, in the very imperfect light, two figures at the foot of it, holding each a bed-post. One of these he half-fancied was his brother Scroope, but the other was the old Squire—of that he was sure—and he fancied that they had shaken him up from his sleep. Squire Toby was talking as Charlie wakened, and he heard him say:

'Put out of our own house by you! It won't hold for long. We'll come in together, friendly, and stay. Forewarned, wi' yer eyes open, ye did it;

and now Scroope'll hang you! We'll hang you together! Look at me, you devil's limb.'

And the old Squire tremblingly stretched his face, torn with shot and bloody, and growing every moment more and more into the likeness of the dog, and began to stretch himself out and climb the bed over the foot-board; and he saw the figure at the other side, little more than a black shadow, begin also to scale the bed; and there was instantly a dreadful confusion and uproar in the room, and such a gabbling and laughing; he could not catch the words; but, with a scream, he woke, and found himself standing on the floor. The phantoms and the clamour were gone, but a crash and ringing of fragments was in his ears. The great china bowl, from which for generations the Marstons of Gylingden had been baptised, had fallen from the mantelpiece, and was smashed on the hearth-stone.

'I've bin dreamin' all night about Mr. Scroope, and I wouldn't wonder, old Cooper, if he was dead,' said the Squire, when he came down in the morning.

'God forbid! I was adreamed about him, too, sir: I dreamed he was dammin' and sinkin' about a hole was burnt in his coat, and the old master, God be wi' him! said—quite plain—I'd 'a swore 'twas himself—"Cooper, get up, ye d——d land-loupin' thief, and lend a hand to hang him—for he's a daft cur, and no dog o' mine." 'Twas the dog shot over night, I do suppose, as was runnin' in my old head. I thought old master gied me a punch wi' his knuckles, and says I, wakenin' up, "At yer service, sir"; and for a while I couldn't get it out o' my head, master was in the room still.'

Letters from town soon convinced the Squire that his brother Scroope, so far from being dead, was particularly active; and Charlie's attorney wrote to say, in serious alarm, that he had heard, accidentally, that he intended setting up a case, of a supplementary deed of settlement, of which he had secondary evidence, which would give him Gylingden. And at this menace Handsome Charlie snapped his fingers, and wrote courageously to his attorney; abiding what might follow with, however, a secret foreboding.

Scroope threatened loudly now, and swore after his bitter fashion, and reiterated his old promise of hanging that cheat at last. In the midst of these menaces and preparations, however, a sudden peace proclaimed itself: Scroope died, without time even to make provisions for a posthumous attack upon his brother. It was one of those cases of disease of the heart in which death is as sudden as by a bullet.

Charlie's exultation was undisguised. It was shocking. Not, of course, altogether malignant. For there was the expansion consequent on the removal of a secret fear. There was also the comic piece of luck, that only the day before Scroope had destroyed his old will, which left to a stranger every farthing he possessed, intending in a day or two to execute another to the same person, charged with the express condition of prosecuting the suit against Charlie.

The result was, that all his possessions went unconditionally to his brother Charles as his heir. Here were grounds for abundance of savage elation. But there was also the deep-seated hatred of half a life of mutual and persistent aggression and revilings; and Handsome Charlie was capable of nursing a grudge, and enjoying a revenge with his whole heart.

He would gladly have prevented his brother's being buried in the old Gylingden chapel, where he wished to lie; but his lawyers doubted his power, and he was not quite proof against the scandal which would attend his turning back the funeral, which would, he knew, be attended by some of the country gentry and others, with an hereditary regard for the Marstons.

But he warned his servants that not one of them were to attend it; promising, with oaths and curses not to be disregarded, that any one of them who did so, should find the door shut in his face on his return.

I don't think, with the exception of old Cooper, that the servants cared for this prohibition, except as it baulked a curiosity always strong in the solitude of the country. Cooper was very much vexed that the eldest son of the old Squire should be buried in the old family chapel, and no sign of decent respect from Gylingden Hall. He asked his master, whether he would not, at least, have some wine and refreshments in the oak parlour, in case any of the country gentlemen who paid this respect to the old family should come up to the house? But the Squire only swore at him, told him to mind his own business, and ordered him to say, if such a thing happened, that he was out, and no preparations made, and, in fact, to send them away as they came. Cooper expostulated stoutly, and the Squire grew angrier; and after a tempestuous scene, took his hat and stick and walked out, just as the funeral descending the valley from the direction of the 'Old Angel Inn' came in sight.

Old Cooper prowled about disconsolately, and counted the carriages as well as he could from the gate. When the funeral was over, and they began to drive away, he returned to the hall, the door of which lay open, and as usual deserted. Before he reached it quite, a mourning coach drove up, and two gentlemen in black cloaks, and with crapes to their hats, got out, and without looking to the right or the left, went up the steps into the house. Cooper followed them slowly. The carriage had, he supposed, gone round to the yard, for, when he reached the door, it was no longer there.

So he followed the two mourners into the house. In the hall he found a fellow-servant, who said he had seen two gentlemen, in black cloaks, pass through the hall, and go up the stairs without removing their hats, or asking leave of anyone. This was very odd, old Cooper thought, and a great liberty; so upstairs he went to make them out.

But he could not find them then, nor ever. And from that hour the house was troubled.

In a little time there was not one of the servants who had not something to tell. Steps and voices followed them sometimes in the passages, and tittering whispers, always minatory, scared them at corners of the galleries, or from dark recesses; so that they would return panic-stricken to be rebuked by thin Mrs. Beckett, who looked on such stories as worse than idle. But Mrs Beckett herself, a short time after, took a very different view of the matter.

She had herself begun to hear these voices, and with this formidable aggravation, that they came always when she was at her prayers, which she had been punctual in saying all her life, and utterly interrupted them. She was scared at such moments by dropping words and sentences, which grew, as she persisted, into threats and blasphemies.

These voices were not always in the room. They called, as she fancied, through the walls, very thick in that old house, from the neighbouring apartments, sometimes on one side, sometimes on the other; sometimes they seemed to holloa from distant lobbies, and came muffled, but threateningly, through the long panelled passages. As they approached they grew furious, as if several voices were speaking together. Whenever, as I said, this worthy woman applied herself to her devotions, these horrible sentences came hurrying towards the door, and, in panic, she would start from her knees, and all then would subside except the thumping of her heart against her stays, and the dreadful tremors of her nerves.

What these voices said, Mrs. Beckett never could quite remember one minute after they had ceased speaking; one sentence chased another away; gibe and menace and impious denunciation, each hideously articulate, were lost as soon as heard. And this added to the effect of these terrifying mockeries and invectives, that she could not, by any effort, retain their exact import, although their horrible character remained vividly present to her mind.

For a long time the Squire seemed to be the only person in the house absolutely unconscious of these annoyances. Mrs. Beckett had twice made up her mind within the week to leave. A prudent woman, however, who has been comfortable for more than twenty years in a place, thinks oftener than twice before she leaves it. She and old Cooper were the only servants in the house who remembered the good old housekeeping in Squire Toby's day. The others were few, and such as could hardly be accounted regular servants. Meg Dobbs, who acted as housemaid, would not sleep in the house, but walked home, in trepidation, to her father's, at the gatehouse, under the escort of her little brother, every night. Old Mrs. Beckett, who was high and mighty with the make-shift servants of fallen Gylingden, let herself down all at once, and made Mrs. Kymes and the kitchen-maid move their beds into her large and faded room, and there, very frankly, shared her nightly terrors with them.

Old Cooper was testy and captious about these stories. He was already uncomfortable enough by reason of the entrance of the two muffled figures into the house, about which there could be no mistake. His own eyes had seen them. He refused to credit the stories of the women, and affected to think that the two mourners might have left the house and driven away, on finding no one to receive them.

Old Cooper was summoned at night to the oak parlour, where the Squire was smoking.

'I say, Cooper,' said the Squire, looking pale and angry, 'what for ha' you been frightenin' they crazy women wi' your plaguy stories? d——me, if you see ghosts here it's no place for you, and it's time you should pack. I won't be left without servants. Here has been old Beckett, wi' the cook and the kitchen-maid, as white as pipe-clay, all in a row, to tell me I must have a parson to sleep among them, and preach down the devil! Upon my soul, you're a wise old body, filling their heads wi' maggots! and Meg goes down to the lodge every night, afeared to lie in the house—all your doing, wi' your old wives' stories,—ye withered old Tom o' Bedlam!'

'I'm not to blame, Master Charles. 'Tisn't along o' no stories o' mine, for I'm never done tellin' 'em it's all vanity and vapours. Mrs. Beckett 'ill tell you that, and there's been many a wry word betwixt us on the head o't. Whate'er I may *think*,' said old Cooper, significantly, and looking askance, with the sternness of fear in the Squire's face.

The Squire averted his eyes, and muttered angrily to himself, and turned away to knock the ashes out of his pipe on the hob, and then turning suddenly round upon Cooper again, he spoke, with a pale face, but not quite so angrily as before.

'I know you're no fool, old Cooper, when you like. Suppose there was such a thing as a ghost here, don't you see, it ain't to them snipe-headed women it 'id go to tell its story. What ails you, man, that you should think aught about it, but just what *I* think? You had a good headpiece o' yer own once, Cooper, don't be you clappin' a goosecap over it, as my poor father used to say; d——it, old boy, you mustn't let 'em be fools, settin' one another wild wi' their blether, and makin' the folk talk what they shouldn't, about Gylingden and the family. I don't think ye'd like that, old Cooper, I'm sure ye wouldn't. The women has gone out o' the kitchen, make up a bit o' fire, and get your pipe. I'll go to you, when I finish this one, and we'll smoke a bit together, and a glass o' brandy and water.'

Down went the old butler, not altogether unused to such condescensions in that disorderly and lonely household; and let not those who can choose their company, be too hard on the Squire who couldn't.

When he had got things tidy, as he said, he sat down in that big old kitchen, with his feet on the fender, the kitchen candle burning in a great brass candlestick, which stood on the deal table at his elbow, with the brandy bottle and tumblers beside it, and Cooper's pipe also in readiness. And these preparations completed, the old butler, who had remembered other generations and better times, fell into rumination, and so, gradually, into a deep sleep.

Old Cooper was half awakened by some one laughing low, near his head. He was dreaming of old times in the Hall, and fancied one of 'the young gentlemen' going to play him a trick, and he mumbled something in his sleep, from which he was awakened by a stern deep voice, saying, 'You weren't at the funeral; I might take your life, I'll take your ear.' At the same moment, the side of his head received a violent push, and he started to his feet. The fire had gone down, and he was chilled. The candle was expiring in the socket, and threw on the white wall long shadows, that danced up and down from the ceiling to the ground, and their black outlines he fancied resembled the two men in cloaks, whom he remembered with a profound horror.

He took the candle, with all the haste he could, getting along the passage, on whose walls the same dance of black shadows was continued, very anxious to reach his room before the light should go out. He was startled half out of his wits by the sudden clang of his master's bell, close over his head, ringing furiously.

'Ha, ha! There it goes—yes, sure enough,' said Cooper, reassuring himself with the sound of his own voice, as he hastened on, hearing more and more distinct every moment the same furious ringing. 'He's fell asleep, like me; that's it, and his lights is out, I lay you fifty—'

When he turned the handle of the door of the oak parlour, the Squire wildly called, 'Who's *there?*' in the tone of a man who expects a robber.

'It's me, old Cooper, all right, Master Charlie, you didn't come to the kitchen after all, sir.'

'I'm very bad, Cooper; I don't know how I've been. Did you meet anything?' asked the Squire.

'No,' said Cooper.

They stared on one another.

'Come here—stay here! Don't you leave me! Look round the room, and say is all right; and gie us your hand, old Cooper, for I must hold it.' The Squire's was damp and cold, and trembled very much. It was not very far from daybreak now.

After a time he spoke again: 'I 'a done many a thing I shouldn't; I'm not fit to go, and wi' God's blessin' I'll look to it—why shouldn't I? I'm as lame as old Billy—I'll never be able to do any good no more, and I'll give over drinking, and marry, as I ought to 'a done long ago—none o' yer fine ladies, but a good homely wench; there's Farmer Crump's youngest daughter, a good lass, and discreet. What for shouldn't I take her? She'd take care o' me, and wouldn't bring a head full o' romances here, and mantua-makers' trumpery, and I'll talk with the parson, and I'll do what's fair wi' everyone; and mind, I said I'm sorry for many a thing I 'a done.'

A wild cold dawn had by this time broken. The Squire, Cooper said, looked 'awful bad,' as he got his hat and stick, and sallied out for a walk, instead of going to his bed, as Cooper besought him, looking so wild and distracted, that it was plain his object was simply to escape from the house. It was twelve o'clock when the Squire walked into the kitchen, where he was sure of finding some of the servants, looking as if ten years had passed over him since yesterday. He pulled a stool by the fire, without speaking a word, and sat down. Cooper had sent to Applebury for the doctor, who had just arrived, but the Squire would not go to him. 'If he wants to see me, he may come here,' he muttered as often as Cooper urged him. So the doctor did come, charily enough, and found the Squire very much worse than he had expected.

The Squire resisted the order to get to his bed. But the doctor insisted under a threat of death, at which his patient quailed.

'Well, I'll do what you say—only this—you must let old Cooper and Dick Keeper stay wi' me. I mustn't be left alone, and they must keep awake o' nights; and stay a while, do *you*. When I get round a bit, I'll go and live in a town. It's dull livin' here, now that I can't do nou't, as I used, and I'll live a better life, mind ye; ye heard me say that, and I don't care who laughs, and I'll talk wi' the parson. I like 'em to laugh, hang 'em, it's a sign I'm doin' right, at last.'

The doctor sent a couple of nurses from the County Hospital, not choosing to trust his patient to the management he had selected, and he went down himself to Gylingden to meet them in the evening. Old Cooper was ordered to occupy the dressing-room, and sit up at night, which satisfied the Squire, who was in a strangely excited state, very low, and threatened, the doctor said, with fever.

The clergyman came, an old, gentle, 'book-learned' man, and talked and prayed with him late that evening. After he had gone the Squire called the nurses to his bedside, and said:

'There's a fellow sometimes comes; you'll never mind him. He looks in at the door and beckons,—a thin, hump-backed chap in mourning, wi' black gloves on; ye'll know him by his lean face, as brown as the wainscot: don't ye mind his smilin'. You don't go out to him, nor ask him in; he won't say nout; and if he grows anger'd and looks awry at ye, don't ye be afeared, for he can't hurt ye, and he'll grow tired waitin', and go away; and for God's sake mind ye don't ask him in, nor go out after him!'

The nurses put their heads together when this was over, and held afterwards a whispering conference with old Cooper. 'Law bless ye!—no, there's no madman in the house,' he protested; 'not a soul but what ye saw,—it's just a trifle o' the fever in his head—no more.'

The Squire grew worse as the night wore on. He was heavy and delirious, talking of all sorts of things—of wine, and dogs, and lawyers; and then he began to talk, as it were, to his brother Scroope. As he did so, Mrs. Oliver, the nurse, who was sitting up alone with him, heard, as she thought, a hand softly laid on the door-handle outside, and a stealthy attempt to turn it. 'Lord bless us! who's there?' she cried, and her heart jumped into her mouth, as she thought of the hump-backed man in black, who was to put in his head smiling and beckoning—'Mr. Cooper! sir! are you there?' she cried.

'Come here, Mr. Cooper, please—do, sir, quick!'

Old Cooper, called up from his doze by the fire, stumbled in from the dressing-room, and Mrs. Oliver seized him tightly as he emerged.

'The man with the hump has been atryin' the door, Mr. Cooper, as sure as I am here.' The Squire was moaning and mumbling in his fever, understanding nothing, as she spoke. 'No, no! Mrs. Oliver, ma'am, it's impossible, for there's no sich man in the house: what is Master Charlie sayin'?'

'He's saying *Scroope* every minute, whatever he means by that, and—and—hisht!—listen—there's the handle again,' and, with a loud scream, she added—'Look at his head and neck in at the door!' and in her tremor she strained old Cooper in an agonising embrace.

The candle was flaring, and there was a wavering shadow at the door that looked like the head of a man with a long neck, and a longish sharp nose, peeping in and drawing back.

'Don't be a d—— fool, ma'am!' cried Cooper, very white, and shaking her with all his might. 'It's only the candle, I tell you—nothing in life but that. Don't you see?' and he raised the light; 'and I'm sure there was no one at the door, and I'll try, if you let me go.'

The other nurse was asleep on a sofa, and Mrs. Oliver called her up in a panic, for company, as old Cooper opened the door. There was no one near it, but at the angle of the gallery was a shadow resembling that which he had seen in the room. He raised the candle a little, and it seemed to beckon with a long hand as the head drew back. 'Shadow from the candle!' exclaimed Cooper aloud, resolved not to yield to Mrs. Oliver's panic; and, candle in hand, he walked to the corner. There was nothing. He could not forbear peeping down the long gallery from this point, and as he moved the light, he saw precisely the same sort of shadow, a little further down, and as he advanced the same withdrawal, and beckon. 'Gammon!' said he; 'it is nout but the candle.' And on he went, growing half angry and half frightened at the persistency with which this ugly shadow—a literal shadow he was sure it was—presented itself. As he drew near the point where it now appeared, it seemed to collect itself, and nearly dissolve in the central panel of an old carved cabinet which he was now approaching.

In the centre panel of this is a sort of boss carved into a wolf's head. The light fell oddly upon this, and the fugitive shadow seemed to be breaking up, and re-arranging itself as oddly. The eye-ball gleamed with a point of reflected light, which glittered also upon the grinning mouth, and he saw the long, sharp nose of Scroope Marston, and his fierce eye looking at him, he thought, with a steadfast meaning.

Old Cooper stood gazing upon this sight, unable to move, till he saw the face, and the figure that belonged to it, begin gradually to emerge from the wood. At the same time he heard voices approaching rapidly up a side gallery, and Cooper, with a loud 'Lord a-mercy on us!' turned and ran back again, pursued by a sound that seemed to shake the old house like a mighty gust of wind.

Into his master's room burst old Cooper, half wild with fear, and clapped the door and turned the key in a twinkling, looking as if he had been pursued by murderers.

'Did you hear it?' whispered Cooper, now standing near the dressing-room door. They all listened, but not a sound from without disturbed the utter stillness of night. 'God bless us! I doubt it's my old head that's gone crazy!' exclaimed Cooper.

He would tell them nothing but that he was himself 'an old fool,' to be frightened by their talk, and that 'the rattle of a window, or the dropping o' a pin' was enough to scare him now; and so he helped himself through that night with brandy, and sat up talking by his master's fire.

The Squire recovered slowly from his brain fever, but not perfectly. A very little thing, the doctor said, would suffice to upset him. He was not yet sufficiently strong to remove for change of scene and air, which were necessary for his complete restoration.

Cooper slept in the dressing-room, and was now his only nightly attendant. The ways of the invalid were odd: he liked, half sitting up in his bed, to smoke his churchwarden o' nights, and made old Cooper smoke, for company, at the fireside. As the Squire and his humble friend indulged in it, smoking is a taciturn pleasure, and it was not until the Master of Gylingden had finished his third pipe that he essayed conversation, and when he did, the subject was not such as Cooper would have chosen.

'I say, old Cooper, look in my face, and don't be afeared to speak out,' said the Squire, looking at him with a steady, cunning smile; 'you know all this time, as well as I do, who's in the house. You needn't deny—hey?—Scroope and my father?'

'Don't you be talking like that, Charlie,' said old Cooper, rather sternly and frightened, after a long silence; still looking in his face, which did not change.

'What's the good o' shammin', Cooper? Scroope's took the hearin' o' yer right ear—you know he did. He's looking angry. He's nigh took my life wi' this fever. But he's not done wi' me yet, and he looks awful wicked. Ye saw him—ye know ye did.'

Cooper was awfully frightened, and the odd smile on the Squire's lips frightened him still more. He dropped his pipe, and stood gazing in silence at his master, and feeling as if he were in a dream.

'If ye think so, ye should not be smiling like that,' said Cooper, grimly.

'I'm tired, Cooper, and it's as well to smile as t'other thing; so I'll even smile while I can. You know what they mean to do wi' me. That's all I wanted to say. Now, lad, go on wi' yer pipe—I'm goin' asleep.'

So the Squire turned over in his bed, and lay down serenely, with his head on the pillow. Old Cooper looked at him, and glanced at the door, and then half-filled his tumbler with brandy, and drank it off, and felt better, and got to his bed in the dressing-room.

In the dead of night he was suddenly awakened by the Squire, who was standing, in his dressing-gown and slippers, by his bed.

'I've brought you a bit o' a present. I got the rents o' Hazelden yesterday, and ye'll keep that for yourself—it's a fifty—and give t' other to Nelly Carwell, to-morrow; I'll sleep the sounder; and I saw Scroope since; he's not such a bad 'un after all, old fellow! He's got a crape over his face—for I told him I couldn't bear it; and I'd do many a thing for him now. I never could stand shilly-shally. Good-night, old Cooper!'

And the Squire laid his trembling hand kindly on the old man's shoulder, and returned to his own room. 'I don't half like how he is. Doctor don't come half often enough. I don't like that queer smile o' his, and his hand was as cold as death. I hope in God his brain's not a-turnin'!'

With these reflections, he turned to the pleasanter subject of his present, and at last fell asleep.

In the morning, when he went into the Squire's room, the Squire had left his bed. 'Never mind; he'll come back, like a bad shillin',' thought old Cooper, preparing the room as usual. But he did not return. Then began an uneasiness, succeeded by a panic, when it began to be plain that the Squire was not in the house. What had become of him? None of his clothes, but his dressing-gown and slippers, were missing. Had he left the house, in his present sickly state, in that garb? and, if so, could he be in his right senses; and was there a chance of his surviving a cold, damp night, so passed, in the open air?

Tom Edwards was up to the house, and told them, that, walking a mile or so that morning, at four o'clock—there being no moon—along with Farmer Nokes, who was driving his cart to market, in the dark, three men walked, in front of the horse, not twenty yards before them, all the way from near Gylingden Lodge to the burial-ground, the gate of which was opened for them from within, and the three men entered, and the gate was shut. Tom Edwards thought they were gone in to make preparation for a funeral of some member of the Marston family. But the occurrence seemed to Cooper, who knew there was no such thing, horribly ominous.

He now commenced a careful search, and at last bethought him of the lonely upper storey, and King Herod's chamber. He saw nothing changed there, but the closet door was shut, and, dark as was the morning, something, like a large white knot sticking out over the door, caught his eye.

The door resisted his efforts to open it for a time; some great weight forced it down against the floor; at length, however, it did yield a little, and a heavy crash, shaking the whole floor, and sending an echo flying through all the silent corridors, with a sound like receding laughter, half stunned him.

When he pushed open the door, his master was lying dead upon the floor. His cravat was drawn halter-wise tight round his throat, and had done its work well. The body was cold, and had been long dead.

In due course the coroner held his inquest, and the jury pronounced, 'that the deceased, Charles Marston, had died by his own hand, in a state of temporary insanity.' But old Cooper had his own opinion about the Squire's death, though his lips were sealed, and he never spoke about it. He went and lived for the residue of his days in York, where there are still people who remember him, a taciturn and surly old man, who attended church regularly, and also drank a little, and was known to have saved some money.

—1870—

STORIES OF LOUGH GUIR

WHEN the present writer was a boy of twelve or thirteen, he first made the acquaintance of Miss Anne Baily, of Lough Guir, in the county Limerick. She and her sister were the last representatives at that place, of an extremely good old name in the county. They were both what is termed 'old maids,' and at that time past sixty. But never were old ladies more hospitable, lively, and kind, especially to young people. They were both remarkably agreeable and clever. Like all old county ladies of their time, they were great genealogists, and could recount the origin, generations, and intermarriages, of every county family of note.

These ladies were visited at their house at Lough Guir by Mr. Crofton Croker; and are, I think, mentioned, by name, in the second series of his fairy legends; the series in which (probably communicated by Miss Anne Baily), he recounts some of the picturesque traditions of those beautiful lakes—lakes, I should no longer say, for the smaller and prettier has since been drained, and gave up from its depths some long lost and very interesting relics.

In their drawing-room stood a curious relic of another sort: old enough, too, though belonging to a much more modern period. It was the ancient stirrup cup of the hospitable house of Lough Guir. Crofton

Croker has preserved a sketch of this curious glass. I have often had it in my hand. It had a short stem; and the cup part, having the bottom rounded, rose cylindrically, and, being of a capacity to contain a whole bottle of claret, and almost as narrow as an old-fashioned ale glass, was tall to a degree that filled me with wonder. As it obliged the rider to extend his arm as he raised the glass, it must have tried a tipsy man, sitting in the saddle, pretty severely. The wonder was that the marvellous tall glass had come down to our times without a crack.

There was another glass worthy of remark in the same drawing-room. It was gigantic, and shaped conically, like one of those old-fashioned jelly glasses which used to be seen upon the shelves of confectioners. It was engraved round the rim with the words, 'The glorious, pious, and immortal memory;' and on grand occasions, was filled to the brim, and after the manner of a loving cup, made the circuit of the Whig guests, who owed all to the hero whose memory its legend celebrated and invoked.

It was now but the transparent phantom of those solemn convivialities of a generation, who lived, as it were, within hearing of the cannon and shoutings of those stirring times. When I saw it, this glass had long retired from politics and carousals, and stood peacefully on a little table in the drawing-room, where ladies' hands replenished it with fair water, and crowned it daily with flowers from the garden.

Miss Anne Baily's conversation ran oftener than her sister's upon the legendary and supernatural; she told her stories with the sympathy, the colour, and the mysterious air which contribute so powerfully to effect, and never wearied of answering questions about the old castle, and amusing her young audience with fascinating little glimpses of old adventure and bygone days. My memory retains the picture of my early friend very distinctly. A slim straight figure, above the middle height; a general likeness to the full-length portrait of that delightful Countess

D'Aulnois, to whom we all owe our earliest and most brilliant glimpses of fairy-land; something of her gravely-pleasant countenance, plain, but refined and ladylike, with that kindly mystery in her sidelong glance and uplifted finger, which indicated the approaching climax of a tale of wonder.

Lough Guir is a kind of centre of the operations of the Munster fairies. When a child is stolen by the 'good people,' Lough Guir is conjectured to be the place of its unearthly transmutation from the human to the fairy state. And beneath its waters lie enchanted, the grand old castle of the Desmonds, the great earl himself, his beautiful young countess, and all the retinue that surrounded him in the years of his splendour, and at the moment of his catastrophe.

Here, too, are historic associations. The huge square tower that rises at one side of the stable-yard close to the old house, to a height that amazed my young eyes, though robbed of its battlements and one storey, was a stronghold of the last rebellious Earl of Desmond, and is specially mentioned in that delightful old folio, the Hibernia Pacata, as having, with its Irish garrison on the battlements, defied the army of the lord deputy, then marching by upon the summits of the overhanging hills. The house, built under shelter of this stronghold of the once proud and turbulent Desmonds, is old, but snug, with a multitude of small low rooms, such as I have seen in houses of the same age in Shropshire and the neighbouring English counties.

The hills that overhang the lakes appeared to me, in my young days (and I have not seen them since), to be clothed with a short soft verdure, of a hue so dark and vivid as I had never seen before.

In one of the lakes is a small island, rocky and wooded, which is believed by the peasantry to represent the top of the highest tower of the castle which sank, under a spell, to the bottom. In certain states of the atmosphere, I have heard educated people say, when in a boat you have reached a certain distance, the island appears to rise some feet from the water, its rocks assume the appearance of masonry, and the whole circuit presents very much the effect of the battlements of a castle rising above the surface of the lake.

This was Miss Anne Baily's story of the submersion of this lost castle:

THE MAGICIAN EARL

It is well known that the great Earl of Desmond, though history pretends to dispose of him differently, lives to this hour enchanted in his castle, with all his household, at the bottom of the lake.

There was not, in his day, in all the world, so accomplished a magician as he. His fairest castle stood upon an island in the lake, and to this he brought his young and beautiful bride, whom he loved but too well; for she prevailed upon his folly to risk all to gratify her imperious caprice.

They had not been long in this beautiful castle, when she one day presented herself in the chamber in which her husband studied his forbidden art, and there implored him to exhibit before her some of the wonders of his evil science. He resisted long; but her entreaties, tears, and wheedlings were at length too much for him, and he consented.

But before beginning those astonishing transformations with which he was about to amaze her, he explained to her the awful conditions and dangers of the experiment.

Alone in this vast apartment, the walls of which were lapped, far below, by the lake whose dark waters lay waiting to swallow them, she must witness a certain series of frightful phenomena, which, once commenced, he could neither abridge nor mitigate; and if throughout their ghastly succession she spoke one word, or uttered one exclamation, the castle and all that it contained would in one instant subside to the bottom of the lake, there to remain, under the servitude of a strong spell, for ages.

The dauntless curiosity of the lady having prevailed, and the oaken door of the study being locked and barred, the fatal experiments commenced.

Muttering a spell, as he stood before her, feathers sprouted thickly over him, his face became contracted and hooked, a cadaverous smell filled the air, and, with heavy winnowing wings, a gigantic vulture rose in his stead, and swept round and round the room, as if on the point of pouncing upon her.

The lady commanded herself through this trial, and instantly another began.

The bird alighted near the door, and in less than a minute changed, she saw not how, into a horribly deformed and dwarfish hag: who, with yellow skin hanging about her face, and enormous eyes, swung herself on crutches toward the lady, her mouth foaming with fury, and her grimaces and contortions becoming more and more hideous every moment, till she rolled with a yell on the floor, in a horrible convulsion, at the lady's feet, and then changed into a huge serpent, which came sweeping and arching toward her, with crest erect, and quivering tongue. Suddenly, as it seemed on the point of darting at her, she saw her husband in its stead, standing pale before her, and, with his finger on his lip, enforcing the continued necessity of silence. He then placed himself at his length on the floor, and began to stretch himself out and out, longer and longer, until his head nearly reached to one end of the vast room, and his feet to the other.

This horror overcame her. The ill-starred lady uttered a wild scream, whereupon the castle and all that was within it, sank in a moment to the bottom of the lake.

But, once in every seven years, by night, the Earl of Desmond and his retinue emerge, and cross the lake, in shadowy cavalcade. His white horse is shod with silver. On that one night, the earl may ride till daybreak, and it behoves him to make good use of his time; for, until the silver shoes of his steed be worn through, the spell that holds him and his beneath the lake, will retain its power.

When I (Miss Anne Baily) was a child, there was still living a man named Teigne O'Neill, who had a strange story to tell.

He was a smith, and his forge stood on the brow of the hill, overlooking the lake, on a lonely part of the road to Cahir Conlish. One bright moonlight night, he was working very late, and quite alone. The clink of his hammer, and the wavering glow reflected through the open door on the bushes at the other side of the narrow road, were the only tokens that told of life and vigil for miles around.

In one of the pauses of his work, he heard the ring of many hoofs ascending the steep road that passed his forge, and, standing in his doorway, he was just in time to see a gentleman, on a white horse, who was dressed in a fashion the like of which the smith had never seen before. This man was accompanied and followed by a mounted retinue, as strangely dressed as he.

They seemed, by the clang and clatter that announced their approach, to be riding up the hill at a hard hurry-scurry gallop; but the pace abated as they drew near, and the rider of the white horse who, from his grave and lordly air, he assumed to be a man of rank, and accustomed to command, drew bridle and came to a halt before the smith's door.

He did not speak, and all his train were silent, but he beckoned to the smith, and pointed down to one of his horse's hoofs.

Teigne stooped and raised it, and held it just long enough to see that it was shod with a silver shoe: which, in one place, he said, was worn as thin as a shilling. Instantaneously his situation was made apparent to him by this sign, and he recoiled with a terrified prayer. The lordly rider, with a look of pain and fury, struck at him suddenly, with something that whistled in the air, like a whip; and an icy streak seemed to traverse his body, as if he had been cut through with a leaf of steel. But he was without scathe or scar, as he afterwards found.

At the same moment he saw the whole cavalcade break into a gallop and disappear down the hill, with a momentary hurtling in the air, like the flight of a volley of cannon shot.

Here had been the earl himself! He had tried one of his accustomed stratagems to lead the smith to speak to him. For it is well known that either for the purpose of abridging or of mitigating his period of enchantment, he seeks to lead people to accost him. But what, in the event of his succeeding, would befal the person whom he had thus ensnared, no one knows.

MOLL RIAL'S ADVENTURE

When Miss Anne Baily was a child, Moll Rial was an old woman. She had lived all her days with the Bailys of Lough Guir; in and about whose house, as was the Irish custom of those days, were a troop of bare-footed country girls, scullery maids, or laundresses, or employed about the poultry yard, or running of errands.

Among these was Mary Rial, then a stout good-humoured lass, with little to think of, and nothing to fret about. She was once washing clothes, by the process known universally in Munster as beatling. The washer stands up to her ankles in water, in which she has immersed the clothes, which she lays in that state on a great flat stone, and smacks with lusty strokes of an instrument which bears a rude resemblance to a cricket bat, only shorter, broader, and light enough to be wielded freely with one hand. Thus, they smack the dripping clothes, turning them over and over, sousing them in the water, and replacing them on the same stone, to undergo a repetition of the process, until they are thoroughly washed.

Moll Rial was plying her 'beatle' at the margin of the lake, close under the old house and castle. It was between eight and nine o'clock on a fine summer morning, everything looked bright and beautiful. Though quite alone, and though she could not see even the windows of the house (hidden from her view by the irregular ascent and some interposing bushes), her loneliness was not depressing.

Standing up from her work, she saw a gentleman walking slowly down the slope toward her. He was a 'grand-looking' gentleman, arrayed in a flowered silk dressing-gown, with a cap of velvet on his head; and as he stepped toward her, in his slippered feet, he showed a very handsome leg. He was smiling graciously as he approached, and drawing a ring from his finger with an air of gracious meaning, which seemed to imply that he wished to make her a present; he raised it in his fingers with a pleased look, and placed it on the flat stones beside the clothes she had been beatling so industriously.

He drew back a little, and continued to look at her with an encouraging smile, which seemed to say: 'You have earned your reward; you must not be afraid to take it.'

The girl fancied that this was some gentleman who had arrived, as often happened in those hospitable and haphazard times, late and unexpectedly the night before, and who was now taking a little indolent ramble before breakfast.

Moll Rial was a little shy, and more so at having been discovered by so grand a gentleman with her petticoats gathered a little high about her bare shins. She looked down, therefore, upon the water at her feet, and then she saw a ripple of blood, and then another, ring after ring, coming and going to and from her feet. She cried out the sacred name in horror, and, lifting her eyes, the courtly gentleman was gone, but the blood-rings about her feet spread with the speed of light over the surface of the lake, which for a moment glowed like one vast estuary of blood.

Here was the earl once again, and Moll Rial declared that if it had not been for that frightful transformation of the water she would have spoken to him next minute, and would thus have passed under a spell, perhaps as direful as his own.

THE BANSHEE

So old a Munster family as the Bailys, of Lough Guir, could not fail to have their attendant banshee. Every one attached to the family knew this well, and could cite evidences of that unearthly distinction. I heard Miss Baily relate the only experience she had personally had of that wild spiritual sympathy.

She said that, being then young, she and Miss Susan undertook a long attendance upon the sick bed of their sister, Miss Kitty, whom I have heard remembered among her contemporaries as the merriest and most entertaining of human beings. This light-hearted young lady was dying of consumption. The sad duties of such attendance being divided among many sisters, as they then were, the night watches devolved upon the two ladies I have named: I think, as being the eldest.

It is not improbable that these long and melancholy vigils, lowering the spirits and exciting the nervous system, prepared them for illusions. At all events, one night at dead of night, Miss Baily and her sister, sitting in the dying lady's room, heard such sweet and melancholy music as they had never heard before. It seemed to them like distant cathedral music. The room of the dying girl had its windows toward the yard, and the old castle stood near, and full in sight. The music was not in the house, but seemed to come from the yard, or beyond it. Miss Anne Baily took a candle, and went down the back stairs. She opened the back door, and, standing there, heard the same faint but solemn harmony, and could not tell whether it most resembled the distant music of instruments, or a choir of voices. It seemed to come through the windows of the old castle, high in the air. But when she approached the tower, the music, she thought, came from above the house, at the other side of the yard; and thus perplexed, and at last frightened, she returned.

This aërial music both she and her sister, Miss Susan Baily, avowed that they distinctly heard, and for a long time. Of the fact she was clear, and she spoke of it with great awe.

THE GOVERNESS'S DREAM

This lady, one morning, with a grave countenance that indicated something weighty upon her mind, told her pupils that she had, on the night before, had a very remarkable dream.

The first room you enter in the old castle, having reached the foot of the spiral stone stair, is a large hall, dim and lofty, having only a small window or two, set high in deep recesses in the wall. When I saw the castle many years ago, a portion of this capacious chamber was used as a store for the turf laid in to last the year.

Her dream placed her, alone, in this room, and there entered a grave-looking man, having something very remarkable in his countenance: which impressed her, as a fine portrait sometimes will, with a haunting sense of character and individuality.

In his hand this man carried a wand, about the length of an ordinary walking cane. He told her to observe and remember its length, and to mark well the measurements he was about to make, the result of which she was to communicate to Mr. Baily, of Lough Guir.

From a certain point in the wall, with this wand, he measured along the floor, at right angles with the wall, a certain number of its lengths, which he counted aloud; and then, in the same way, from the adjoining wall he measured a certain number of its lengths, which he also counted distinctly. He then told her that at the point where these two lines met, at a depth of a certain number of feet which he also told her, treasure lay buried. And so the dream broke up, and her remarkable visitant vanished.

She took the girls with her to the old castle, where, having cut a switch to the length represented to her in her dream, she measured the distances, and ascertained, as she supposed, the point on the floor beneath which the treasure lay. The same day she related her dream to Mr. Baily. But he treated it laughingly, and took no step in consequence.

Some time after this, she again saw, in a dream, the same remarkable-looking man, who repeated his message, and appeared displeased. But the dream was treated by Mr. Baily as before.

The same dream occurred again, and the children became so clamorous to have the castle floor explored, with pick and shovel, at the point indicated by the thrice-seen messenger, that at length Mr. Baily consented, and the floor was opened, and a trench was sunk at the spot which the governess had pointed out.

Miss Anne Baily, and nearly all the members of the family, her father included, were present at this operation. As the workmen approached the depth described in the vision, the interest and suspense of all increased; and when the iron implements met the solid resistance of a broad flagstone, which returned a cavernous sound to the stroke, the excitement of all present rose to its acme.

With some difficulty the flag was raised, and a chamber of stone work, large enough to receive a moderately-sized crock or pot, was disclosed. Alas! it was empty. But in the earth at the bottom of it, Miss Baily said, she herself saw, as every other bystander plainly did, the circular impression of a vessel: which had stood there, as the mark seemed to indicate, for a very long time.

Both the Miss Bailys were strong in their belief hereafterwards, that the treasure which they were convinced had actually been deposited there, had been removed by some more trusting and active listener than their father had proved.

This same governess remained with them to the time of her death, which occurred some years later, under the following circumstances as extraordinary as her dream.

THE EARL'S HALL

The good governess had a particular liking for the old castle, and when lessons were over, would take her book or her work into a large room in the ancient building, called the Earl's Hall. Here she caused a table and chair to be placed for her use, and in the chiaroscuro would so sit at her favourite occupations, with just a little ray of subdued light, admitted through one of the glassless windows above her, and falling upon her table.

The Earl's Hall is entered by a narrow-arched door, opening close to the winding stair. It is a very large and gloomy room, pretty nearly square, with a lofty vaulted ceiling, and a stone floor. Being situated high in the castle, the walls of which are immensely thick, and the windows very small and few, the silence that reigns here is like that of a subterranean cavern. You hear nothing in this solitude, except perhaps twice in a day, the twitter of a swallow in one of the small windows high in the wall.

This good lady, having one day retired to her accustomed solitude, was missed from the house at her wonted hour of return. This in a country house, such as Irish houses were in those days, excited little surprise, and no alarm. But when dinner hour came, which was then, in country houses, five o'clock, and the governess had not appeared, some of her young friends, it being not yet winter, and sufficient light remaining to guide them through the gloom of the dim ascent and passages, mounted the old stone stair to the level of the Earl's Hall, gaily calling to her as they approached.

There was no answer. On the stone floor, outside the door of the Earl's Hall, to their horror, they found her lying insensible. By the usual means she was restored to consciousness; but she continued very ill, and was conveyed to the house, where she took to her bed.

It was there and then that she related what had occurred to her. She had placed herself, as usual, at her little work table, and had been either working or reading—I forget which—for some time, and felt in her usual health and serene spirits. Raising her eyes, and looking towards the door, she saw a horrible-looking little man enter. He was dressed in red, was very short, had a singularly dark face, and a most atrocious countenance. Having walked some steps into the room, with his eyes fixed on her, he stopped, and beckoning to her to follow, moved back toward the door. About half way, again he stopped once more and turned. She was so terrified that she sat staring at the apparition without moving or speaking. Seeing that she had not obeyed him, his face became more frightful and menacing, and as it underwent this change, he raised his hand and stamped on the floor. Gesture, look, and all, expressed diabolical fury. Through sheer extremity of terror she did rise, and, as he turned again, followed him a step or two in the direction of the door. He again stopped, and with the same mute menace, compelled her again to follow him.

She reached the narrow stone doorway of the Earl's Hall, through which he had passed; from the threshold she saw him standing a little way off, with his eyes still fixed on her. Again he signed to her, and began to move along the short passage that leads to the winding stair. But instead of following him further, she fell on the floor in a fit.

The poor lady was thoroughly persuaded that she was not long to survive this vision, and her foreboding proved true. From her bed she never rose. Fever and delirium supervened in a few days, and she died. Of course it is possible that fever, already approaching, had touched her brain when she was visited by the phantom, and that it had no external existence.

1870

MADAM CROWL'S GHOST

I'M an old woman now; and I was but thirteen my last birthday, the night I came to Applewale House. My aunt was the housekeeper there, and a sort o' one-horse carriage was down at Lexhoe to take me and my box up to Applewale.

I was a bit frightened by the time I got to Lexhoe, and when I saw the carriage and horse, I wished myself back again with my mother at Hazelden. I was crying when I got into the 'shay'—that's what we used to call it—and old John Mulbery that drove it, and was a good-natured fellow, bought me a handful of apples at the Golden Lion, to cheer me up a bit; and he told me that there was a currant-cake, and tea, and pork-chops, waiting for me, all hot, in my aunt's room at the great house. It was a fine moonlight night and I eat the apples, lookin' out o' the shay winda.

It is a shame for gentlemen to frighten a poor foolish child like I was. I sometimes think it might be tricks. There was two on 'em on the tap o' the coach beside me. And they began to question me after nightfall, when the moon rose, where I was going to. Well, I told them it was to wait on Dame Arabella Crowl, of Applewale House, near by Lexhoe.

'Ho, then,' says one of them, 'you'll not be long there!'

And I looked at him as much as to say, 'Why not?' for I had spoke out when I told them where I was goin', as if 'twas something clever I had to say.

'Because,' says he—'and don't you for your life tell no one, only watch her and see—she's possessed by the devil, and more an half a ghost. Have you got a Bible?'

'Yes, sir,' says I. For my mother put my little Bible in my box, and I knew it was there: and by the same token, though the print's too small for my ald eyes, I have it in my press to this hour.

As I looked up at him, saying 'Yes, sir,' I thought I saw him winkin' at his friend; but I could not be sure.

'Well,' says he, 'be sure you put it under your bolster every night, it will keep the ald girl's claws aff ye.'

And I got such a fright when he said that, you wouldn't fancy! And I'd a liked to ask him a lot about the ald lady, but I was too shy, and he and his friend began talkin' together about their own consarns, and dowly enough I got down, as I told ye, at Lexhoe. My heart sank as I drove into the dark avenue. The trees stands very thick and big, as ald as the ald house almost, and four people, with their arms out and finger-tips touchin', barely girds round some of them.

Well, my neck was stretched out o' the winda, looking for the first view o' the great house; and, all at once we pulled up in front of it.

A great white-and-black house it is, wi' great black beams across and right up it, and gables lookin' out, as white as a sheet, to the moon, and the shadows o' the trees, two or three up and down upon the front, you could count the leaves on them, and all the little diamond-shaped winda-panes, glimmering on the great hall winda, and great shutters, in the old fashion, hinged on the wall outside, boulted across all the rest o' the windas in front, for there was but three or four servants, and the old lady in the house, and most o' t'rooms was locked up.

My heart was in my mouth when I sid the journey was over, and this, the great house afore me, and I sa near my aunt that I never sid till noo, and Dame Crowl, that I was come to wait upon, and was afeared on already.

My aunt kissed me in the hall, and brought me to her room. She was tall and thin, wi' a pale face and black eyes, and long thin hands wi' black mittins on. She was past fifty, and her word was short; but her word was law. I hev no complaints to make of her; but she was a hard woman, and I think she would hev bin kinder to me if I had bin her sister's child in place of her brother's. But all that's o' no consequence noo.

The squire—his name was Mr. Chevenix Crowl, he was Dame Crowl's grandson—came down there, by way of seeing that the old lady was well treated, about twice or thrice in the year. I sid him but twice all the time I was at Applewale House.

I can't say but she was well taken care of, notwithstandin', but that was because my aunt and Meg Wyvern, that was her maid, had a conscience, and did their duty by her.

Mrs. Wyvern—Meg Wyvern my aunt called her to herself, and Mrs. Wyvern to me—was a fat, jolly lass of fifty, a good height and a good breadth, always good-humoured, and walked slow. She had fine wages, but she was a bit stingy, and kept all her fine clothes under lock and key, and wore, mostly, a twilled chocolate cotton, wi' red, and yellow, and green sprigs and balls on it, and it lasted wonderful.

She never gave me nout, not the vally o' a brass thimble, all the time I was there; but she was good-humoured, and always laughin', and she talked no end o' proas over her tea; and, seeing me sa sackless and dowly, she roused me up wi' her laughin' and stories; and I think I liked her better than my aunt—children is so taken wi' a bit o' fun or a story—though my aunt was very good to me, but a hard woman about some things, and silent always.

My aunt took me into her bed-chamber, that I might rest myself a bit while she was settin' the tea in her room. But first she patted me on the shouther, and said I was a tall lass o' my years, and had spired up well, and asked me if I could do plain work and stitchin'; and she looked in my face, and said I was like my father, her brother, that was dead and gone, and she hoped I was a better Christian, and wad na du a' that lids.

It was a hard sayin' the first time I set my foot in her room, I thought.

When I went into the next room, the housekeeper's room—very comfortable, yak (oak) all round—there was a fine fire blazin' away, wi' coal, and peat, and wood, all in a low together, and tea on the table, and hot cake, and smokin' meat; and there was Mrs. Wyvern, fat, jolly, and talkin' away, more in an hour than my aunt would in a year.

While I was still at my tea my aunt went upstairs to see Madam Crowl.

'She's agone up to see that old Judith Squailes is awake,' says Mrs. Wyvern. 'Judith sits with Madam Crowl when me and Mrs. Shutters'—that was my aunt's name—'is away. She's a troublesome old lady. Ye'll hev to be sharp wi' her, or she'll be into the fire, or out o' t' winda. She goes on wires, she does, old though she be.'

'How old, ma'am?' says I.

'Ninety-three her last birthday, and that's eight months gone,' says she; and she laughed. 'And don't be askin' questions about her before your aunt—mind, I tell ye; just take her as you find her, and that's all.'

'And what's to be my business about her, please ma'am?' says I.

'About the old lady? Well,' says she, 'your aunt, Mrs. Shutters, will tell you that; but I suppose you'll hev to sit in the room with your work, and see she's at no mischief, and let her amuse herself with her things on the table, and get her her food or drink as she calls for it, and keep her out o' mischief, and ring the bell hard if she's troublesome.'

'Is she deaf, ma'am?'

'No, nor blind,' says she; 'as sharp as a needle, but she's gone quite aupy, and can't remember nout rightly; and Jack the Giant Killer, or Goody Twoshoes will please her as well as the King's court, or the affairs of the nation.'

'And what did the little girl go away for, ma'am, that went on Friday last? My aunt wrote to my mother she was to go.'

'Yes; she's gone.'

'What for?' says I again.

'She didn't answer Mrs. Shutters, I do suppose,' says she. 'I don't know. Don't be talkin'; your aunt can't abide a talkin' child.'

'And please, ma'am, is the old lady well in health?' says I.

'It ain't no harm to ask that,' says she. 'She's torflin' a bit lately, but better this week past, and I dare say she'll last out her hundred years yet. Hish! Here's your aunt coming down the passage.'

In comes my aunt, and begins talkin' to Mrs. Wyvern, and I, beginnin' to feel more comfortable and at home like, was walkin' about the room lookin' at this thing and at that. There was pretty old china things on the cupboard, and pictures again the wall; and there was a door open in the wainscot, and I sees a queer old leathern jacket, wi' straps and buckles to it, and sleeves as long as the bed-post, hangin' up inside.

'What's that you're at, child?' says my aunt, sharp enough, turning about when I thought she least minded. 'What's that in your hand?'

'This, ma'am?' says I, turning about with the leathern jacket. 'I don't know what it is, ma'am.'

Pale as she was, the red came up in her cheeks, and her eyes flashed wi' anger, and I think only she had half a dozen steps to take, between her and me, she'd a gov me a sizzup. But she did give me a shake by the shouther, and she plucked the thing out o' my hand, and says she, 'While ever you stay here, don't ye meddle wi' nout that don't belong to ye,' and she hung it up on the pin that was there, and shut the door wi' a bang and locked it fast.

Mrs. Wyvern was liftin' up her hands and laughin' all this time, quietly in her chair, rolling herself a bit in it, as she used when she was kinkin'.

The tears was in my eyes, and she winked at my aunt, and says she, dryin' her own eyes that was wet wi' the laughin', 'Tut, the child meant no harm—come here to me, child. It's only a pair o' crutches for lame ducks, and ask us no questions mind, and we'll tell ye no lies; and come here and sit down, and drink a mug o' beer before ye go to your bed.'

My room, mind ye, was upstairs, next to the old lady's, and Mrs. Wyvern's bed was near hers in her room and I was to be ready at call, if need should be.

The old lady was in one of her tantrums that night and part of the day before. She used to take fits o' the sulks. Sometimes she would not let them dress her, and other times she would not let them take her clothes off. She was a great beauty, they said, in her day. But there was no one about Applewale that remembered her in her prime. And she was dreadful fond o' dress, and had thick silks, and stiff satins, and velvets, and laces, and all sorts, enough to set up seven shops at the least. All her dresses was old-fashioned and queer, but worth a fortune.

Well, I went to my bed. I lay for a while awake; for a' things was new to me; and I think the tea was in my nerves, too, for I wasn't used to it, except now and then on a holiday, or the like. And I heard Mrs. Wyvern talkin', and I listened with my hand to my ear; but I could not hear Mrs. Crowl, and I don't think she said a word.

There was great care took of her. The people at Applewale knew that when she died they would every one get the sack; and their situations was well paid and easy.

The doctor come twice a week to see the old lady, and you may be sure they all did as he bid them. One thing was the same every time; they were never to cross or frump her, any way, but to humour and please her in everything.

So she lay in her clothes all that night, and next day, not a word she said, and I was at my needlework all that day, in my own room, except when I went down to my dinner.

I would a liked to see the ald lady, and even to hear her speak. But she might as well a' bin in Lunnon a' the time for me.

When I had my dinner my aunt sent me out for a walk for an hour. I was glad when I came back, the trees was so big, and the place so dark and lonesome, and 'twas a cloudy day, and I cried a deal, thinkin' of home, while I was walkin' alone there. That evening, the candles bein' alight, I was sittin' in my room, and the door was open into Madam Crowl's chamber, where my aunt was. It was, then, for the first time I heard what I suppose was the ald lady talking.

It was a queer noise like, I couldn't well say which, a bird, or a beast, only it had a bleatin' sound in it, and was very small.

I pricked my ears to hear all I could. But I could not make out one word she said. And my aunt answered:

'The evil one can't hurt no one, ma'am, bout the Lord permits.'

Then the same queer voice from the bed says something more that I couldn't make head nor tail on.

And my aunt med answer again: 'Let them pull faces, ma'am, and say what they will; if the Lord be for us, who can be against us?'

I kept listenin' with my ear turned to the door, holdin' my breath, but not another word or sound came in from the room. In about twenty minutes, as I was sittin' by the table, lookin' at the pictures in the old Æsop's Fables, I was aware o' something moving at the door, and lookin' up I sid my aunt's face lookin' in at the door, and her hand raised.

'Hish!' says she, very soft, and comes over to me on tiptoe, and she says in a whisper: 'Thank God, she's asleep at last, and don't ye make no noise till I come back, for I'm goin' down to take my cup o' tea, and I'll be back i' noo—me and Mrs. Wyvern, and she'll be sleepin' in the room, and you can run down when we come up, and Judith will gie ye yaur supper in my room.'

And with that away she goes.

I kep' looking at the picture-book, as before, listenin' every noo and then, but there was no sound, not a breath, that I could hear; an' I began whisperin' to the pictures and talkin' to myself to keep my heart up, for I was growin' feared in that big room.

And at last up I got, and began walkin' about the room, lookin' at this and peepin' at that, to amuse my mind, ye'll understand. And at last what sud I do but peeps into Madame Crowl's bed-chamber.

A grand chamber it was, wi' a great four-poster, wi' flowered silk curtains as tall as the ceilin', and foldin' down on the floor, and drawn close all round. There was a lookin'-glass, the biggest I ever sid before, and the room was a blaze o' light. I counted twenty-two wax-candles, all alight. Such was her fancy, and no one dared say her nay.

I listened at the door, and gaped and wondered all round. When I heard there was not a breath, and did not see so much as a stir in the curtains, I took heart, and I walked into the room on tiptoe, and looked round again. Then I takes a keek at myself in the big glass; and at last it came in my head, 'Why couldn't I ha' a keek at the ald lady herself in the bed?'

Ye'd think me a fule if ye knew half how I longed to see Dame Crowl, and I thought to myself if I didn't peep now I might wait many a day before I got so gude a chance again.

Well, my dear, I came to the side o' the bed, the curtains bein' close, and my heart a'most failed me. But I took courage, and I slips my finger in between the thick curtains, and then my hand. So I waits a bit, but all was still as death. So, softly, softly I draws the curtain, and there, sure enough, I sid before me, stretched out like the painted lady on the tomb-stean in Lexhoe Church, the famous Dame Crowl, of Applewale House. There she was, dressed out. You never sid the like in they days. Satin and silk, and scarlet and green, and gold and pint lace; by Jen! 'twas a sight! A big powdered wig, half as high as herself, was a-top o' her head, and, wow!—was ever such wrinkles?—and her old baggy throat all powdered white, and her cheeks rouged, and mouse-skin eyebrows, that Mrs. Wyvern used to stick on, and there she lay grand and stark, wi' a pair o' clocked silk hose on, and heels to her shoon as tall as nine-pins. Lawk! But her nose was crooked and thin, and half the whites o' her eyes was open. She used to stand, dressed as she was, gigglin' and dribblin' before the lookin'-glass, wi' a fan in her hand, and a big nosegay in her bodice. Her wrinkled little hands was stretched down by her sides, and such long nails, all cut into points, I never sid in my days. Could it ever a bin the fashion for grit fowk to wear their fingernails so?

Well, I think ye'd a-bin frightened yourself if ye'd a sid such a sight. I couldn't let go the curtain, nor move an inch, not take my eyes off her; my very heart stood still. And in an instant she opens her eyes, and up she sits, and spins herself round, and down wi' her, wi' a clack on her two tall heels on the floor, facin' me, ogglin' in my face wi' her two great glassy eyes, and a wicked simper wi' her old wrinkled lips, and lang fause teeth.

Well, a corpse is a natural thing; but this was the dreadfullest sight I ever sid. She had her fingers straight out pointin' at me, and her back was crooked, round again wi' age. Says she:

'Ye little limb! what for did ye say I killed the boy? I'll tickle ye till ye're stiff!'

If I'd a thought an instant, I'd a turned about and run. But I couldn't take my eyes off her, and I backed from her as soon as I could; and she came clatterin' after, like a thing on wires, with her fingers pointing to my throat, and she makin' all the time a sound with her tongue like zizz-zizz-zizz.

I kept backin' and backin' as quick as I could, and her fingers was only a few inches away from my throat, and I felt I'd lose my wits if she touched me.

I went back this way, right into the corner, and I gev a yellock, ye'd think saul and body was partin', and that minute my aunt, from the door, calls out wi' a blare, and the ald lady turns round on her, and I turns about, and ran through my room, and down the back stairs, as hard as my legs could carry me.

I cried hearty, I can tell you, when I got down to the housekeeper's room. Mrs. Wyvern laughed a deal when I told her what happened. But she changed her key when she heard the ald lady's words.

'Say them again,' says she.

So I told her.

'Ye little limb! What for did ye say I killed the boy? I'll tickle ye till ye're stiff!'

'And did ye say she killed a boy?' says she.

'Not I, ma'am,' says I.

Judith was always up with me, after that, when the two elder women was away from her. I would a jumped out at winda, rather than stay alone in the same room wi' her.

It was about a week after, as well as I can remember, Mrs. Wyvern, one day when me and her was alone, told me a thing about Madam Crowl that I did not know before.

She being young, and a great beauty, full seventy years before, had married Squire Crowl of Applewale. But he was a widower, and had a son about nine year old.

There never was tale or tidings of this boy after one mornin'. No one could say where he went to. He was allowed too much liberty, and used to be off in the morning, one day, to the keeper's cottage, and breakfast wi' him, and away to the warren, and not home, mayhap, till evening, and another time down to the lake, and bathe there, and spend the day fishin' there, or paddlin' about in the boat. Well, no one could say what was gone wi' him; only this, that his hat was found by the lake, under a haathorn that grows thar to this day, and 'twas thought he was drowned bathin'. And the squire's son, by his second marriage, by this Madam Crowl that lived sa dreadful lang, came in for the estates. It was his son, the ald lady's grandson, Squire Chevenix Crowl, that owned the estates at the time I came to Applewale.

There was a deal o' talk lang before my aunt's time about it; and 'twas said the step-mother knew more than she was like to let out. And she managed her husband, the ald squire, wi' her whiteheft and flatteries. And as the boy was never seen more, in course of time the thing died out of fowks' minds.

I'm goin' to tell ye noo about what I sid wi' my own een.

I was not there six months, and it was winter time, when the ald lady took her last sickness.

The doctor was afeared she might a took a fit o' madness, as she did, fifteen years befoore, and was buckled up, many a time, in a strait-waistcoat, which was the very leathern jerkin' I sid in the closet, off my aunt's room.

Well, she didn't. She pined, and windered, and went off, torflin', torflin', quiet enough, till a day or two before her flittin', and then she took to rabblin', and sometimes skirlin' in the bed, ye'd think a robber had a knife to her throat, and she used to work out o' the bed, and not being strong enough, then, to walk or stand, she'd fall on the flure, wi' her ald wizened hands stretched before her face, and skirlin' still for mercy.

Ye may guess I didn't go into the room, and I used to be shiverin' in my bed wi' fear, at her skirlin' and scrafflin' on the flure, and blarin' out words that id make your skin turn blue.

My aunt, and Mrs. Wyvern, and Judith Squailes, and a woman from Lexhoe, was always about her. At last she took fits, and they wore her out.

T' sir (parson) was there, and prayed for her; but she was past praying with. I suppose it was right, but none could think there was much good in it, and sa at lang last she made her flittin', and a' was over, and old Dame Crowl was shrouded and coffined and Squire Chevenix was wrote for. But he was away in France, and the delay was sa lang, that t' sir and doctor both agreed it would not du to keep her langer out o' her place, and no one cared but just them two, and my aunt and the rest o' us, from Applewale, to go to the buryin'. So the old lady of Applewale was laid in the vault under Lexhoe Church; and we lived up at the great house till such time as the squire should come to tell his will about us, and pay off such as he chose to discharge.

I was put into another room, two doors away from what was Dame Crowl's chamber, after her death, and this thing happened the night before Squire Chevenix came to Applewale.

The room I was in now was a large square chamber, covered wi' yak pannels, but unfurnished except for my bed, which had no curtains to it, and a chair and a table, or so, that looked nothing at all in such a big room. And the big looking-glass, that the old lady used to keek into and admire herself from head to heel, now that there was na mair o' that wark, was put out of the way, and stood against the wall in my room, for there was shiftin' o' many things in her chambers ye may suppose, when she came to be coffined.

The news had come that day that the squire was to be down next morning at Applewale; and not sorry was I, for I thought I was sure to be sent home again to my mother. And right glad was I, and I was thinkin' of a' at hame, and my sister, Janet, and the kitten and the pymag, and Trimmer the tike, and all the rest, and I got sa fidgetty, I couldn't sleep, and the clock struck twelve, and me wide awake, and the room as dark as pick. My back was turned to the door, and my eyes toward the wall opposite.

Well, it could na be a full quarter past twelve, when I sees a lightin' on the wall befoore me, as if something took fire behind, and the shadas o' the bed, and the chair, and my gown, that was hangin' from the wall, was dancin' up and down, on the ceilin' beams and the yak pannels; and I turns my head ower my shouther quick, thinkin' something must a gone a' fire.

And what sud I see, by Jen! but the likeness o' the ald beldame, bedizened out in her satins and velvets, on her dead body, simperin', wi' her eyes as wide as saucers, and her face like the fiend himself. 'Twas a red light that rose about her in a fuffin low, as if her dress round her feet was blazin'. She was drivin' on right for me, wi' her ald shrivelled hands crooked as if she was goin' to claw me. I could not stir, but she passed me straight by, wi' a blast o' cald air, and I sid her, at the wall, in the alcove as my aunt used to call it, which was a recess where the state bed used to stand in ald times, wi' a door open wide, and her hands gropin' in at somethin' was there. I never sid that door befoore. And she turned round to me, like a thing on a pivot, flyrin' (grinning), and all at once the room was dark, and I standin' at the far side o' the bed; I don't know how I got there, and I found my tongue at last, and if I did na blare a yellock, rennin' down the gallery and almost pulled Mrs. Wyvern's door, off t' hooks, and frightened her half out o' her wits.

Ye may guess I did na sleep that night; and wi' the first light, down wi' me to my aunt, as fast as my two legs cud carry me.

Well, my aunt did na frump or flite me, as I thought she would, but she held me by the hand, and looked hard in my face all the time. And she telt me not to be feared; and says she:

'Hed the appearance a key in its hand?'

'Yes,' says I, bringin' it to mind, 'a big key in a queer brass handle.'

'Stop a bit,' says she, lettin' go ma hand, and openin' the cupboard-door. 'Was it like this?' says she, takin' one out in her fingers and showing it to me, with a dark look in my face.

'That was it,' says I, quick enough.

'Are ye sure?' she says, turnin' it round.

'Sart,' says I, and I felt like I was gain' to faint when I sid it.

'Well, that will do, child,' says she, saftly thinkin', and she locked it up again.

'The squire himself will be here to-day, before twelve o'clock, and ye must tell him all about it,' says she, thinkin', 'and I suppose I'll be leavin' soon, and so the best thing for the present is, that ye should go home this afternoon, and I'll look out another place for you when I can.'

Fain was I, ye may guess, at that word.

My aunt packed up my things for me, and the three pounds that was due to me, to bring home, and Squire Crowl himself came down to Applewale that day, a handsome man, about thirty years ald. It was the second time I sid him. But this was the first time he spoke to me.

My aunt talked wi' him in the housekeeper's room, and I don't know what they said. I was a bit feared on the squire, he bein' a great gentleman down in Lexhoe, and I darn't go near till I was called. And says he, smilin':

'What's a' this ye a sen, child? it mun be a dream, for ye know there's na sic a thing as a bo or a freet in a' the world. But whatever it was, ma little maid, sit ye down and tell us all about it from first to last.'

Well, so soon as I med an end, he thought a bit, and says he to my aunt:

'I mind the place well. In old Sir Oliver's time lame Wyndel told me there was a door in that recess, to the left, where the lassie dreamed she saw my grandmother open it. He was past eighty when he telt me that, and I but a boy. It's twenty year sen. The plate and jewels used to be kept there, long ago, before the iron closet was made in the arras chamber, and he told me the key had a brass handle, and this ye say was found in the bottom o' the kist where she kept her old fans. Now, would not it be a queer thing if we found some spoons or diamonds forgot there? Ye mun come up wi' us, lassie, and point to the very spot.'

Loth was I, and my heart in my mouth, and fast I held by my aunt's hand as I stept into that awsome room, and showed them both how she came and passed me by, and the spot where she stood, and where the door seemed to open.

There was an ald empty press against the wall then, and shoving it aside, sure enough there was the tracing of a door in the wainscot, and a keyhole stopped with wood, and planed across as smooth as the rest, and the joining of the door all stopped wi' putty the colour o' yak, and, but for the hinges that showed a bit when the press was shoved aside, ye would not consayt there was a door there at all.

'Ha!' says he, wi' a queer smile, 'this looks like it.'

It took some minutes wi' a small chisel and hammer to pick the bit o' wood out o' the keyhole. The key fitted, sure enough, and, wi' a strang twist and a lang skreeak, the boult went back and he pulled the door open.

There was another door inside, stranger than the first, but the lacks was gone, and it opened easy. Inside was a narrow floor and walls and vault o' brick; we could not see what was in it, for 'twas dark as pick.

When my aunt had lighted the candle the squire held it up and stept in.

My aunt stood on tiptoe tryin' to look over his shouther, and I did na see nout.

'Ha! ha!' says the squire, steppin' backward. 'What's that? Gi'ma the poker—quick!' says he to my aunt. And as she went to the hearth I peeps beside his arm, and I sid squat down in the far corner a monkey or a flayin' on the chest, or else the maist shrivelled up, wizzened ald wife that ever was sen on yearth.

'By Jen!' says my aunt, as, puttin' the poker in his hand, she keeked by his shouther, and sid the ill-favoured thing, 'hae a care sir, what ye're doin'. Back wi' ye, and shut to the door!'

But in place o' that he steps in saftly, wi' the poker pointed like a swoord, and he gies it a poke, and down it a' tumbles together, head and a', in a heap o' bayans and dust, little meyar an' a hatful.

'Twas the bayans o' a child; a' the rest went to dust at a touch. They said nout for a while, but he turns round the skull as it lay on the floor.

Young as I was I consayted I knew well enough what they was thinkin' on.

'A dead cat!' says he, pushin' back and blowin' out the can'le, and shuttin' to the door. 'We'll come back, you and me, Mrs. Shutters, and look on the shelves by-and-bye. I've other matters first to speak to ye about; and this little girl's goin' hame, ye say. She has her wages, and I mun mak' her a present,' says he, pattin' my shoulder wi' his hand.

And he did gimma a goud pound, and I went aff to Lexhoe about an hour after, and sa hame by the stagecoach, and fain was I to be at hame again; and I never saa ald Dame Crowl o' Applewale, God be thanked, either in appearance or in dream, at-efter. But when I was grown to be a woman my aunt spent a day and night wi' me at Littleham, and she telt me there was na doubt it was the poor little boy that was missing sa lang sen that was shut up to die thar in the dark by that wicked beldame, whar his skirls, or his prayers, or his thumpin' cud na be heard, and his hat was left by the water's edge, whoever did it, to mak' belief he was drowned. The clothes, at the first touch, a' ran into a snuff o' dust in the cell whar the bayans was found. But there was a handful o' jet buttons, and a knife with a green handle, together wi' a couple o' pennies the poor little fella had in his pocket, I suppose, when he was decoyed in thar, and sid his last o' the light. And there was, amang the squire's papers, a copy o' the notice that was prented after he was lost, when the old squire thought he might 'a run away, or bin took by gipsies, and it said he had a green-hefted knife wi' him, and that his buttons were o' cut jet. Sa that is a' I hev to say consarnin' ald Dame Crowl, o' Applewale House.